❀

Yellow
Flowers
in the
Antipodean
Room

JANET FRAME

Yellow
Flowers
in the
Antipodean
Room

GEORGE BRAZILLER

New York

This book was written while the author held the Robert Burns Fellowship at the University of Otago, Dunedin, New Zealand.

Yellow
Flowers
in the
Antipodean
Room

1

A SKILLED CLERICAL WORKER, EUROPEAN OF British birth, twenty, single, not a convicted criminal, not suffering from physical or mental illness, politically placid, beardless, Godfrey Rainbird was well qualified to be accepted as an assisted immigrant to New Zealand. He chose New Zealand as a home because someone in the London office (Continental Travel) knew someone who had emigrated to Australia and liked it, and because all those posters of painted cows generously yielding their milk into suncolored butter and cheese made him feel well fed and warm, and when he started to think about feeling warm he guessed that perhaps Britain was not the place to marry and bring up a family; also, in another country his skin would not be so pale and there would not be as much rain as in the Trossachs where he spent the war years as an evacuee.

The Trossachs haunted him. In London, when the memory of his mother's death in the bombing came to him, with the image of the lonely raining valley and its mountain clouds and indistinct faces seen as lofty as clouds from the height of a five-year-old boy, Godfrey would panic and take a bus or the tube to Camden Town to visit Lynley, his sister. While he was a mere child in the Trossachs, she was already one of the privileged grownups whose talk came out of their mouths at a level beyond him. She could deal with fears—with loneliness in the night, and nightmares. She had called him Goff. My Goff, she would say, though she was careful not to say it now he was grown up. When God-

3

frey told her of his plan to emigrate she showed in her eyes that she watched a ship with a tiny white sail go down down below the horizon.

"Emigrate? And why not?"

"You could too," Godfrey said.

"Don't be silly. Out to that wilderness."

"It's not a wilderness. It's a new start in life."

Lynley looked puzzled. "But you're only a kid. You've scarcely had your first start." She clasped her hands. "Where's your girl-friend?"

Godfrey knew she was waiting for him to say, I haven't a girl-friend. Then she would ask him to stay to tea and watch the telly.

He frowned, looked sour. He invented Edna. "You mean Edna? She's waiting for me."

"Oh! It's Edna is it?"

Lynley unclasped her hands, and bending her elbow she rested her chin upon her right hand like someone standing on a station platform waiting for the train; just standing there as if her head became too heavy and had to be propped up; one hand under her chin; nothing to rest her elbow on; looking restless, unanchored.

"You'll come to see me when you've made your arrangements, then?"

"Sure."

Lynley invited him to tea and the telly. She knew there was no Edna but she was quite happy to play makebelieve if he would, too. The ship with its tiny white sail stayed in her eyes as she dropped the teabags into the pot, poking at them sharply with a spoon to speed the infusion.

One month and fifteen days later Godfrey was living at Number Three Dahlia Terrace Carroll Street Dunedin, working as a booking clerk in the Tourist Bureau, and apart from his occasional annoyance when he was teased about his accent, and the questions he could not answer about the secrets of the Football

4

Pools, he felt cautiously content. New Zealanders, they told him in London, will remind you how their food helped to win the Second World War. He found his workmates had other things to talk about. They too had been children during the war. They looked on it as a topic for Councils, Heads of Government, Old Men, and visiting Generals who, touching down at Christchurch, had the energy and impertinence, without coming to Dunedin, to tap its people on the shoulder with a long braided arm of remembered fellowship in suffering.

2

BEATRICE MULDREW OF MATUATANGI, SOUTH Island, was twenty-two. Twenty-one and the golden key on the kewpie-ridden, six-tiered cake had not brought the promised rewards. She was waiting for a fascinating young man to come her way. She would marry him, settle down with him for life, cook his meals, give him pleasure in bed, give him as an end or by-product of that pleasure, sons and daughters.

Beatrice waited.

How could this man find her and know her when he found her? She was not an unusual person. She had an imagination that grew about her like natural vegetation sunned and rained on and as much a part of her as hair or fingernails or skin. She had left school early to help her father in his paint and wallpaper shop downtown. Though her parents had vague ideas made clearer by the advice of her teachers that she should have "more education," they suppressed the misgivings that sprouted from these ideas, using the popular herbicide: "She'll only get married, so what's the use."

Beatrice had some knowledge prized for its apparent uselessness. She could quote French verbs and latin mnemonics. She had read *Wuthering Heights*. In the fourth form she had "done" *Jane Eyre*, grinding Jane's soul to death with a précis pestle. But the men of Matuatangi and now of Dunedin where Beatrice worked as a doctor's receptionist seemed far away from the heroes of Charlotte Brontë. Their speech was utilitarian, immediate,

6

unflattering; not captivatingly fluent and picturesque. Also they could not be expected to tell the lies that men used to tell when one half of the world was ignorant of the other half. Their travelers' tales could be no taller than the tourist posters—bold in color, factual, exaggerated with the exaggeration of emphasis rather than invention. So what hope was there, Beatrice wondered, for her future? She was ready to burst out over her fascinating young man the way broom pods in the sun go pop-pop-pop, scattering their ripeness.

She wanted her dream to come true, at once, now—or tomorrow morning, not on any later tomorrow—now, sharp sharp while the fog lay on Flagstaff Hill and the puddle of morning sunlight shone in the ditch that was St. Kilda, oilsheen of drainwater held between the palm of the peninsula and the mainland. If only, she felt, she could wake in her boarding house near the Oval to a new full life where the heroines of the novels would not be out of place, nor the heroes either, where she could walk along George Street and Princes Street on a Friday afternoon, arm in arm with her fascinating husband, and eavesdrop upon witty charming sentences spoken miraculously by the white-hatted, white-gloved women and the sheep-haunted men!

One evening at the Town Hall Dance, when Godfrey Rainbird stood with the other arrogant young men "looking over" the girls from a leaning post near the door, Beatrice, noticing him, decided without much thought or evidence that here at last was her fascinating young man.

3 FAMILY GROUP 1964. FLEET DRIVE, ANDERSONS Bay, the last house facing the harbor, next to a steep gorse and broom-covered slope that while it gave shelter from the Peninsula's northerly winds, hid the sunlight all morning and most of the afternoon and lay in the path of the bitter southerlies and rain and snow-filled westerlies. It was Sunday evening. The rain rained a dark February sample of June weather. Sonny Rainbird, six, lay on the hearthrug with a picturebook of airplanes. Teena, eight, busily crayonned a red rose.

"I'm drawing people with my rose. Robin Hood. Daddy, when are we going to get a television?"

"A television costs a lot of money."

"But you've lots of money. You're rich."

Sonny looked up from his airplanes. "When are we going to get a television?"

The darkness outside, the steady falling of the rain, the coal fire twisting its flames, tortured by its bright fluidity yet unable to escape from it by freezing into one permanent form, Godfrey reclining in his armchair, his eyes shut, his face that had grown tanned in eleven southern summers, now pale again, Sonny up in the air with his V-Jets, Teena smudging the red petals of her rose—big petals like outsize ruby dewdrops, Beatrice dreaming, her former pout of complaint changed to a rich pout of satisfaction—all seemed to be contained in the moment of asking as if

8

the scene were the drawstring around the top of a treasure bag and Teena and Sonny had pulled the string tight, imprisoning and controlling the contents.

"Please Daddy, everyone. . . ."

Godfrey opened his eyes.

"I know," he said, smiling. "Everyone in the street has a television."

"Everyone at school too. Aren't we rich enough?"

"There are lots of things to do besides watching television," Beatrice said. "Snakes and Ladders, Draughts. . . ."

But that's only when Grandma and Grandad Muldrew come to stay!

The little ritualist. Like her father, Beatrice thought, suddenly jealous that Godfrey had been divided thus into two almost while she was not looking, like those lower forms of pond life that without effort or fuss in the flick of an instant reproduce themselves. Beatrice felt cheated as if her laborious carrying and bearing of the children had been a side-issue only while the true reproduction had taken place elsewhere, swiftly, invisibly, almost without her knowledge or help or indeed her pleasure.

"Not games."

"There are books," Godfrey said, pointing to the two full shelves lining the wall on either side of the fireplace.

"But hardly anyone has *books* at home. The Passmores haven't any books. They've got shelves like ours but with ferns and a tank of fish, live fish. Fish are better than books. They're all colors. Gold, too. And there's an angelfish with black stripes. You can feed them and they swim and swim and sometimes go to sleep under the weeds with their eyes open."

Teena paused, coming to her conclusion. "Books are alright. I like books. But fish are better."

Just then Sonny looked up from his airplanes. "Mummy, will this year be the same as last year?"

"How?"

"Will Grandma and Grandad Muldrew come and bring wallpaper and chocolate biscuits?"

"Perhaps."

"I wish Daddy had his mother and father here. Will there be a parcel from Aunty Lynley?"

"Sure to be," Godfrey said.

Lynley had "adopted" the children, sending parcels of sweets and toys wonderful in their foreignness that were played with and played with, and broke. Sometimes Lynley wrote that she planned a trip to New Zealand for which she had been saving for years but she would wait until the time was ripe.

What did she mean? Godfrey wondered. A ripe time, an overripe time, a rotten time, and what was the secret season?

The rain rained on and on. Teena continued with her rose and Robin Hood, Sonny with his airplanes.

"What are you thinking about Godfrey?"

Here autumn and winter were not the beginning of doom as in England. Godfrey could see again the rusted sodden slimy leaves on the pavements, the rim of soot on the window ledge. He could smell the cold London room, the leaking gas ring in the corner, the furniture polish and stale waterbuckets in the corridor. He remembered the hunger in the eyes of those who punctually at the beginning of autumn drifted like leaves forced by the prevailing wind into the Tourist Office, and seized the free travel folders. (The clerks knew these dream-travelers by heart. At this time of year they took care to remove the free but expensively printed brochures.) They would demand complicated timetables of trains they knew they would never catch, flight numbers and routes of planes they would never fly in; yet persistent, earnest, they leaned over the counter while the harassed clerks explored the intricate timetables, trying to discover the right ship train or plane for the sunstarved dreamers. As a clerk in the Continental Office, Godfrey had suffered much from these travelers, yet he understood them for he himself had been one who became a clerk thereby cunningly getting to the heart and control of the matter.

The Trossachs. The Hostel for Young Men Business and Clerical and the room overlooking the mortuary of the Cancer Hospital. The old home in Camden Town and Lynley fussing around her three men boarders. Though it was all so far away now, Godfrey had brought much of it with him, in his luggage, on his back, in his heart; often its heaviness weighed on him. Already, not long past his thirtieth birthday, he walked with a slight stoop and this past summer he'd become immune to the sun's burning; one might have supposed he lived now in a world without sun, but how ridiculous that would be when he had come at last to a land of milk butter wool and honey; annual holidays; the beach at his front door.

"What are you thinking about, Godfrey?"

"Nothing. I was almost asleep. This rain!"

So he had been thinking about the rain. "Perhaps we ought to have television," she said. "It would keep us from getting too gloomy."

She seemed commonplace at this moment, Godfrey thought. She looked, fleetingly, like her mother in Matuatangi, that God-forsaken place. He thought of Matuatangi in this way because everyone he knew, including Beatrice, described it thus. It was a favorite description of any small town, especially if you had been born and bred there and left it to go to the city. Dunedin as a city was smaller than Godfrey had known and in his country it would have been named such only if the population numbers were a census also of the leaves and twigs on the trees in the Town Belt, the seagulls in the harbor, in the Queens and Botanical Gardens, over the University, the Oval, Forbury and Logan Park, the numerous billowing white clouds traveling above Swampy and Flagstaff and Signal Hill, the ducks in the Leith Stream, the flowerheads in the Octagon in spring. Yet it could

11

still be a place of apprehension for anyone leaving home for the first time, it could still be as strange, with the transport and the street names as confusing, the dread of being set down in a strange place as paralyzing as in a city where the population did not depend for its numbers on seagulls leaves crocuses and clouds shifting and dividing above the seven hills.

"I was so scared," Beatrice told Godfrey, "when I first came to Dunedin. Everyone but me seemed to know something about the city. Some had even been to Wellington and Auckland. And all the names were so strange; they kept going over and over in my mind. Balmacewen, Mornington, Shiel Hill, Dalmore. Don't you think so, Godfrey?"

Godfrey started. "You mean the television? I was thinking of the rain. The front path will be a mess where I put the gravel. I'll slope it when I get the time. Petersens have done theirs that way. A television? Can we afford it?"

They bought a television. They replaced the coal fire by an electric fire with flames frozen into permanent shape, and only the night wind rising from the Bay moaning like a swarm of bees in the chimney gave evidence that an oldfashioned coal fire once burned there. At night the children played pillow games, taking the television pictures in their head to see them again when their eyes were tightly shut against their pillow.

One night Teena said, "I'm taking the wicked witch to my pillow."

"I'm taking her too," Sonny answered. "I'll see her flying with her broomstick, flying flying through the sky."

Beatrice spoke fondly. "Will you, dear?"

She did not say, "I'll see her too, sharp and fierce and bright, but Beware; and not only Beware; May you have much joy, for it was in my pillow world that I first saw your father and peeled and hammered to shape him into my favorite pillow dream."

When the children had gone to their rooms Beatrice could hear them calling to each other, "What can you see? What can you see?"

"I can see an iceberg."

"I can see an airplane."

There was a cry, and Teena came running from the room to where Godfrey sat reading the evening paper. Her face pale, her body trembling, she ran to him and put her arms around him.

Godfrey, trying to concentrate on the newspaper, annoyed with himself for reading the same sentence over and over, not having heard the talk of the television pictures, misinterpreted Teena's demands in one of those mood-collisions that are common in families. Godfrey wanted to receive comfort, not give it. His mind had become obstinately haunted by one or two phrases in the newspaper—a company's loss and the reason given as their decision to sell pine logs. All these pine forests. There were so many pine forests in New Zealand, honored like prophets from another country and what a melancholy sighing these trees made in concert in the wind! Last year in the crib up north they spent their holidays next to pine forests and as it was high summer there were storms—thunder, lightning, torrential rains, gale force winds, and day after day they sat in the crib, looking out at the trees, listening to their sighing and moaning.

It's a wonder we didn't pack up last Christmas when the rain began, Godfrey thought.

Then with Teena still clinging to him and crying and with him pushing at her to get away he called to Beatrice.

"I say, isn't it a wonder we didn't pack up last Christmas as soon as the rain started?"

Beatrice came out of their bedroom. "What did you say?"

Godfrey repeated his question. He spoke sharply.

How pale he is, Beatrice thought. Then she saw Teena and the tears running down her face. She bent over her.

"Teena, whatever's the matter? What did you do to her, Godfrey?"

13

"Do? Why should I do anything to her?"

Beatrice encircled Teena with a comforting arm. "Something's upset the child." (Teena ached with the pleased warmth of being called "the child.") "She was happy as larry a moment ago. What did you say to her?"

Godfrey was indignant. "As far as I know all I said was, 'Isn't it a wonder we didn't pack up last Christmas when the rain came?' "

"Stop crying, Teena," Beatrice said sharply. "She's probably thinking of last Christmas. The children were bored, inside all the time with all that rain. Yes we should have packed up. The Robinsons did. And the Carters. And that couple, you know the loudvoiced one who tried to boss everyone in the camp kitchen, hogging the gas ring—they went home on the third day. And we just stayed behind in the rain to rot."

"It won't happen again," Godfrey said loyally, as if he had been responsible for the weather and would take care this Christmas to provide sun.

"But I wasn't thinking so much of the weather as of the pine trees. I've never seen so many in my life. And when the wind blew . . ."

Beatrice looked with sudden understanding. "You've frightened the child, talking of the wind in the pine trees. She and Sonny were playing at witches. It's something on television."

Teena stopped crying. "It's not on television and it's not the silly old pine trees. It's a secret."

This idea appealed to her. A confession of a secret, if made to other children, could result in the coercion of a twisted arm or pulled hair but mothers and fathers didn't have the same longing to find out secrets, or if they did they did not show it. With her head in the air Teena went out of the room.

"I've got a secret."

"Shoreward and McLeod have run their company at a loss since they went into *pinus radiata*."

14

"Oh Godfrey what's the sudden interest in *pinus radiata?*"

"I'm just glancing at the newspaper. This year let's go somewhere away from all those pine trees."

"Why of course, let's," Beatrice said, thinking: He and Teena are so alike. I wonder what he said to frighten her? "What did you really say to Teena?"

"If you want to know, nothing, absolutely nothing. She came crying out of the bedroom and grabbed hold of me as if she thought I'd be lost for ever. As I suppose I shall be, some day," he said, smiling, screwing up his eyes as if the sun were shining into his face.

Beatrice was gay. "Don't be morbid. I hate all thought of dying, anywhere, at any place. I think some people are born not to die. I'm not going to die."

She knew she sounded childish, trying to convert the will of life and death to her own use, but she felt she had to voice her wishes. If she did not make them known, how could any man or God take enough pity on her to grant them? Which they do, they must do, she told herself, certain that her needs in their very abundance would always be satisfied.

4   ONE NIGHT WHEN GODFREY WAS LATER THAN
usual at his meeting of the Fellowship Society, a travel club with
vague ideas of universal goodwill through travel, Beatrice went to
bed, and as she lay with her face in the pillow she found herself
remembering and playing the children's pillow game, shutting
her eyes tight and frowning at the hideous purple stripes that
trisected the scene. *Pinus radiata? Pinus insignus?* A dark candle-
shaped blot, a forest of flickering blots; and then there was only
a thin empty envelope of darkness with the light shining through
it, and then the glare of light as if the envelope had caught fire
and then someone was ringing the chimes of the new doorbell
that Godfrey was so proud of because it played two whole lines
of an old German folksong.

> My pigeon house I open wide
> to set my pigeons free.

Suddenly awake, Beatrice listened intently to the chimes completing the song under her breath,

> My pigeon house I open wide
> to set my pigeons free.
> They fly o'er the fields to the other side
> and light on the tallest tree.

And then, realizing the meaning of the chiming song Beatrice
sprang out of bed, put on her dressing gown and went, wondering, to the front door. It was late. Godfrey should have been home

16

hours ago. Was it wise to open the door at this time? Still, the neighbors were up, she could see their lights and they could see hers. Perhaps Godfrey had lost his key.

The caller was a woman, a stranger.

"I'm Miss Hendry. May I come in?"

Beatrice waited curiously for more information.

"Are you Mrs. Rainbird, Mrs. Godfrey Rainbird?"

The formal "Mrs. Godfrey Rainbird" gave Beatrice a stir of alarm.

The woman persisted. "Do you mind if I come in?"

"Well, it's late. I was in bed." Beatrice waited. She had a feeling of limitless time as if her investigation of the strange Miss Hendry could take all night and the next day and the next night and nobody would mind; and yet a stream of thoughts began to run inside her, then to rush, gathering momentum, on fire like a comet, separating itself from her outward calm. She felt two streams, one of fire, one of ice, meeting at the crossroads where her heart was beating and now her heart in its pounding pounding kept time with the fiery stream, yet still she waited, staring stupidly at this woman in the dark gabardine and the small black felt hat like the school "winter" hat at Matuatangi High School.

"Yes. I'm the Police Matron. There's been an accident."

Conventionally Beatrice should have clasped her hands over her breast and whispered, Godfrey? She had often wondered how she would receive bad news. Now she did not speak. She stood aside for Miss Hendry to come in. And once in the sitting room, taking command of it and of the dead fixed flames of the electric fire and that of the frost-gray television, and of Beatrice, Miss Hendry spoke exactly the often imagined words and phrases. Be brave. You have my sympathy. Bear Up.

So it was Godfrey, then.

How absurd! Godfrey walking home along the shore near where the land was being reclaimed. Godfrey being struck down by a car, killed instantly.

Instantly. That was how they were all killed. That was how they all seemed to prefer to die: like coffee.

"Let's go home this instant," Beatrice wanted to say to Godfrey as with Teena and Sonny they looked out of the crib window at the rain raining and the pine trees sighing; *pinus insignus; pinus radiata*; Shoreward and McLeod; Shoreward.

"Let's go home this instant and never come here again."

But no one answered her. Instead the chimes rang their hideous purple stripes and tried to tell her about a sunny day, a wooden house full of messenger birds, a child taking pity on them and opening the door whereupon *instantly* they were flying away moon-silver into the sun.

And that was Godfrey's death ringing its folksong in Beatrice's head; only she was not in a sunny land in a house full of pigeons, she was here in the dark and all was quiet with the sea almost unheard in its long crawl up the harbor, slipping gently over the mudflats, lying calm in its sleep between the mainland and the peninsula like a child safe between its parents in the "big bed" at home.

Home. That was where Beatrice longed to go now. Home to Mum and Dad in Matuatangi. She tried to recollect what the police matron had said. Wasn't it only old people who were struck by cars? Godfrey was far from old—yet even as the thought came to her she found it was an effort to remember clearly whether Godfrey was old or young, as if already the memory of him were being snatched away, as if death did not come alone but as head of a gang of thieves with death taking charge of the main treasure while the others lurked near to seize the rest of the loot, picking over the dead man's essence, stealing the thoughts and memories of him held by others, his past deeds, the story of his life.

"Near where they're reclaiming the land," Miss Hendry said.

Reclaimed land. Miss Hendry spoke bitterly as if the land were being reclaimed and she'd not had her fair share. Who owned the land? Who stole it in the first place? Was it a matter between the sea and the Harbor Board but what an unlikely negotiation for the sea to make when the sea could not write its own name on a document, and yet its mark was more powerful than its name.

And now Miss Hendry was asking if she could help, send telegrams to parents, relations. And what about the arrangements?

"But the children? And Godfrey?"

Miss Hendry frowned disapproval at Beatrice for putting the living so close to the dead. There was such a process as contamination.

"Have you good neighbors?"

"The Baldwins."

"I'll ask if they'll keep an eye on the children while I take you to Mr. Rainbird. Or is there anyone else you'd rather call?"

Beatrice longed to be one of those people who are relative-minded, whose time is devoted to visiting relatives, sharing news about them, writing and receiving letters, going on holiday to their homes and inviting them in return, giving them the guest room with its guest soap and hemstitched guest towels and embroidered pillow shams (shams!): such people made a skilled profession of being a relative. At the same time Beatrice wanted to be alone without this police matron observing her state of shock. She wanted to think but her head kept chiming with the doorbell and she kept seeing the pigeons set free, flying into the tallest tree, *pinus insignus, pinus radiata*; and there was a sensation in her head as of whirring springs like the sound inside a clock after it has struck the hour.

She looked at Miss Hendry. "Mrs. Baldwin might help. She's young. About my age. (*It is only old people who get killed at night.*) They're home. I saw their lights. And my parents at Matuatangi will come at once."

She was relieved when Miss Hendry went next door to the Baldwins. For a moment she stood free, yet bogged deep in the place

19

where she stood, that is, in her husband and children. Her feet and hands were as cold as layers of clay upturned from the deepest level of earth where it lies smooth, mottled, waterlogged with no hint in its heaviness and coldness that the center of the earth is fire. The one moment was precious. She absorbed the news and quickly put aside belief in it. Godfrey dead? Ridiculous, a mad mistake. How did they know it was him? Someone, seeing him, probably exclaimed, "Oh, that looks like Godfrey Rainbird, you know, the clerk in the Tourist Office."

What proof had they? These things had to be proved. And who had proved that the center of the earth was fire? Somewhere, everywhere, there was a terrible deception.

And then Beatrice's mind and body were encoiled by a slowly tightening realization that all care was taken with the dead, for death, concerning and touching everyone, had to be seen clearly, a truth held up to the light to detect the counterfeit markings.

"I must go to the children," Beatrice said aloud.

She went to Teena's room and was startled to find that she was not in bed. She went to Sonny's room where Teena and Sonny, white-faced with big night-eyes, were sitting on the edge of the bed waiting for her to tell them what they already knew. She sat on the bed between them with an arm around each and Teena pressed her face into her side, and Sonny whimpered, pressing his face under her heart, and each of her breasts lay a little over each head. The children enclosed her tightly as if trying to get in.

"We heard you, Mummy," Teena said at last. "We heard what that wicked woman told you."

"A nasty woman," Sonny echoed. "I don't like her."

"We've been planning what to do with her," Teena said. "We're going to ambush her and take her down to the sea and drown her. Don't you think that's a good way to get rid of her, Mummy?"

Quelling her own primitive resentment against the bringer of bad news, Beatrice said sharply but unconvincingly, "She's a nice woman. She's going to talk to Mrs. Baldwin and you're going next door and perhaps Charley and Bonny will be awake, and I've something from the Secrets Cupboard for you." She hoped this bribery in the face of death would help. It did. Children are ready, at any age, to be corrupted into sharp emotional practices.

Beatrice congratulated herself on having thought of the Secrets Cupboard where she had arranged a number of surprises for special occasions. She never dreamed of using it as it was to be used now with Teena being given a china breakfast set and Sonny a black-and-red plastic airplane to make them forget their father was dead. Watching them go happily next door clutching their "secrets," ready to receive the envious attentions of Charley and Bonny, she felt that she had cruelly whittled away their grief, distorted their idea of death and rewards, and in the mixing of so many incongruous feelings into their first experience of death, she felt she had poured on them the "boiling moment" that would cool and set in a permanent shape and they would never know "pure" grief, they would always look to the Secrets Cupboard for consolation.

Beatrice took her duties as a mother seriously, though she had not always put her theories into practice. She'd grown up since the days of her longing for the "fascinating young man," and having found him she possessed a new world, became owner, trustee of the human equivalent of many continents, and when her feelings were roused Beatrice could be a harsh cunning imperialist sending troops to quell rebellions setting up her kingdom shamelessly exploiting the inhabitants with glass beads, silver paper, ticking toy watches of love, and noting with pride how the land developed under her care, how thoroughly it was explored, mined, sown under her direction, with Godfrey and the children always in residence as the king and the prince and the princess.

Yet until now Beatrice had not known death so close to her. She wondered again, Where were the relatives that came, always, in life and fiction to share grief? Caring for Godfrey and the children, keeping in touch only with her parents, occasionally with her brother and his wife and family in the North Island, and with Lynley (she must send a cable at once to Lynley), she had made herself a kingdom but it was an island kingdom. I must phone, cable, send messages, she thought. Godfrey would wish me to get in touch with Lynley.

One must respect the wishes of the dead, she said to herself, accepting the platitudes of bereavement in the sievelike condition of mind in which the news had put her, allowing for the moment her own thoughts and feelings to fall through to the bottom of her heart so that when the remnants of the time had been thrown away her own thoughts and feelings would remain as sediment in her heart.

"Why am I not surrounded by people—neighbors, councilors, doctors, lawyers, old witch women bringing prophecies, herbal comforts, applying the juice of exotic plants to all wounds?"

She went with Miss Hendry in the car to the hospital.

"Wear your hat," Miss Hendry said, and meekly Beatrice obeyed her.

She felt strange in a hat. All the women in George Street and Princes Street in their garden party meringues, she thought.

She was afraid, a novice in death, in grief. People she had known did not die. Her grandparents had died before she was born and the family reference, "Before you were born," had set death at a comfortable distance. How did one cope with the ritual of death? What lay behind the wreaths, the letters, the death notice in the newspaper (North Island papers please copy No flowers by Request), the mourning, the procession to the grave?

22

North Island papers please copy. The urge to have the news repeated, duplicated, came to her again and again. There must be some way of letting the whole world know!

Arrived at the hospital she was led to the room where Godfrey lay with closed eyes pale face and clasped hands, the classical picture of the dead man. Did a pulse flutter under his eyelid? Oh no, it was madness not to believe the dead were dead. His only disfigurement was a plaster-covered wound (why cover it with plaster if he were dead?) over his left cheek; healed, it would have left a scar, she thought, reaching forward and touching the plaster for it was not human material, like skin, and she could bear to touch it. Her fingers pressed upon it and would not obey her longing to touch the skin of his cheek and forehead. Therefore she did not touch him. She moved back, abruptly, as if he startled her with a movement or expression. She did not cry. She said in a matter-of-fact way, "It is—was—Godfrey, my husband."

She was led from the room. Then feelings came raining down on her, raining down from the sky and there was nowhere to put them and no one to ask, Will you hold my feelings for me while I think, while I breathe? No cousins, aunts, grandparents. Mum and Dad Muldrew were coming from Matuatangi, on the midnight train; and a cable had been sent to Lynley; and there were the arrangements to think of; and there were the children with their toy cups and saucers and cream jug and teapot and the red-and-blue plastic airplane; and the neighbors to explain to; and the lawn to mow; and the sea to keep at bay; *at bay.*

And then there was Godfrey in the small room; a man made of paper with a tiny dream-pulse fluttering under his eyelid like a breath of wind blowing a petal or paper scrap through the street on a Sunday morning.

"You mustn't give way," Miss Hendry said.

"I shan't," Beatrice said firmly, her mind shaping its plans that kept being dislodged by the feelings that came down now like hailstones on a circus tent collapsing the tent flooding the standing-place crashing against the cages that held the wild tigers, letting the wild tigers escape to prowl with their sunfire-filled eyes among the people and the vegetation that waited to receive the favors of the sunfire but were caught instead between the claws of ice.

Beatrice shivered. She felt sick. *North Island papers please copy. North Island papers please copy.* But why should the North Island be interested when it never knew ice, it had no glaciers tremendous in their century-slow urging toward the Tasman Sea.

"You must face it," Miss Hendry said.

Then the ice changed to a chalk quarry like the one at Matuatangi where Beatrice used to play as a child, breaking pieces of chalk to make hopscotch lines and write scores and initialed winning stars and, later, the heart-piercing love-arrows. What a privileged place Matuatangi was to have writing materials as part of its landscape!

Oh, if only we could stay contained in ourselves, Beatrice thought, remembering the overwhelming material evidence of Godfrey—his clothes, books, the objects surrounding him.

She thought of chalk and ice, of faces drawn with chalk, marked with ice, of old and new skin, of burning, of the witches' cry, Fire Burn.

Then she and Miss Hendry went home. She sat in the sitting room while Miss Hendry, the haunting "other self," stayed with her while the children slept safely at Baldwins. Then at half-past five when morning had begun to streak and stain the sky Beatrice went to the railway station to meet Mum and Dad on the midnight from Matuatangi. The engine's arriving breath burst over her; the soot and smoke pierced her eyes like grains of sleep after waking. Then, at last, the happy bustle of crying. The sweetness of advice given with the sweet tea brewed by someone else, of scones made in a twinkling and no flour spilled; of people, Mum

24

and Dad but seeming many, a stockade of flesh, blood, tea, flour, words, tears, protecting from the sad, the unpleasant, the shocking. All the contents of the Secrets Cupboard poured out at once!

5

WHEN BEATRICE AND GODFREY WERE PLANNING to marry it was the question of their ages that worried Mum Muldrew, Cora.

"He's two years younger than you. A man should be older than his wife. It takes longer for a man to mature. They should be several years older."

Dad Muldrew (Wally), hearing this had looked amused and said nothing.

"But what about you?" Beatrice cried. "You're older than Dad!"

"That kind of thing doesn't matter these days. Besides (as if this made Godfrey more qualified to be her husband, for how much more fascinating a fascinating young man might be if he were born and brought up in another country!)—besides, he's not a New Zealander!"

Her mother looked puzzled, her own reasoning in love long forgotten.

"Yes, you're older than Dad," Beatrice said again, whereupon her mother with the final quelling argument used by all parents when their behavior is questioned, replied, "It's different with your father and me."

And perhaps it had been. Beatrice had not thought again of the difference between her age and Godfrey's until now at the time of his death. It seemed that suddenly she packed into her two extra years a superior wisdom and endurance that Godfrey had

26

never shown. She thought of him as having been a mere boy. Then a conviction that was quickly stained with shame spread in her mind that it was fitting for Godfrey to have died, as if their life together had been a battle in which she was now the victor and it was right that she should be. Thinking this way she began to accept Godfrey's death as inevitable and it was by this devious path that the belief in his death as a certainty at last came home to her and was given shelter inside her and she was able to think. He's dead. That's that. Now let me enjoy his death.

She baked a cake to provide, she said, for the extra mouths to be fed, as if death were a multiplication instead of a subtraction. The children were surprised and pleased to have dark fruitcake, not iced like Christmas cake and not decorated with tiny silver shoes and horseshoes and with wedding rings and threepences inside it, but almost as exciting as Christmas cake. They hoped for a pudding, too, like a Christmas pudding, but it seemed that their mother's thoughts did not follow the same logic as theirs. She cried in her bedroom and she baked a cake.

Meanwhile Mum and Dad Muldrew, whose education in death was more advanced and who had been deprived for many years of the opportunity of practicing what they had learned and remembered, were setting in motion the proper ritual. The wreaths already beginning to arrive (bad news travels swifter than good) were put in the "front" room, the sitting room, arranged in a row along the wall. Though the undertaker had a chapel on his premises and had suggested keeping the coffin there, Mum Muldrew remembered that the coffin was always brought home and put in the front room with the wreaths surrounding it. The blinds were drawn, the furniture covered with dark drapes, and at the appointed hour (for Godfrey's funeral Wednesday at two thirty), following a family service, the procession would leave the house for the cemetery. Mum Muldrew described it so vividly and convincingly that all were won to her opinion. Beatrice, at first apprehensive in case the children were upset or she herself might not be able to bear the presence of a dead body in the house, then remembered her longing for the time she had not known, the death of her grandparents, and her brother's teasing—You weren't there. Before you were born; and her sense of loss warring with her gratitude that she had not been there. She remembered the china teacups and saucers and plastic airplane and her misgivings that she had adulterated the children's "fair share" of "pure" grief.

She agreed with her mother. Yes. Godfrey was to be brought home.

With one more arrangement settled there was almost an atmosphere of subdued rejoicing. Everything was going very smoothly for a funeral. The telegrams, letters, cards were beginning to arrive, with more wreaths. Mary Collins would be working overtime, Beatrice thought, in the back room of Petal Bowl Wedding and Funeral Florists.

The children, on holiday from school, or rather "away" from school because their father was dead, stayed down by the gate, hanging over it, watching with pride and dignity while their friends went running and skipping to and from school; and knowing that when they stopped outside the Rainbird's place and stared with fear or curiosity, whispering to one another, that they were saying, "The Rainbirds' father's dead. He was killed. Their father's dead."

Teena, who had thought about having a father banished or in exile or in prison but never really *dead*, kept hearing in her mind what the children might be saying.

Their father's dead. They're staying away from school because their father's dead. They're going to miss Nature Study today and they won't see the tadpole in its warm pool turn into a frog, Mr. Coleville said it would happen today, the tadpole would think it was springtime, but their father's dead and they won't see it. They won't have skipping in the playground and peanut butter sandwiches for lunch and they won't see the film this afternoon or be allowed to broadcast over the school radio because their father's dead. See, their father's dead.

Teena hung over the gate staring wistfully at everyone who passed, feeling important and proud and yet knowing that tomorrow or the day after or the day after that or perhaps weeks after the funeral something terrible was going to happen and that something terrible would be that their father was *really* dead. Why wasn't he dead now when they said he was? What was going to happen to make him really dead? Teena knew that it might have something to do with his clothes, for she had heard her mother and Grandma Muldrew talking about his clothes, saying what they would do with them and who would have them, and her mother held up their father's brown sweater with the wool coming undone at the edges.

"I'd rather his clothes were out of the house at once. I can't bear to see them. If things like this are any good to Dad . . . I'd rather have everything away, otherwise I'll be reminded. And then there's the future to think of. A widow's pension isn't much. I'll have to get a job. Then there's the TV set. And the children, their education. I want them to go on. Godfrey would have wanted them to go on."

What was it like, "going on"? Teena wondered. Had their mother "gone on"? And if you went on, where did you get to? If I go on, she thought, hanging over the gate, I'll go right into the sea into Andersons Bay.

"Sonny!"

"What?"

"If we go on, we'll go right into the sea. Do you want to go on?"

Sonny was suspicious. "Go on where?"

"Just on. Everyone goes on. Daddy wanted us to go on, and now Mummy is going to let us go on."

Sonny knew she was teasing him but he did not know how to take the teasing. He began to cry. "I don't want to go on!"

Some children passing the gate stopped and looked in awe at

them, and one whispered to the other (Teena *knew*)—Their father's dead. Sonny Rainbird is crying because their father's dead and being buried on Wednesday.

Pale, solemn, Teena stared back at them thinking, The tadpole has turned into a frog and I never saw it. It's not fair!

And she too began to cry and the watching children, curious, said, Teena Rainbird is crying because her father's dead and being buried on Wednesday.

Then together hand in hand, both crying, Teena and Sonny went up the path and inside the house where everything smelled of flowers and cooking and another smell that they hadn't known before; and then there was Grandad's smell, and Grandma's. Grandma had a black handbag that she carried with her wherever she went and when she wanted to blow her nose she opened her handbag, took out her hanky, and blew her nose. She didn't keep her hanky up her sleeve or up her pants leg or down between her titties, but in a handbag; carrying it up and down and around all the time; and when she sat down to the table to eat she put it beside her on a chair or on the sideboard. Perhaps it had gold in it. I wish I had a handbag, Teena thought. I wish I had a handbag with a pretty handkerchief inside it to carry up and down and around and put beside me on a chair or on the sideboard while I have my tea!

Another thing about Grandma and Grandad that Sonny and Teena enjoyed was the wallpaper. Twice when they had been to Matuatangi for holidays Grandad had let them go to the shop and choose leftovers, as many as they wanted, to make pictures with or cover their books with or draw on. Now, even coming in the middle of the night by the Limited and being tired and all over smoke from the train, Grandad had not forgotten to bring some wallpaper. He called it Remnants. One piece that Sonny claimed had a sailing ship and one had elves and the other had irises, tall and dark blue with pointed green leaves. Teena decided to cover her school exercise books with irises—but where was there room? Every place in the house seemed full even when there was nothing there, and their mother made it seem more crowded by saying every now and again, "What with the extra mouths."

Grandma and Grandad had Sonny's room with Grandad on the stretcher that they used for camping, Mummy was in the big bed in her and Daddy's room, and Sonny and Teena were in Teena's room, Sonny in the sleeping bag because he had cried to be. So where was there room to spread wallpaper and paste and exercise books? The kitchen was full of Grandma and Mummy and dinner. The sitting room was full of flowers. Therefore Teena decided to sit in her bedroom on the bed and cover her books. Sonny came too, unhappy because he did not have so many books to cover but triumphant because of the ship wallpaper. Once when Grandma looked in and said as a matter of habit, "What on earth are you two doing," and Teena and Sonny said they were pasting, Grandma said, "Here's the paste? Don't make a mess," and when they showed her the bottle of Woolworth's paste she looked annoyed.

"In my day," she said, "paste was made out of flour and water. You did not *buy* paste."

She made it sound like a punishment, like "bread and water."

"But you buy everything, Grandma," Teena said politely. "That's how you *get* things."

"Flour and water," Grandma said. "It suited me, in my day. And your mother too, in *her* day."

She sighed then and smiled at them to forgive them for buying paste. Then she went back into the kitchen.

Grandma must be very old, Teena thought. It must have been sad to have to make paste when you can buy it at Woolworth's. I wonder if Daddy, when he was little in England, had flour and water paste?

Lots of people die, Teena said calmly to herself as she smoothed the blue iris into position at the back of her social studies book. She flipped the pages, looking at the project she had made about Australia. There was a picture she had pasted in of Sydney at night labeled Kings Cross Sydney.

"Kings Cross," she murmured. "Kings Cross. Would you like to be a king, Sonny?"

Sonny did not answer. He was not interested. Teena turned the pages of her book and pointed to the picture of a church and the words beneath it, "That kings for such a tomb would wish to die." What did it mean?

She did not know what it meant, she did not really care either, and she felt suddenly tired and cheated, and thrusting out her arm she tipped over the pot of paste on to her bed, all over her project and Sonny's ships, and Sonny began to cry.

"Mum," he called. "Come an' see what Teena did. Look what Teena did! Deliberately." Sonny relished the word. It was a word that brought certain punishment. Deliberately.

"My arm slipped," Teena said when their mother, indulgent because their father was dead, came at Sonny's call. "Truly. My arm slipped."

She rejoiced inside when her mother said, "Never mind. Don't tell tales, Sonny. Be good children. Be good because ..."

"I know why," Sonny said. "Because Daddy's dead."

Beatrice took them both in her arms and began to cry, and Teena, feeling a sudden wild unhappiness, moved her arm again, accidentally on purpose, tipping the remainder of the paste over the bed and Sonny's pictures and her Australian project. There, she said inside herself. There. *It serves it right.*

6 A DAY CROWDED WITH TALKING, PLANNING, coming and going, with scarcely time to take up grief like a new piece of embroidery, to work designs in it, match or contrast colors, see what use it could be put to when it was finished, who might welcome it as a present or if it would be more suitable for draping at home, constantly in view! Such a day left everyone in the Rainbird household exhausted. Dad and Mum Muldrew almost unable to keep awake after their midnight journey and bustling day had gone to bed early. The children were now fast asleep, and when Beatrice looked in at them she noticed how much their sleep resembled the happy oblivion that might have told of a hot summer's day at the beach—sightseeing, picnicking, bathing. When the energy was spent and sleep came at last who could tell whether the time had been used in grieving or loving or playing? Who could say, This is the aftermath of death and grief, Beatrice thought, as she brushed the clinging tiredness from her forehead.

She sat by the fire, the two-bar electric fire in the kitchen. She had just decided she would go to bed when the phone rang. She went to the hall and lifted the receiver. I'm standing in the *hall*, she thought. In Matuatangi I would have said *passage*. Why have I changed my name for it? Who has changed it? Why has everything changed? Why are words so different? Where is Dr. Findling, where are the girls at the Town Hall Dance, the old women in the Evening Star home?

"Hello."

"Mrs. Rainbird? A call from London."

She gasped. "London?"

"London. Rainbird calling. I'll put you through."

London. Direct. She had thought you would have to fight your way through wires as through a barbed wire entanglement to get to London!

"Hello."

"Hello. Is that Mrs. Rainbird? Beatrice? I got your cable. You know how I feel for you."

"Lynley?"

"Yes. How clear your voice is! I'm taking the plane today."

"The plane?"

"The plane. It leaves at noon. You're ahead of us."

"Godfrey's dead."

"I'll be in Dunedin for the funeral."

When Beatrice sent the cable she had mentioned the time of the funeral because she could think of little else to say.

"I'm emigrating, Bea, coming out for good."

Beatrice had a feeling of shock, of being threatened. How old was Lynley? She tried to remember.

"Godfrey was all I had."

"Emigrating?"

"Keep up your courage Bea. See you on Wednesday."

Silence. Then the click-clicking noise that telephone wires make when they are recovering from a transmitted conversation. Bea! I've never been called that in my life, Beatrice thought. Lynley emigrating! It seemed an insult to Godfrey. Why emigrate when he was dead? How ridiculous to end a phone call from London with the words, See you on Wednesday! Perhaps these English people had an obsession about funerals, Beatrice thought, reverting to her early suspicions about "foreigners." These English, she thought. I wonder where Lynley is finding the money to emigrate. What is she going to do? Where is she going to stay?

34

I've never met her! She can't be arriving so soon, not on Wednesday.

Beatrice leaned her head in her hands and began to cry. After all this, after the accident, and seeing Godfrey, and meeting Mum and Dad at the station, getting a taxi at that hour with the taximen ignoring them, they were all alike those taxi-drivers, they had got worse too, and then getting home and all the bother of baking the fruitcake, three hours, no three and a half hours in the oven and not daring to look at it because she'd been taught that if you looked at a cake it became bashful or despairing or something and sank to the bottom of the tin; and then Dad Muldrew wanting the morning paper sewn together so that he could read it properly—he was always so pernickety about the paper, and reading out the Death Notice, Overseas paper please copy, North Island papers please copy, and not knowing why she had said that, for what did Overseas or the North Island care and what was the North Island anyway but a colony of the Mainland . . . and then to have Lynley telephoning, sounding as if she talked from the next room; Lynley emigrating, flying, See you Wednesday. Forty-eight was no age to settle in a new country. (Here Beatrice grasped her own age, her youthful thirty-two, so carefully in her hands as if it were a precious golden bowl.) Lynley's letters had always been impersonal notes, not revealing many details of her life. At birthdays and Christmas her greetings and their neat italic handwriting had a medieval appearance as if she wrote from a convent, yet she had been living in a house in Hampstead, near the Heath, since she sold the home in Camden Town. But what is that to me? Beatrice thought jealously, knowing that Lynley and Godfrey had known Hampstead Heath. It's only a name, she told herself. Heaths, moors, commons, downs, fells, fields, they're not part of my life.

She stood up, patted her hair into place, blew her nose and made herself ready to face the night—the bedroom and the lonely double bed. She wished now that she had let Mum and

Dad Muldrew sleep in her room. She had made the bed, putting the usual number of pillows, but she had hidden Godfrey's clothes and his dressing gown and slippers and his hairbrush with the strands of dark hair clinging to it, and his shaving gear; and yet, removing them she had felt guilty as if Godfrey watched her as in one of those plays where the ghost appears to the guilty, Ah! Removing all trace of me so soon?

Oh, she did not know what to do! She could not imagine his death. She felt as if she had committed a crime in agreeing to the arrangements made to bury him. If only burial were not such a hasty process, if only he could have lain embalmed, yet not so bound or stopped as to be unable to spring to life if life were suddenly restored to him. If only he could have been kept "by" as part of the family, to let everyone grow used to his death, even to draw sustenance from it! Oh, the ancient peoples knew what they were about when they allowed the dead to be a part of living and the living to take their full part in dying and death! This hasty dispatch was unseemly, a Christian urge to put the dead out of sight, concealing the body while pretending one could draw comfort from the hovering immortal soul when the only comfort was that of improved hygiene!

Beatrice lay on her side of the bed in the attitude of a corpse, almost as if to entice Godfrey to return, as if to say, See, I am like this also. She felt that this pose relaxed her. She breathed deeply, shut her eyes, knitting her brows against the oppression of the day's events and thoughts. After nine years she was alone again, a wounding slice cut from her life; and now she must wait for the edges to draw together to heal as if the nine years had never been; yet that would not be so; the edges would not fit; one rejected the other as the body rejects a foreign substance; nine years ago and today were not of the same pattern or direction of growth; if she tried to draw them together as if the nine years had never been, her life would be cobbled, unsightly; yet if she kept the years, perhaps she could use the memory of them as a—

golden mushroom?—to carry the darning thread from one edge of her life to the other, completing a harmonious pattern?

With the thoughts of the golden mushroom, of princes, of fascinating young men, of hates in George Street and Princes Street and Matuatangi High School, of Miss Hendry who had vanished almost like an ingredient that disintegrates when it is used, of Mum and Dad Muldrew, of North Island papers please copy, of Sonny and Teena, of how life would seem after the funeral when, as if it were not Godfrey's death that was being mourned now, his death would come *home* to her when all was quiet and the loud exclamations of sympathy were over and people forgot Godfrey's death to return to their own death and their ways of avoiding it—other deaths, other sensations, other pleasures—the Easter Holidays, the television, the Forbury Trots . . . with all thoughts sharpened by the pervading thought of Godfrey, Beatrice tried to go to sleep but her thoughts encircled sleep, and, a prisoner of waking, she was forced to scale the high wall of that waking, to meet and feel, before she could escape, the separate pinnacles of sharp glass that were the thought of Godfrey's death.

At last she slept deeply, waking once only when she put her hand under the sheet to Godfrey's side of the bed and felt, her hand spread flat, the cold lack, the unattended level and chill of his absence. Her skin ached all over to touch his skin as if he and she had been worms or plants that breathe and feel and survive through their skin. Then she withdrew her hand, made a fist of it, and thrust it with the other, fist to fist against her cheek, turned facing the wall, away from Godfrey's side of the bed, and slept.

7

GULLS WITH WINGS OF ICE BEAT DOWN UPON HIM, their red feet flashing like rubies, their claws grasping rubies that reflected a red-and-green world, a light-and-dark world; tundra— "a barren arctic region where the subsoil is frozen." Oil and mud; and the reclaimed land fighting against its reclamation crying, Who owns me? Who is first owner, where is the origin of the dispute of possession?

He thought, I'll move the television to another room for the winter. Winter in New Zealand is not as it used to be at home. Home? This reclaimed land that I never claimed yet am given a share of, here where a factory is to be built, and garages, cemeteries for secondhand and dead cars, already the flags are flying green and blue and yellow in a festival of cars and the smell of oil lingers on the reclaimed land. Soon the tankers will creep up the harbor, outsized saucepan containers will appear around the dear blue bays, our feet will be stained black where the oil and mud flow and the sinus in our head will be white as cream, common with the common cold; people die.

Then the doors swung to and fro. They were iron with a lucky horseshoe nailed upon one, the shoe from Lucky Lady or Delphinium, both winners of the Saturday double; all those photographs in the newspapers of the country's distinguished people, the breeders, breeders of Lucky Lady, Delphinium, Peter's Oracle: stout women in costumes and hats, with preserved faces: famous breeders.

38

His head raced with its hoofs flying, tipped with pain. Pain hammered like a horseshoe into the iron door that swung open and shut while the Wildlife Program, the giraffes grazed in his eyes, crossing the screen, in peace, making patterns in the tall golden grass.

And then he wondered, Who will reclaim me? My mother lies dead in Balham Tube Station beside three hundred others, a light brigade in the dark, never found or claimed or reclaimed. Oh, Lucky Dunedin Harbor, lucky water at the mouth of the peninsula, Oh, lucky water, Lucky Lady, Peter's Oracle, Delphinium, Larkspur, spur to the racing horses and the head, spur of iron, iron door, great iron door swinging to and fro the claim at last set, arranged, like the world within the ruby.

He fought off the seagulls but they crowded his face, cleaving wings of ice. A larkspur, a delphinium grew tall, alone, deep blue upon the reclaimed land. It was not fair, to die. How could anyone die without reclaiming life while there was still time?

He lay in a deathlike coma for thirty-six hours. When at last he opened his eyes the fact that he made personal and local history was overshadowed by the immediate fact of the shrieks and faints that afflicted the attendants in the hospital mortuary, and the disruption of routine, temper, credulity, and reputation in the hospital itself. It appeared that only Godfrey could afford to be jubilant at such a time, but even his joy was diminished by his exhaustion and confusion, the pain of the wound in his cheek, and the shock of identifying his surroundings.

Ten o'clock Tuesday morning. Morning teatime. An inconvenient time in any institution. Fifteen minutes before Godfrey's preparation to go home. Not understanding why suddenly he should be pronounced alive with as much certainty and ceremony as if he were being pronounced dead, Godfrey followed the example of the mortuary attendants and fainted.

When he woke again he was in bed in a hospital ward. He

was content to imagine that the bed was a white surfboard floating gently on inland waters while he lay in peace on it looking up at the sun and the sky. He felt a stillness in his body as if it had been hushed by an agent whose orders, seldom given, were obeyed under the penalty of—death?

He lay still, feeling warmth awakening in his body, wondering where this warmth had been that it should waken only now and be different from the warmth he imagined (for he could not remember) that he had known before. Before what and when? Then with great effort, as if he hauled two stones from the mouth of an unfathomable cave, he lifted his arms; then freeing himself from the two iron cannonballs that pinned him on either side he moved his legs; then, blowing away the bubbles of snow from his lips he tried to speak and did speak, whispering, asking what had happened, and they answered again and again that he'd been in an accident.

"I must go home," he said. "I promised not to be late."

People with looks of horror on their faces kept coming to his bed and staring at him. Why? And why did men in long white coats form a semicircle about him, inclining their heads, not speaking, their eyes filled with horror and disbelief? Too exhausted almost to breathe or move Godfrey could accept only one thought at a time and then his thoughts had not their usual coherent form; they kept crumbling, as if they had been long in storage and exposed to decay.

It seemed as if someone were delivering to him, under the door of his mind, as a postman slips mail under the door, a special thought in a foreign language with a foreign postmark that he could not translate, not knowing the grammar, the syntax, the vocabulary, nor even the common phrases of the language— please, thank you, hello, good-bye. Will you kindly show me the way?—that are stock passports from strangeness. Taking up this special thought he slit it open to extract the essence of it and was alarmed to find that the essence had disappeared. The

40

thought was delivered again. He approached it with more cunning, like a fisherman surprising a fish, reeling it in, seizing it, killing it, plunging his hand in at once to clean and gut it. Again his hand took hold of nothing. Why?

Then rejecting all incoming thought he gave his time to the awareness of his body, sensing that the blood seemed to be flowing in its usual reassuring way, that the lymph in its marshy world wandered at its sluggish pace while the swiftly streaming blood coursed to shallow places to drop into the chamber-tunnels of his heart; that somewhere, at intervals, a phagocyte with bulging mouth crept through vessel walls to digest its meal. He could feel the message of warmth circulating in his body, being taken up, developed, strengthened, like a rumor; he could feel it trying to melt clusters of icicles while his blood assisted by roaring upon them as if they were particles of steel in the grip of a foundry furnace.

"What happened?" he asked again.

"An accident," they told him. All had the same look of horror and curiosity as if to say, Tell us, tell us everything you know that we may be able to face it. We are desperate to know!

The inquisiting eyes were sharp. They dug like needles into his mind, trying to withdraw the desired thread.

And then when a nurse came to tell him that his wife would be with him soon, and urged him to be calm for it had been a great shock to everyone, he felt that at last he knew what had happened. The thing that many dread and some must suffer had come to him. He'd been in an accident where his face had been disfigured: this explained the frightened gaze of those who dared to let their eyes look into his. He moved his hands across his face, touching the wound there, wondering why they had not given him a mirror when they washed him. Was he a faceless man? He had read about such men, how many that had been afflicted during the war now crept about in darkness, turning their face away so as not to terrify. Some, he had read, wore masks that were unexpectedly torn from their faces to reveal their deformities in blazing light. Others had new skin grafted to their face, had become patchwork indentities.

Why, he wondered, was the light dimmed above his head? Why were the curtains drawn?

He moved his hand again slowly over his face. The injuries, he thought, must be frightful yet I cannot feel them. Here was a nurse passing his bed, peeping through the curtains, staring with that look of fear. Why?

He whispered to her. "Nurse, have you a mirror?"

She looked shocked. "A mirror?"

Then she smiled. "Oh, a mirror. I'll get one."

How brave she was, he thought. She returned at once with a large handmirror which she held in front of him and though she was smiling the horrified, curious look did not leave her face.

"Making yourself pretty for your wife?"

He shut his eyes, opened them, and stared at his face. He could recognize it. It was *his face*. He felt the pure bliss of ownership. No one had sewn borrowed skin on him. There was no disfigurement apart from the strip of bandaid on his left cheek. There was nothing to explain the strange behavior of those around him.

He smiled at his face and his face smiled back at him.

"Oh!" the nurse cried suddenly, and snatching the mirror from him, she fled.

Why?

A moment or two later she returned, trying to smile. "I'm sorry Mr. Rainbird, but it's all been so unexpected and you see, I was in Casualty when they brought you in. I have to get used to it, that's all; I have to get used to it."

"There was an accident?"

She looked doubtful. "Do you remember?"

"Yes, there must have been an accident. I must get home. Beatrice, the children . . ."

42

He plunged suddenly, sliding downhill, into memories of Beatrice and the children. He sighed, shut his eyes, heard from far away the nurse saying, "Your wife is coming to see you. Naturally it has been a shock to her."

"Have I been unconscious long?"

"No . . . No."

"I think I must have dreamed the Wildlife Program. On Safari. I can't remember much of what happened."

He slept, and when he woke again he heard the murmur of voices, the rustle of paper. Something dropped from the bed next to him and rolled under his bed. He wondered what it was. He felt rested. He had not had such a deep drifting sleep since he was a child; yet unlike then, when his parents came and went about the house, when he slept deeply yet knew without waking that doors were opening and shutting, people were talking, cars were starting in the street, the Underground was rocketing every few minutes beneath the house, this recent sleep had been strangely unattended. No one came or went. No trains whistled, cars started, no planes throbbed overhead; no one had cared. His sleep had been that of one whom the world has deserted, abandoned alone on the plains under a sky empty but for the hovering waiting birds of prey. He had seen their shadow cast over his body. Or had the shadow been in the Wildlife Program? On Safari. The Hooded Buzzard—had he been sleeping inside a television? No wonder the children had such dreams at night! The children!

"Excuse me."

A woman with a hat like a latticed veranda stooped to pick up an orange from under his bed and as she returned to the patient in the next bed she gave Godfrey a swift horrified glance that made his bones go chill and the tips of his fingers and toes set like ice. He knew his face had gone pale. Why had she looked at him in that way? What was the mystery surrounding him?

8

LYNLEY HAD ALWAYS ENJOYED LOOKING AFTER her boarders in Camden Town. She was happy knowing they were fond of her and as some women do who never marry she had grown into a teasing relationship with each man, exchanging harmless jokes and references in a tone that implied he and she were being very wicked and daring when in fact their references and jokes were as harmless as milk without its strontium 90. With this habit of jocularity she acquired a permanent jauntiness that was mistaken for natural cheerfulness. A cheerful soul, Miss Rainbird, was the general verdict. A good housekeeper, cook, receiver of confidences: a "good sort." When she sold the home in Camden Town and became housekeeper for old Daniel Wandling, she missed her three young men, and yet when in response to their invitation to "come round and see us once in a while for old time's sake" she did at last go to visit them, they spent an embarrassing evening. There was no time to regain the old jocularity; and without the jokes and veiled references Lynley found she had little to say; she sat stiffly in her armchair in the front room while Jack, Henry, and Hilary served tea, Hilary pouring out because he was adept at such things; all very comfortable and homely but there was nothing to say. Lynley looked primly at them. They were men, they were strangers, something had diverted the path from her to them; they were out of her reach. With a slight flush in her cheeks and a haughty expression in her

44

eyes she stared them up and down, feeling safe yet stranded in her distance from them—as if she wore chafing gloves while she forked and weeded among the gross earth of the human garden: Jack, Henry, Hilary.

"It was a lovely evening," she said, as she was leaving. And in a way it had been for despite her silence and her embarrassment she had felt in herself a simplicity she had not known before as if for the first time with Jack Henry and Hilary she had worn instead of the cluttered cumbersome jewelry of false jokes and smiles, a single string of best pearls: her own pearls. Oh, Jack, Henry and Hilary had not noticed them but they were her own pearls and they shone in the light and no one would ever penetrate their opaque secrecy and loveliness.

She did not go again to visit Jack Henry and Hilary, and her manner changed toward old Daniel Wandling. Where before she lost patience with him now she accepted his complaining and once when he asked her, as people sometimes did, Why have you never married, Lynley?, she did not as before smile mysteriously as if to say, Ah, I'm not telling but maybe there's a man in my life! Instead, she answered directly, "The opportunity has never come my way, and it's too late now."

And when Daniel Wandling protested, "Oh, no, it's not too late, Lynley," she did not blush and murmur, conceding, "Perhaps not; oh well; maybe some time. . . ."

Again she said directly, "Yes, it's too late. I don't care to be married now."

And Daniel Wandling believed her for she spoke the truth, she was satisfied to live her life alone. Wearing gloves one at least escaped the thorns in the roses and the sting of the flying insects; one was less healed, renewed, strengthened; one was also less harmed. One sacrificed the roses—though often, from a distance, their scent came blowing through the door that in spite of all protests the wind of desire kept pushing open. Besides, there were

45

people to care for—Daniel Wandling, and Godfrey out in New Zealand with his wife and family. His daughter Christina was taking after him, Godfrey had said in a letter.

Christina. An attractive name. Lynley planned to go to New Zealand when old Daniel Wandling died and left her that legacy for a lifetime. She had told him so, for he had asked her and there had been no pretense about his dying; she had wished, guiltily, that he would go on dying for ever; the arrangement was so peaceful and she was not anxious to get the legacy and Daniel Wandling's son and daughter knew about it and were generous in their feelings, not because generosity was their characteristic but because they could afford to feel generous. So when Daniel Wandling died, Lynley began to receive her allowance (far more than her salary while he lived), and at the son's request she stayed for two years with the Wandling household, postponing her visit to New Zealand.

It was the cable with news of Godfrey's death that forced her to decide and act. There was no time to think of Godfrey's death as a death. There were too many plans to make, a seat to book on the plane, travel documents to collect, luggage to pack, all in an exhausting urgency in which any feelings of shock and grief were bundled confusedly into her heart, her suitcases, her handbag, between the veined pages of her passport and in her passport photograph which alone could not conceal them. Who was that woman staring out at her with a face blurred with tears or too sudden exposure and a neck wrinkled like a cabbage leaf?

Then there was the phone call to Dunedin and hearing Beatrice speak, and wondering about her and the children and why she hadn't given more details of Godfrey's death, for Godfrey, a little boy crying in the rain of the Trossachs, had died, and all this coming and going and paying and signing and being photographed and buying new clothes (yes, even buying new clothes to travel in and being excited and afraid at the thought of the new life), all had been prompted by Godfrey's death. And

46

Lynley had had experience in death! Here she knew a feeling of triumph over Beatrice, for no experience Beatrice had known in New Zealand would have taught her as much as Lynley knew about dying and being buried, and not only conventional death, but sudden ghastly explosions of bombs, mass killing and mass burial; and then there'd been this past slow, quiet inevitable death of an old man who'd not loved life or people with much passion and whom few in their turn had known or cared for. Lynley felt superior in all her knowledge and prepared with the condescension of one sixteen years older to teach Beatrice what she had learned. She knew an excited anticipation followed by guilt, for Godfrey was dead, and his death should have lain a dark numbing hand on such feelings of pleasure; yet without his death she might not have decided to go to New Zealand, she might never have been as she was now, posing as a seasoned traveler ready to step aboard the Boeing 707 and fly nonstop to Christchurch, New Zealand, and from there to Dunedin Airport and to the terminal, to Fleet Drive, Andersons Bay. They say there's so much room in New Zealand, she thought.

She looked out of her window from the spacious fog-shrouded Hampstead Heath to the cramped crowded buildings of London with its millions of people thrust together like lice on a penny, and she thought of the acres of grass and mountains and lakes and rivers, the sheer abundance of room that awaited her in New Zealand, and she shivered with eagerness to enjoy her new life. Then her guilt returned. She was flying to New Zealand to see Godfrey before he was buried. How strange it would be to arrive and find him gone, to know that moment after moment beneath all that Antipodean Room his body would be decaying, mingling with the dust of the Room, so that if she met a speck of dust on the side of the road she would never know how close it had been to Godfrey, or if it had *been* Godfrey, or if she picked a wheatstalk from the fields and found earth clinging to the stalk, she would never know, and if she

47

climbed one of the high mountains she had read about, and grasped a clod of snow wrapped in earth, nothing could tell her if it had touched or lain close to Godfrey. She would never know how to recognize and claim his dust. She, his nearest relative, nearer than his wife—sharing the same bed was nothing to sharing the same womb—might not even recognize his dead body, for he would have changed, he would have (she thought with sudden anger) *dared* to change.

Her reason told her then, icily, that she was no longer Godfrey's nearest relative, for the law spoke of beds, not of wombs. Yet she *mattered*, and the matter was blood. She would make Beatrice realize this, that as Godfrey's only sister she had come to exercise her right to preside over his burial.

At half-past twelve, then, on the second Monday in March Lynley boarded the plane for New Zealand. She wore her official matronly uniform—a pleated Dacron skirt and white blouse: best dress and pearls were judged not to be "coping" material for a first flight of twelve thousand miles. It was one of the first spring days of the season. A warm current of wind blew from the newly opened store of spring, the grass in the fields shone with a glossy new coat, and the trees were tipped with light green buds. The plane made a perfect takeoff, one moment squatting back on its wings like a bird paralyzed with fear, the next moment, with a scream that no bird ever made, disappearing beyond the layers of cloud toward New York, San Francisco, Honolulu, Fiji, Christchurch, with a day to be lost in flight, dropped between the horizon and the sky where only the sun could follow to probe for it with bleeding fingers; now or never up so close to the sun and the birthplace of day and light and time one must think of these things; but one does not think of these things, one chevies a slab of wet fish with a fork, and begins to eat, trying not to remember the difficulty in following the Safety Directions printed in five languages or to think of the emergency oxygen hidden in the

48

light-panel above the seat, and of what might happen were the doors and windows to fly open and the passengers be sucked out into the sky; for encircling all with a devilish boundary that exercises more magical power in the unfamiliar element of sky is the imperative, *Imagine.*

Lynley was tired. She slept, waking from time to time to observe and marvel at the nonchalance of her fellow passengers. Waking, she remembered that Godfrey was dead, and it did not seem to matter that he was dead. She wondered if all these years she had cared for and loved a dead person, as the mallard ducks when their ducklings are taken from them may care for and keep warm a block of wood or a stone, their maternal love blinding them to the difference between the living and the dead. She began to regret not having said good-bye to Jack, Henry, Hilary. And she dreamed of old Daniel Wandling in his silk dressing gown, sitting in his bedchair in the room that overlooked the Heath. The Heath, he complained, is not what it used to be. The sheep were legends. Did Lynley understand?

Yes, Lynley had said, she understood. But she did not care for "nature." She preferred asphalt and concrete to earth and often wondered why others did not share her views. She was sure that though there might be more earth than concrete in New Zealand she would have no difficulty in indulging her preference, on wet days at least; living was inconvenient enough without allowing it to be ruled by wet earth. She hoped that with all the "uncovered earth" in New Zealand there would not be too much rain, not as there had been in the Trossachs when Godfrey had been put in her care. What a dull aching mist-ridden time it had been, with news, bad news wreathing the hills as ceaselessly as the mist. Mother dead. The flying bombs like giant cigars in the sky thrust with lethal aim from the mouth of some malignant God; and then there was Churchill sucking his cigar and not seeming to know how it resembled a torpedo or flying bomb; an explosive man, Churchill, muddled but modern in his mythology, siren-suited with word music that certainly lured the enemy to destruction.

The enemy? The enemy wanting "living-room" for his superior race? Oh, but there was so much room in New Zealand, Lynley thought again. There, she thought, there will be a special kind of room for me, for I dream now in the spacious sky that I've never had room in my life, that perhaps my life may be accounted a failure because I never had room to breathe, move, grow, love. It's too late to find in my life the necessary "early" room, the kind that children possess or that Adam and Eve knew in the Garden of Eden; but perhaps I may yet find "late" room. It may be Godfrey's legacy to me that when I supervise his burial in the contracted room allotted to him I may be able to take both his and my space to make up for what I never had. I shall see him buried with appropriate dignity and ritual as we never saw our mother buried. His grave shall be refined, private, impenetrable and no tourists arriving ten years later to hear recounted the history of his death and burial and no accidental discovery by County Council workmen digging drains, repairing gas mains, laying sewers, of his uncertainly identified bones.

And so Lynley is in the sky close to the imagined heaven source of light, the Boeing 707 conferring on her for a time the supposed privileges of the dead.

9 BEATRICE, TIRED ON HER TUESDAY WAKING, IS finding the presence of Mum and Dad Muldrew a strain. Dad Muldrew inserting himself like a driven screw into Godfrey's "place" by the fire and at the table, talks now in a more commanding tone, usurping Mum Muldrew's role of settling arguments about whether the clock is fast or slow, what time the milkman came, who muddied and ruffled the morning paper, was Labor Day last year wet or fine, when is Easter, what did we have for dinner when the Stevensons came, both the first course and the pudding, has the coal bill been paid, where shall we spend Christmas, when shall we be able to go for that long-planned holiday to Australia?

Mum Muldrew is placid, consoling, so different from her usual self. This Tuesday morning she is being an oldfashioned grandmother to the children, playing Snakes and Ladders with them and not heeding Beatrice's superior remark, No one these days plays Snakes and Ladders; entering the fun of the game and distributing from time to time the windfall apples brought from Matuatangi that taste of scent and trainsmoke. Mum Muldrew peels them, cuts out the core, makes quarter-boats that rock when put on the table, rowed by two brown polished pips. Usually the children eat their apples whole. Is it because their father is dead, Teena wonders, that Grandma is peeling their apples?

And when they are tired of Snakes and Ladders there's a pirate game with numbered squares and colored counters, TV pirates that board ships, find treasure, are trapped in caves, rescued, captured, rescued, and in the end allowed to go Home to a square so small you might wonder if there were room; such a small blank square without furniture or fire or mother and father, but it's a part of every game and everyone has to get there, and that's the meaning of the game, First Home Wins.

And now Teena gives a delighted cry as she promotes her red counter to the skimped square that hardly allows room for her counter to get in. "I'm home, I'm home, I've won!"

Even Grandma Muldrew is pleased. Everyone looks with admiration and envy.

"Teena is home!"

Teena, blushing with pride, presses her red counter within the four walls of the safest place she knows where alone, before the others with their green and yellow counters come rushing in to disturb and overcrowd her possession, she may enjoy sovereignty of her kingdom.

Outside the weather is chilly with fog though the sun may appear later and the sky turn blue but there'll be no swimming in the sea, no visit to the Portobello Aquarium, no bus ride to see the peacocks at Glenfalloch or the carvings of bats and dragons at Larnach's Castle. Soon everyone is Home, then all are out in the wilderness again, threatened with capture, captured, rescued, then Home again, and no one seems to tire of playing. It is as if the children recognize a propriety about the table-games that makes them suitable for playing by children whose father is dead; just as it is suitable for their grandmother to peel and core their apples into boat-shapes, for their mother to make them an orange Jell-o with slices of banana in it, eaten with cream on top, not whipped cream for that would be too like a feast, but thin trickles poured from the top of the jug around and about the hills and valleys of Jell-o, like mild white streams set to flow on beds of golden glass.

10

A NURSE CAME, DRAWING ASIDE THE CURTAIN. "YOUR wife is here," she said.

Beatrice bent over him, her golden hair brushing against his face, her shoulders moving with sobs though her eyes were dry and bright. She clung to him, breathing quickly, her face flushing. He could feel the warmth of her body, so different from his own newly acquired unfamiliar warmth; it seemed as if her skin had grown fur. He felt naked, unproviding; should a storm come with snow and ice he would be unable to house them both.

She sat back, upright against the hard bars of the hospital visiting chair. She clasped her hands and combining a smile with a frown of unshed tears she whispered, glancing quickly about her as if talking to him were a shameful practice, "Mum and Dad Muldrew are here."

"Here?"

"I mean at home. And Lynley's coming."

"Lynley? Quite a family party!"

She did not return his smile. "Yes, by plane, tomorrow at twelve. The children are terribly confused, poor things—but so excited! And the phone's been ringing and ringing since the news came about you.

A blissful thought came to Godfrey, the kind of thought he would have rejected, normally, for its futility, exaggerated fantasy and grandiose expectations—He, Godfrey Rainbird had in some way played the role of Hero. He had saved a life, perhaps dragged

53

someone from behind the wheel of a burning car or from that stretch of sea near the reclaimed land. He was a hero. The horrified glances everyone had given him were to be interpreted as, Thank God it was you and not I who risked death to save another's life. The marvel is that you are alive.

"It's a marvel that you are alive," Beatrice said, confirming his dream. "Though the television people have heard about it already."

And why not? Godfrey thought. This may be the opportunity I've waited for. Mr. Galbraith at the Tourist Office might welcome the publicity. Everyone will be interested to know that the young man who advises on tours of the North Island and the Southern Lakes has lived dangerously, had wide experience of life and almost of death.

Yet Godfrey still did not know what had happened and no one seemed willing to tell him. "Have I been very ill?" he asked and was startled to see the look of horror in Beatrice's eyes.

She spoke shrilly, leaning forward and clutching him. "*Ill?*"

Then she sat back calmly in the chair. "*Ill?* You were dead! Are you listening? Your funeral . . ."

She stopped speaking and began to tremble.

What about his funeral? he wondered. He must have been very close to death for them to start thinking about his funeral. What a joke! Well he hadn't been quite close enough, just not close enough!

"Are you listening, Godfrey? I know it's been frightful for you. I mean if you . . ."

He was modest. "It's over now. Let's forget it."

Her horrified glance returned. Her voice became shrill. "*Forget it?* How can we ever forget it? You've been *dead!*"

"But only figuratively speaking."

She recoiled from him as if he were a corpse. "*Dead!*"

"You mean *dead?*"

"*Pronounced dead.*"

How fearful, irrevocable pronouncements were! The Air Ministry has made a pronouncement. The War Office. Pronouncements, Bulletins, the details of the raids; the casualties; all the official words webbing themselves about the idea of *pronounced death*. That was that. Dead. No further words to waste or web.

Beatrice bent over him and kissed him. He did not respond to her kiss. He had been dead. He had heard of people who were able to say, Everything is changed, nothing will ever be the same. He had been skeptical about this lamentation that was also a secret hope for too often nothing changed, all remained the same, but how could anything remain, different or the same, after you had been *pronounced dead*?

The pronouncement of death would cling to him, close as his skin, while his heart persisted in its beating.

"You haven't heard what I said, Godfrey."

"I'm sorry, Beatrice," he said calmly, plunging the barrier like a thin sheet of unbreakable glass between them. He smiled.

Her voice was happy. "Oh, Godfrey you're your old self again! I knew it as soon as I saw that smile! They say there's not a thing wrong with you now, that you can come home—tomorrow if you like—and rest there. Lazybones! You could come with me now, I'm sure, if I asked, only . . ."

"Only what?"

She frowned. "I have to prepare the house. I mean . . ."

She burst into tears. "It's terrible. You'll never forgive me. I sent your clothes to Corso this morning. There was a special collection—oh, please understand, Godfrey, I couldn't bear to see your clothes, knowing—you're not angry, Godfrey? You understand?"

"No, I'm not angry. Of course not."

"You understand?"

"Yes, I understand."

"I've brought some mints. Isn't that silly? Have one?"

"No, thanks. My new suit, and those new shoes?"

55

"Not your shoes. The suit, yes—well you'd been *in* it, Godfrey!"

"The coat as well as the trousers?"

"The whole suit. Oh, Godfrey isn't it awful? But you're here again. Everything was so—so . . ."

"Changed?"

"Yes, changed."

Godfrey looked secretive. "In what way has everything changed?"

"Oh, that was *then*. This is now. It's the same now . . . only when that happens you have to set to work to make so many changes; it takes control of you, directs you."

"*It?*"

"What they said about you. The pronouncement."

Godfrey wanted to shout, You mean my death, *my death*?

"We'll soon be back to our old life, Godfrey, and rid of this nightmare. I told you Lynley's coming tomorrow?"

"Yes, you told me. Does she know?"

"She knows about *that*, but not about *this*. I'll cable her en route. The papers had something about it, you know, and I told you about the TV people."

A bell rang in the ward.

"With Mum and Dad Muldrew to help we'll soon have things as they were and you'll be home again. We will, Godfrey! I've read of this sort of thing happening in olden times."

Olden times! What romantic dream, Godfrey wondered, was Beatrice trying to recreate from the facts. He had been pronounced dead, almost made ready for burial, had awakened, and was now giving himself and his family (and the hospital authorities) the practical and emotional inconvenience of an arduous exercise in an extreme form of adaptability. It was not only his best suit (the coat as well as the trousers!) that they'd given away to the door-to-door collectors. Other collectors, other scavengers were at work ceaselessly inside the human heart and mind

56

ready to snatch what had been cast away—the concerns of the dead having become an embarrassment to the living. If it were not too late the Corso collector could be phoned and the suit recovered but it was likely that a different suit would be returned, one that would not fit. There'd be little hope of finding what had been thrown to the Invisible scavengers, for those who'd worn it close to their heart might not be able to identify it. What had Beatrice given to these secret scavengers, Godfrey wondered, as from the dividing distance of his time spent dead he watched her pick up her handbag, put the untouched bag of Minties on his locker, kiss him good-bye and promising to come for him the next day, join the group of visitors leaving the ward.

Coughs good-byes oranges rolling beneath those high beds with their special levers and attachments then whispers, the day's human reckoning, profit or loss, and silence as the ward settled down to pursue its illnesses, striking them intensely, like the ringing of iron into each detail of the inflexible routine, while Godfrey lay, the ward marvel and monster, trying to remember what had happened and when the effort failed, trying to set out his experiences and touch each one as if wandlike to restore life to it, as a child strikes or embraces others when he himself has been struck or embraced. Then finding the effort of memory too great, he swept all the arrayed treasures and totems from his mind and was left with a gray void like a huge waste of pumice that received on its porous surface the simpler details falling like rain about him—the light, the time, the bowl of egg custard, the polished linoleum on the floor.

The doctor making his rounds stopped in front of Godfrey's bed. "How's our miracle today? What's it like to be alive again, eh? You lucky so-and-so!"

Godfrey detected the envious note in his voice, as if the doctor himself were not alive, yet how could that be, how could it be that one had to die, to be resuscitated, before one was alive?

"Well how's our miracle?"

Godfrey did not answer. He was thinking—a miracle certainly, bringing with it what is seldom mentioned about miracles—their inconvenience, the fact that even life may be resented if it disturbs the arrangements made for death and burial. Godfrey supposed that his coffin had been ready—plush, polished, not paid for. No bonfire or change of ownership would destroy it now. Going to bed each night he would climb into the dream of his coffin, sleep against its white satin, and waking in the morning, climb from it a resurrected corpse, pursued by the nightmarish comfort of his white satin world.

"Yes, you lucky bastard!" The doctor looked guiltily around him. He had been greatly daring.

"I'm fine," he said, as the doctor waited.

"You'll be home in a day or two when everything's ready for you so they tell me?"

They. Who were *they*? Why did the doctor not know at firsthand? Godfrey smiled and said nothing. He would need to clear a space in his mind, a retreat where he could try to remember and plan.

He felt confused, fearful, grateful. He learned to take in good humor the jokes being made about him by other patients who unable and untrained in their convention of feeling to face the horror of his experience, found relief in teasing him, stressing what they called "the lighter side," unwilling to realize that there was no "light side," that the cunningly evasive lanterns in their minds, heavily loaded with the event, projected through its darkness on to the ice-white sheet of death only what they could bear to see and laugh at. And as Godfrey lay accepting this uneasily jubilant mood of those around him, he was aware of a stray idea, some part of the retinue of his experience that had not yet come home to him as his guest. He did not know why it had been delayed. His mind was already overcrowded with the attending ideas. He could feel the stranger coming close, encircling him, waiting to get in. Then there was a storm in his eyes

58

and ears and head, and the idea broke in, and seeing it and recognizing it Godfrey gave a shriek that brought the staff nurse to his bedside and quelled the humorous byplay of the other patients. He gasped, breathed deeply, then smiled the kind of smile that, he suspected, would become in future his expressive uniform.

"The matter? I'm sorry I alarmed you. Nothing, nothing at all." His heart jerked and thudded against his ribs like a huge wave punishing the framework of a fragile ship. "Nothing at all."

"The smile, see! He's his old self, aren't you Mr. Rainbird?"

Under the blankets the sweat poured into his clenched fists, running in the groove of his life line, heart line, line of deceit, line of happiness.

The idea of burial alive. He'd read of men being buried alive through mine disaster, earthquake, avalanche, and he'd enjoyed sensing the pleasantly distant tumult of their experience. Yet his mother's death had been such a burial. The thought of it used to torment him as he looked up at the misty Trossachs and feared with his head spinning that the mountains would fall on him, might bury him in their playful avalanche as the collapsing building of the bombed station had buried his mother. That street and the underground station had been built by men. Men had cared for the street, patched its skin, in winter lit their charcoal braziers by its pavement, warming their hands before they mended a broken paving stone or gas pipe or water pipe; and beneath the innocent street that directed (as the label on the fairy-tale bottle said Drink Me) Walk On Me, the intestines of the city of Westminster lay, planned and nursed by men; and further below them the tube station and the railway lines; the white tiles seamed with soot; the hooded tunnels; the advertisements like New Age cave-paintings; bleak surroundings like the inside of a sooty skeleton, yet how much a blessing during the raids! How safe they said it was down there, with rugs and tea and people lying side by side, head to the tiles against, perhaps, a poster of Spain or a woman's legs and torso gripped by Berlei; each person sharing body warmth with his neighbor. All over London these dormitories of death had been arranged with the hope of escaping death and almost all escaped but Balham Tube Station. After the war Godfrey went one day to inspect the site of his mother's grave, the rebuilt station. Even the thought that the road had been repaired above where hundreds of bodies still lay buried did not rouse the horror that he felt now at *his* death and burial alive.

Burial alive. All men have known it in waking imagination and in dreams: the mounds of earth pressed upon the living body into mouth, eyes, ears, nose, over flesh, arms, and legs; pressing until a man's chest unable to rise in breathing, caves in, becomes a human cavern of darkness where he lies spinning yet immobile like a distantly viewed star. Death comes. The earth does not say to itself, It is all over, he is dead. Clod to clod does not say, We can rest now. The earth continues to press, waiting for the decay of the body, the withering of the flesh, with the pages of skin made more fragile until their writing of existence is erased and they fall apart; and then perhaps an eye explodes in the darkness, slipping like a jelly from its perfectly shaped bowl, and the tidal earth, flooding in, fills the bowl forces its way through it until earth touches earth; and finally when the body is a skeleton only, gaping in its barrenness and thingness, the earth quietly sets about breaking each bone, first into large pieces, then into smaller, then minutely to dust, to earth, until at last the meal the horrible digestion of death is completed and what was once a man in its turn allies itself to the weight of earth pressing down down upon the other dead, passing through the dead as through doorways, for ever pressing toward the fire, the true nest and depths of the earth, the crematorium of living.

"Mr. Rainbird, where's that smile again?"

That smile! His old self!

He could feel clearly the change wrought by his experience; he found he knew of his "old self," but could not remember what it had been, had thought, or known.

The depth of his new experience was something he himself could not gauge. He was like the manager of an oil company who, while supervising the sinking of the shafts, and pleased to contemplate the gusher in the sky when oil is struck, would never dream of sinking *himself* and emerging bathed and blackened in his precious oil. And like the manager who has faith in his ultimate discovery and moves from province to province bringing hope of prosperity to the settlers, so Godfrey felt that within his new experience he would move from point to point, shafting here, shafting there, to tap the wealth of meaning while taking care that it did not spurt out to engulf and suffocate him. His interest in tourism was suddenly diverted from geothermal power, big game fishing, tours of the Southern Lakes and Fiordland to the newly developing territory of himself and his death. He guessed that his experience might become a forbidden topic: was it not as embarrassing, impolite, unseemly to draw attention to one's private death as to one's private life? He hoped he might be able to talk to Beatrice. He would have to "pave the way," knowing that a paved way was not inviting if beforehand it had been strewn with his own wreaths.

"Everyone, now, will be too far away," he said aloud.

A nurse overheard him.

"Nonsense. This sort of thing happens every day. Always some poor devil thinking he's dead or about to die—that's worse, you know, for if you know you're going to die you have to think about it, but with you—why, you never knew a thing! It was instantaneous."

Instantaneous! Godfrey shuddered. When would it be realized that everything takes so much more time than people care to admit? Dying takes time. Living takes more time than is allotted to it. As for the meagre nine months associated with birth—a man and woman and child could testify how much longer it is than nine months.

"Yes," the nurse said. "You were lucky, I'll tell you that. A year ago we had a woman with only six months to live. They believe in letting them know if they're balanced enough. You have to be balanced."

"Balanced? The thought of death would unbalance anyone."

"Yes indeed. But we tell those people whom *life* does not unbalance."

"Oh?"

"This woman was calm. She said she'd be able to plan her six months like a budget, do the things she wanted to do, tidy her business affairs, perhaps go for a world tour."

"Did she?"

"Go on a world tour? No. But it would be hard to find someone happier than she was. She didn't want to die, she wept when they told her, but she recovered and had a wonderful six months." The nurse bent, whispering to Godfrey. "People will recover from anything even if it means dying to recover."

"What happened to the woman?"

"Well, six months later they said they'd made a mistake, that she'd live as long as anybody might expect to. And do you know what she did? At first she refused to believe it. She was like a spoilt child, angrily disappointed and depressed. Her plans had gone awry. The extra delight and anguish went from her life. People didn't bother about her anymore. She'd lost the only thing that made her life worth living—her death in six months. And a month later she *was* dead. Suicide. She couldn't face the idea of living."

"Oh?" Godfrey said thoughtfully.

The nurse looked worried. "I don't know whether I should have told you that," she said. "But I'm from England too, up Manchester way. And after all, you're a married man with children."

62

A married man with children! What a multitude of privileges and condemnations was accorded him, as if being thus he gained a rank and responsibility in so many unrelated causes. He dies—a married man with children! He is indiscreet—a married man with children! He is heroic—a married man with children! Godfrey smiled at the nurse's reasoning.

"You're your old self again."

So people will presume in their knowledge of others, Godfrey thought, and was surprised at the new trend of his thinking. He'd not been a man to generalize or elaborate and had grown less so in a country where a man's actions brought more esteem than his ideas. He had the feeling of having "emigrated" a second time. He was no tourist looking over the new country of his experience; he had settled in it.

He could see against the sky the first dark flowering fountain of oil. He looked down at his arm in its nest by his side. Did he dream that he saw spreading slowly through the hospital pajama sleeve a dark stain of oil?

11

HIS HOMECOMING, HE TOLD HIMSELF, WOULD BE a happy oldfashioned family affair with Mum and Dad Muldrew, Lynley, the children, Beatrice and himself. Tea round the fire or the telly. Cakes, sweets. Would cakes do the trick, he wondered; help them to forget his death? For no matter how elaborate his mind had become in its excursions to the interior, ferrying back and forth from idea to idea, overloaded with possibilities and anxieties, he held clear unadorned knowledge that he had been dead and was now alive but separated by his death from the old family lands.

Perhaps cakes might be successful where ordinary roads to forgetfulness had failed? Yet how undignified, inadequate it all seemed as an expression of joy that he was alive. Was it joy? He wondered whether after coasting along for a few months on the memory of his absorbing personal drama he would be left high and dry on the dull sands of ordinary existence—mowing the lawn in the weekends, renewing washers in the taps, mending fuses, taking the kids in the bus to the Aquarium, watching the telly, borrowing books from the library—handyman books, travel books, novels, with "dives" into deeper literature from which he emerged saturated, gasping for breath, and refreshed, though he bore away with him little of the element in which, briefly, he had floundered and survived. And what would life at work be now—booking people on their five-, seven-, ten-day excursions here and there, when he knew that he alone had made the most hazardous journey of all, and that it was only by good fortune that a return

64

booking had been made available for him at, or rather, *beyond* the last minute.

Then he began to worry about going home. He did not want to face Lynley or the children making pigs of themselves with sweets and jelly, nor Mum and Dad Muldrew from Godforsaken Matuatangi, nor Beatrice with her offerings and celebrations. He worried because he might not be able to take advantage of his death because his own being was not deep or wide enough: the weekend mowing of lawns might come between him and his experience; or the tapwashers, the refund of the unused fare to Here or There; everything in daily life would act as a brake to his inner journeying. But now had he not "lived in the country as one of the people," made his new migration?

In New Zealand he had found that the equivalent of a "wicked weekend in Paris" was spent in the company of a lawnmower or with hammer, nails, and paint. He was satisfied enough with the attractions of lawnmower and housepaint; and with the attractions of his wife! He would think sometimes, however, of how he might have spent his leisure in England. No lawn to mow, garden to weed, house to paint; all the untidiness and wild growth of earth controlled under concrete. He would have spent his days indoors with the telly, at the pictures or theater, and when the dark winter came and evening began at three o'clock, he might have taken classes in art, a language, the ancient Greeks, How to plan a nation's economy, hoarding these interests as defense against the invasion of winter. In the northern hemisphere he might have been better equipped to face death. Here in the South he had been overwhelmed by the greenness of the world, by the sun, the sea. The benign climate encouraged ease, relaxation, the urge to "give a hand" to help the grass to grow, and when it started to assert its growth and power, to put it in its place by cutting it down. Here, man and the natural scene were "cobbers" with nature, still giving a reminder several times a year that being "just good friends" is as it states and is not an encouragement to take liberties with untamed personal snows and self-absorbed remote bush.

Godfrey knew that not everyone spent the weekend mowing and painting. A few enjoyed occupations that might have helped them to face death and resurrection, to give to them and take from them a meaning that, Godfrey felt, he could not find in the front and back lawn, in spite of his devoted care and control of the grass; nor had he found the necessary jewel inside a tin of housepaint. And yet, he knew, the search would never drive him back to London. The children playing in the sun on the beach were gathering a different store of experiences of different deaths. They were acquainted early with the bleached bones of animals, the overturned dinghy in the tidal river, the drowned classmates. Not that it was necessary to experience death in order to face it; only a trained constantly used imagination had hope of "facing" the terrors of being and not being. Beatrice had imagination, Godfrey knew, but it was a blossoming self-indulgent kind intent on giving pleasure to herself or others. Godfrey's imagination had been more carefully thinned, though it came from the same plant; it did not, or had not until now indulged in remote self-sown luxury, blossoming at the risk of being struck down by drought or storm far from its natural environment.

He groaned, lying in his hospital bed. The sun commands, Don't think, he said aloud. The grass—Be at ease. The garden— Herbaceous borders are more precious than a display of bright ideas in the head.

But he became confused. He needed time to collect himself, so much of him lay now in outposts and corners and inaccessible places. He must remember to practice his uniform smile, the apparent legacy from his "old self."

He slept deeply. He did not wake until the next morning when he remembered that he was going home. He felt the joy of anticipation until the thought came to him: Wednesday. Today is the day of my funeral.

66

12

aside the curtain and looked out. A still March day when the gray
buildings of the city collect and store the gray of the sky, the
shady side of the street stays damp all day, smoke goes straight
up with a flourish at the top like an Indian rope trick, and the
weather, the world say, Wait, Wait. It will happen soon. Only to
set everything moving—the empty air, the sky, the trees, to pour
rainbows into the gray world!

The tide was out leaving the sleek mud shining in its gray
sheen, ruffled like silk in folds and pleats where the night wind
had lain and gone, leaving its bed rumpled and unmade.

Even if it had rained, Beatrice thought, it would not have
been a long drive to the cemetery.

The cemetery was near, in Anderson's Bay. She had often
walked by it and stopped to stare at the old weed-covered
graves and the newer neat ones with their jam jars of cut flowers
or gardens filled with dahlias, polyanthus, pansies. Godfrey's plot
had not been arranged before his death. When they'd made their
wills and in a solemn mutually enjoyable but unrealistic session
talked about mortgages, insurance, death, they decided to defer
the buying of a family plot until Godfrey had lived in Dunedin
long enough to qualify for a citizen's right to be buried in the
cemetery.

He must arrange it soon, she thought. We don't want to be left
again not knowing what to do. He must put his will in order,

67

say whether he wants to be cremated, leave his insurance papers where I can find them. And now that I've had to buy a family plot in the cemetery we must keep it weeded as the weeds will grow faster than ever now the earth has been disturbed by the digging of the grave.

But he's alive! she reminded herself.

One moment she rejoiced in his being alive and wished she knew a God who would know how to accept her abundance of gratitude; the next moment she felt unable to rejoice. She kept thinking of trivial things—of his best suit that she claimed from Corso while the woman at the depot said sarcastically, "Some people will never make up their minds about anything."

The suit smelled like the sack it had been stowed in. Every time Beatrice opened the wardrobe where it hung ready for her to take to Godfrey, the sack-smell surged out at her and she sprayed Wild Gardenia Air Freshener in the wardrobe, and now the suit, the wardrobe, the bedroom reeked of Wild Gardenia. What will Godfrey think? Beatrice wondered, if he smells it in the sitting room where his coffin would have lain?

Her head ached. She looked at the clock. A quarter past eight. An hour ago it had been dark. She could not hear the children, but she smelled toast and guessed that Mum Muldrew was in the kitchen getting breakfast, bustling about like a woodcutter's wife or a red hen, in a way she hadn't been used to.

I can tell Godfrey the smell of toast was so strong I sprayed Wild Gardenia everywhere, Beatrice thought. Decaying flesh appalled her; people were no different from the cattle she'd seen in the paddocks, when she'd held her nose—What a pong!

But Godfrey is alive, she told herself again.

Embarrassed and unhappy at the indelicate thoughts that kept displacing her feeling of sweet rejoicing, she sat in her bedroom armchair, put her head in her hands, and began to cry, not because Godfrey had died and come alive but because already she was hiding from him, planning to tell lies so as not to embarrass him. She had never dreamed of deceiving him until now when she was faced with the absurd and tragic inconvenience of his resuscitation. The ache brought by his death was still with her; she did not know how to accommodate it now; she had shaped her heart to fit her bereavement as a piece of metal is twisted and shaped in fierce heat; and like the metal withdrawn from the fire, her heart, withdrawn from the news of Godfrey's death, had set, refusing to be untwisted or reshaped. Perhaps she would live the rest of her life with her heart in a widow's shape. And what of Godfrey? Would he, in his turn, have the heart of a dead man?

She stopped crying and made herself ready for Grandma Muldrew's breakfast. The children, quiet as hedgehogs with their occasional sniffle and snuffle and whisper, had dressed and gone to the kitchen. How quiet they were! Their multitude of spines pricked up ready to be snapped at further devastating news.

"What will Daddy be doing now?" Sonny asked.

Since Godfrey's death Teena and Sonny had pursued Beatrice with questions. "What is Daddy doing now?" "Where is Daddy now?" "What does he look like?" "Is he smiling or crying?"

"Everything is all right," Beatrice had told them when she heard the news. "Daddy is awake in the hospital and sends his love and he's coming home soon."

The children had been overjoyed, then critical first of their mother and grandma and grandad for saying they would never see their father again, and then of their father for not being dead when he was supposed to be. But their rejoicing won! They didn't want their father to be buried among the dead people, cold and lonely and wet in the rain raining and no one to let him inside in the warm and no one to dry him and no fire to sit by. It was terrible to be without warm, to have it stolen from you in bed or to lose it by being killed.

"What will Daddy be doing now?" Teena echoed.

Grandma Muldrew setting the plates and cups and knives and

eggspoons on the breakfast table looked over at Beatrice as if to say, Answering is up to you. I can deal with breakfast. You deal with their questions.

Grandad Muldrew looking up from Godfrey's chair near the two-bar electric fire stared at Beatrice as if to say, Well, what is your answer?

"Your father will be getting ready to come home now. I'm going in the taxi to get him and you and Grandma and Grandad will stay home ready to welcome him. And then, after lunch, Aunty Lynley's coming. All the way from England."

"Will she bring us presents?"

"No," Beatrice said sharply.

Grandma corrected in a mild tone. "She might, you know."

"But how could she have thought of that?" Beatrice cried, beset by everyone in the kitchen, wanting to sit in peace and enjoy being a child again with Mum Muldrew taking the boiled egg out of the pot, sliding it into the eggcup, telling her and her brother Bob to tap it with a spoon and slice off its head and not to quarrel if Beatrice had a brown egg and Bob a white one; and the clock ticking; and the fire glowing bright through the slits of the grate, like light shining, enticing, under the door of other people's houses; and Dad Muldrew getting ready to go to the shop and promising to bring home some wallpaper; everything simple and comfortable and everyone cared for; and the eggshell warm against the hand and the curl of steam from the yolk when the head toppled off; and the toast with a wet dent in the middle where the butter ran downhill; and the kitchen warm with steam on the windowpane; and yesterday's wet coats hung up in the scullery, dry again, warm again; and the thought of school; and going for a last-minute wash and finding you'd missed a patch of dirt behind your knees or on the wrong side of your arm where washing didn't reach naturally.

Beatrice gasped with homesickness for the romantically remembered *then*. She looked at Grandma and Grandad Muldrew, Teena, Sonny, and she hated them for interfering with her comfortable dream. She hated Mum Muldrew for being an old woman with an old woman's limitations, complaints and anxieties, and shrinking of interest. In your life you were your own warmth until age washed you in cold water and you shrank. She hated Dad Muldrew for talking about his "rheumaticky knee" as if he were playing a caricature of an old man; and each time he said, "I'm finding it harder to walk with this leg," standing up and demonstrating his difficulty, he looked appealingly at her as if he expected her to do something about it, and why didn't she, in the flush of her youth, only thirty-two years old?

She hated the children for not understanding what had happened to their father; too sharp and shrewd in their unanswerable questions, then too silent and pale, not revealing what whirled in their minds; Teena with her nightmares a mixture of television fare and recent events, Sonny with his literal shafting of tender places in her armor, like a child-sized medieval knight engaged in an adult tournament.

She hated Godfrey for choosing to walk part of the way home that night, for being dead and coming alive, for so disrupting everything with his death and now with his restored life; for the preparations and rituals that accompanied his death and could never be forgotten; for Lynley's visit—what was to be done with her? How would she feel when she received the cable at Honolulu telling her that Godfrey was alive?

Finally she hated herself—for hating everyone else, for wishing one moment that Godfrey was dead, for rejoicing the next that he was alive, for feeling and knowing that a frightening change had invaded their world. Change is inevitable, the only known security, a standing place as firm as the earth in its imperceptible spinning; yet the change from death to life defying the laws of gravity set the dreamers wheeling and spinning in their wakefulness.

She must be calm, she told herself. She must cancel ceremonies prepared in the final cancellation of Godfrey. She must write to thank people for wreaths, explain that Godfrey was now alive and that the wreaths would be given to a "good cause." It might be more simple to put a notice in the newspaper (*North Island papers please copy*) adding, *Please accept this as a personal acknowledgement.* She knew the convention and the wording just as those who had written their bereavement notes had used, naturally, words they would never have spoken—"your friend and partner," "your sad loss," "deeply grieved." She was ashamed of her enjoyment of the letters and telegrams; as soon as Godfrey died she found herself wondering who would write, who would send wreaths or cut flowers, who would choose cards rather than letters. She had noticed in herself a feeling of pride in having, after only two days, a full "bereavement's worth" of condolences.

Then there was the coffin to be paid for. They had engraved it with Godfrey's name. She was afraid that if he were lying in his grave and the cemetery were suddenly unearthed or the dead recalled to life there would be no means of knowing which was Godfrey; with the illogical thinking of grief she had forgotten that everything, even the smart gold letters, would decay.

Grandad Muldrew who thought more often about his own death had said, "What about putting the coffin aside for when he does need it? It's no disgrace to be prepared."

The undertaker suggested this also, assuring Beatrice that all would be completely confidential, that in time she too would forget it and need give no thought to it until the day it was needed again. As the firm, Perpetual Undertakers Limited, carried from generation to generation, everything would be kept up to date. Beatrice agreed. I'll forget it, she thought, and Godfrey need never know. I'll pay for it so much a week out of the child allowance.

And now there was Godfrey to think about—the source of all this inconvenience and turmoil; oh, how unfair she was being toward him! She remembered how, alone in the big bed, she slipped her hand between the sheets over to his side, and how she felt the chill fall on her hand, how it had seemed that all that first night and the next day while she knew that he was dead her hand would not warm itself, how she thought that if she thrust it into a fire it still would not get warm, nor would it burn; her grief was such that her chilled hand might have conferred holiness or magical power. But that was changed now, Godfrey was alive, her hand would grow warm again, and tonight before she and Godfrey went to bed they would sit by the fire and talk, and he would tell of his plans at the Tourist Office, an idea for the next weekly conference that might earn him a bonus; and she would sort out his clothes ready for work and the children would have their baths and be lying on the floor in their nightclothes watching television, and it would be just as well Grandma and Grandad had gone home by the afternoon train, otherwise they would complain—The floor's no place . . . When your mother was little . . . And Lynley would be there. Lynley? And perhaps they would plan their Christmas holidays, whether they should rent the crib near the motorcamp or find a place around the Bay or even go to the North Island to the exciting places shown on the travel folders that Godfrey brought home for the children: Rotorua, Mount Maunganui, the Giant Kauri Forest.

And then with everything as it used to be, no hurrying (she might even say, Wait till I finish this chapter), she and Godfrey would go to bed and be made warm again, and soon the whole frightening time would be forgotten.

Then why was she crying?

Why had she burst into tears here in the kitchen in front of the children who looked afraid and ran to their bedroom, in front of Mum and Dad Muldrew and everyone, for the number in a group seems never to be known exactly and there are always one or two extra when there are outbursts of feeling that one is ashamed of and can't control.

"I'll take an aspirin," Beatrice said, drying her eyes. "I've a frightful headache."

The children returned moving jerkily to their places at the table. Silently they scooped their egg from its shell, eating it slowly, opening their mouths in lowercase o's.

"It's turned out to be a whale not a sea monster," Dad Muldrew said looking up from the paper.

"A whale?"

"Yes, they thought it was a sea monster on that beach."

"The blue whales are rare these days," Beatrice said calmly.

"There's mass killing of them, I'm told," Grandma Muldrew said with disapproval, in the role of universal mother.

Who has been talking about whales? Beatrice wondered.

"A Monster!" Grandad Muldrew said contemptuously. "Always looking for something out of the ordinary like a monster."

"The taxi," Beatrice said, getting up from the table, "is coming at half past nine."

13

LYNLEY SAT AT HONOLULU AIRPORT WAITING FOR the flight to Fiji. She had not joined the party spending the day at Waikiki Beach, dining at beachside hotels, entertained with music from Hawaiian guitars. She had not the undisciplined curiosity that prompts the tourists to see all the sights in all weathers and all moods as long as their eyes are able to focus and their heads to turn. Except for her time caring for evacuees in the Trossachs, she had lived all her life in London and found there enough interest and variety without making trips to the Continent, wandering sore footed from gallery to gallery, borne from capital to capital in a bus where the amber-tinted glass ceiling threw an ovengold glare on the faces of the passengers all the long, hot Continental summer day. Lynley, had the faculty of elevating her surroundings and the people in them to make a personal architectural construction from which she had a wider view over the landscape. She had enclosed Jack, Henry, Hilary, Daniel Wandling, and of course Godfrey and his family, with spacious thoughts, slender soaring beams with glass between, the whole structure arched above the people she knew and cared for, to enclose as much coming and going, adventure, foreign lands, as if she had built Victoria or St. Pancras Station round her world. What was the need then to go abroad on a fashionable holiday tour, thirteen capitals a week? Until she hastily made her plans to emigrate to the South, she had not realized how much Godfrey meant to her. That is, Godfrey's death.

Now, with anger and dismay and a smaller amount of relief than she would have thought possible she was reading the cable that told of his revival. The relief grew. But why had they spoken so certainly of his death? If only it had been Beatrice who had died! Fantasies came. Lynley would have gone to stay with Godfrey and the children, would have taken over, with sisterly propriety, most of the duties of wife and mother. What confusion had there been that she was now flying to New Zealand to attend his funeral? These New Zealanders, she thought. Surely they know nothing about death! Then a feeling of powerlessness came over her. Godfrey was alive and complete with his family. She would have to find somewhere to live, something to work at. When they met her at the airport she must not demonstrate herself in a tiresome way, she must remain controlled, almost aloof, for Beatrice, she was sure, would be ready to pounce on any emotional dishevelment or any sign of inability to "cope" at her age with life in a new land. She had been irritated by Beatrice's reference in her phone call to her age. Suddenly remembering this she felt forlornly near to tears. It's all very well for Godfrey, being alive, she thought with inexplicable envy.

The passengers were beginning to gather for the flight, loitering near the duty-free shop that was doing a brisk trade in watches, transistors, cameras. In the other shops, too, the souvenirs were selling fast as the passengers, fearing future loss of memory, panicked, trying to decide which souvenir would encompass their holiday—a miniature canoe, a muumuu, a pair of sandals, key rings?

Lynley wandered restlessly up and down and into the shops. The glitter depressed her. She thought and stifled the thought that she wished she had followed old Daniel Wandling to his grave. Or that Godfrey had stayed dead. Why had he not stayed dead? She would have arrived in Dunedin knowing so much more than the others about death and the ceremonies of burial. Beatrice in her grief would have listened eagerly to details of

76

Godfrey's life in England, details that only Lynley could relate or, touching the pressure points of Beatrice's grief, withhold, pretending she had forgotten them. How satisfying it would have been if for once she had been a "key" figure in a human pattern! She'd never been of first importance to Jack, Henry, Hilary. If old Daniel Wandling had not been so absorbed in his memories of Hampstead Heath she might have been the first person in his life. She knew that once, in the Trossachs, she had been first in Godfrey's life. She wondered how many memories of her he had shared with Beatrice and the children. If he had stayed dead, she thought, I would have been *in sole possession* of his early memories. She had a feeling of warmth, of wealth, of discovering a long-forgotten bank account. Would Beatrice have envied her then? Did she need envy from Beatrice? She did not think so. The cheerfulness that for so long others had spread over her nature was her own furnishing now, a useful carpet to deaden the footsteps of gloom, shock, and suffering. She was efficient in living, she had an income, she was disciplined in her desires; she knew how to choose good material for her clothes, to carry herself well. She spoke sharply to children but she got on well with them. She grew fond of people and as she grew fond of them they retreated and that was her fault, in spite of her dignity in pursuit and retreat. She valued her dignity. It was one of the few possessions she felt she had salvaged from the robbery of the passing years. Her hair was gray, she suffered the discomforts of her age, naturally, as children suffer the discomfort of learning to walk, not protesting, but humanly hitting out sometimes at the obstacles. She had an eye on God, but He was not always there because she did not believe consistently in Him though she had longed sometimes to say to Him, peeling away the formality and ritual to reveal the purpose of prayer, "This thing that is between us. . . ."

In the tropical heat she sweltered in her "coping" costume. Her beads carefully chosen to match were boulders around her neck. The Hawaiian and Japanese women walked with such ease, treading softly in their sandals, holding big tropical flowers that brushed the air with their perfume. Lynley had never seen such big flowers except the rhododendrons and ranunculus that leaned soot-bitten against the back fence in Camden Town, their flowers turning brown as the foul air snatched their color from them as soon as they opened. They were always faded, their limpness a sign of their death, whereas these tropical flowers hung naturally limp, at ease like the women who carried them and who themselves moved as rhythmically as bright flowers in cool water. Beside them Lynley felt thick, treetrunk-wide, immobile, in her heavy costume. She was relieved to climb into the plane; she decided she did not care for the tropics.

She wondered what she would do if she did not "care for" New Zealand, for this Dunedin away in the south near the Antarctic with penguins and seals and ice floes in the harbor and a freezing wind blowing yearlong from the ice. Godfrey had not mentioned these discomforts, but she thought she had read of them somewhere. She had heard that New Zealand was not the wilderness she had imagined it to be: it had people; it exported butter and cheese and lamb and race horses; it had the world's champion shearers and runners; and it had a dead writer who had written about a Garden Party, so perhaps it had garden parties? Sitting in the plane, her seat belt fastened, her table adjusted ready for the meal, she thought, smiling in a self-satisfied way, that she would be able to "cope," she was adaptable though the hinges of her adaptability were getting rusty and creaked when the great doors swung open to reveal the new habit, environment, experience. But why should she think of "great doors" and castles, she wondered, when she sat in a jet?

The plane torpedoed on its way. Lynley revolved the air conditioner above her head and felt refreshed, at home in the icy air, assured once more that her heavy costume was the correct uniform for travel. She felt her brow and the hot wondering thoughts inside it grow cool as this air from thousands of feet above the earth touched her skin with its chill-grained palm. One more step. Fiji. Then Christchurch, Dunedin, so far south, level with South America. And then—Godfrey alive when she had been traveling to his funeral. What a whirl of shock and strangeness! Suddenly she felt sympathy for Beatrice, her own personal sympathy as well as the kind she would have expressed in "deeply grieved," "deeply shocked" (for Lynley also knew the language of bereavement). When she arrived in Dunedin and had seen Godfrey and rejoiced at his being alive and had met and was at home with everyone, with everyone bustling around talking and excited, asking questions without waiting for them to be answered; then, when Godfrey went with the children into the garden to swing them on the swing (had they a swing?) and Beatrice would talk and Beatrice would tell her the intimate details that women tell other women, describing how she had met Godfrey, their marriage, what kind of "time" she had when the children were born, at what age they sat up, walked, and talked, how bright they were, and what they were going to be when they grew up.

It would be like that, Lynley thought, remembering the women who had been with their children in the Trossachs, and how they talked and what they talked about, and Lynley had talked with them, for she was like a mother to little Godfrey. Since that time in the Trossachs with the rain forever raining outside, she had not talked to other women in this way. She'd heard them talking mysteriously, intimately, in buses and trains, in railway stations, in waiting rooms; women talking about their husbands, their children, their doctors. And after Daniel Wandling's funeral, when there was a need to affirm, by talking, that everyday existence continued, his sister and sister-in-law had related the family saga—births, easy and difficult; deaths; intimate details, a kind of beauty salon of the emotions—that was not part of Lynley's life. She had spent her days in banter with men, trying to get to them and not succeeding, but pretending she had reached them; finally, being stranded further away from them, in the land of larking where no dignified woman lives and from where, once in, she finds it hard to escape. That will be changed now, Lynley thought. Beatrice will talk to me, tell me of her life with Godfrey, and I, as Godfrey's elder sister will advise her. At this prospect of homeliness she felt a new surge of warmth toward Beatrice. Her own share of the intimate details would be far from small— she had early memories of Godfrey; and she'd had a cyst of some kind, quite complicated, a few years ago.

Fiji. A quick transfer along flower-bordered paths to the waiting plane. A moustached air hostess distributing sweets and pamphlets in a nursery atmosphere. Christchurch. Strange accents. Dunedin. View of a blue sea and sky that appeared to have been smashed by light on the rampage with the pieces flying into the sun and returning to their original shape, retaining the glittering evidence of their shattering in the streaks of cloud that formed a mosaic in the sky and in the surface glaze and polish of the blue air.

Descent through cloud to a gray day. Strange accents like broken guitar strings strummed with the tongue in the back of the mouth. Bright clothes, people with rosy cheeks and crowded hair like overleaved trees in the park. The airport. Godfrey. Godfrey! Beatrice. Sonnleigh. Christina.

Lynley got down from the bus. Yes, there they were, she recognized them. Godfrey must have seen her in the bus and pointed her out to Beatrice and Christina and Sonnleigh, for she saw them watching her, waiting for her to do something foreign, their faces lit with small smiles that prepared to expand. She felt the sweat running down her inner arms and its chill on her skin, then a flush incisive and visible as a rainbow came sweeping up from her neck, waving up through her cheeks to her forehead when it vanished leaving her face damp and pale. There's God-frey, she thought. How married he looks, yet how independent. Is he going gray? Why, he's pale and looks sick. No wonder. Why have they let him out of hospital so soon? I'll complain about this, I'll certainly complain—yes, there's Godfrey.

Then forgetting her resolve not to "demonstrate" herself she went to Godfrey, put her arms around him, and began to cry. "Oh Godfrey isn't it terrible isn't it awful, what have they done to you?"

"Hello, Lyn."

She thought he looked preoccupied. He did not return her embrace.

"So you've made it at last. You'll like it here, Lyn." He did not refer to why she had come. He spoke as if he had prepared his speech; with a drawl, not like the old Godfrey. She saw there was a wound on his left cheek and his left eyelid kept jumping in his skin, like a miniature frog. He shook his head as if to stop it but it kept jumping. Poor Godfrey. He was pale. He was not as tall as she remembered. His nose was longer, his eyes darker. His face had a haunted, hunted look.

"Meet Beatrice and the children."

Lynley and Beatrice smiled at each other.

"It's been awful."

"Hasn't it been awful?"

"You got the cable?"

"Yes, isn't it awful what things happen?"

Then Lynley turning to the little girl standing shyly near said brightly, "So this is Christina. Hello, Christina."

"Teena," the child corrected sharply.

"Yes, we call her Teena."

Lynley felt her heart contract, like snow freezing round a stone.

Godfrey never called her Teena, she thought. In the letters he

81

had written at birthdays and Christmas time he never referred to *Teena*. He said *Christina*. Formally. Christina and Sonnleigh. She must remember not to make that mistake again.

"And you are Sonny?"

Sonny nodded that he certainly was.

Lynley laughed nervously, turning to Beatrice. "I suppose I ought to call you Bea, then?"

Beatrice looked horrified. "Really!" She tried to speak gently, "I've never been called Bea in my life, except by you on the phone the other night. I hope no one's going to start calling me *Bea*."

No one was Lynley.

Godfrey led the way to the taxi, explaining that Mum and Dad Muldrew couldn't come. Mum was preparing something to eat and they didn't want to have to rush for the train. "No one," he said, "had had time to think." Then, contradicting himself, he seemed to lapse into deep thought. Lynley wanted to draw him aside to demand Tell me, tell me *first* how you felt, but instead she walked slowly without speaking. Godfrey had never told her. He had not wanted to share his family with her. She did not even know their correct names! She felt as if she were making herself part of the confusion of people whose names and natures she would never know because no one wanted her to know, and now it was too late.

"Mummy, Aunty Lynley's crying."

"It's enough to make us all cry, what's happened," Beatrice said.

And it was too, Lynley thought. I never knew it was Teena and Sonny. They're nearly grown up and I never knew them. Godfrey, looked after by me in the Trossachs, helped through school by me after the war, given everything that a mother would have given, didn't want me to know, share his children. All the parcels I've sent at birthdays and Christmas, addressed to Christina and Sonnleigh, were sent to strangers even in name.

82

And they never told her! "I'll sit in the back with the children," Lynley said as they got into the taxi. She had a feeling of martyrdom and nobility. She did not look out at the streets of Dunedin. She looked at Beatrice and Godfrey sitting close, at the backs of their heads, their hair, shoulders, clothes, at Godfrey's shoulder blades like thin propellers fastened under his sport coat, at Beatrice's plumper shoulders; but her gaze kept returning to Godfrey. I wonder if it has left a mark on him somewhere, she thought, and suddenly blushed, unaware at first where her imagery led her. Hastily retreating, she looked out of the window.

Godfrey pointed to a stretch of wasteland by the sea.

"It was there," he said. "I was just walking along . . ."—Oh, the harmlessness of "just walking along"! Oh, the harmlessness and the harm!—". . . when it happened. And that's all I know. I remember seeing those heaps of earth they're stacking along there as part of the reclamation. They look like giant molehills."

He half-turned to Lynley who smiled with touching eagerness that he saw and recognized and resented. Poor Lyn, he thought. She hasn't changed. She'll be wanting to tuck me in bed tonight. "You remember, Lyn, on the back lawn in Camden Town, how we used to watch for the moles but never saw one?"

"I've read of moles," Beatrice said, sensing a first communion she could not share.

"I have too," Teena said.

"I have too," Sonny echoed.

To Lynley, it seemed as if they mocked her. "We all know what molehills look like," she said, dropping her firsthand knowledge lightly like a treasure she could afford to share because her supply (and Godfrey's) was endless.

"What's it really like in this country, Goff?" she asked, insinuating his and her foreignness and common experience like a demand note into an unpaid bill, while Beatrice, sensitive to her

mood, in imagination tore up the envelope—We'll not waste anything on *that one*.

"We never call him Goff. He doesn't like Goff."

"Speaking for myself," Godfrey said, settling the matter and
ownership, "I don't. It's a great land, Lyn. I'd never go back."

"No, of course not. I've come to stay, too."

Beatrice spoke casually. "Mum and Dad Muldrew are going
home by train late this afternoon. There's a bed with us for a
while, if you want to get your bearings. Do stay with us!" She
spoke warmly and Lynley felt ashamed of her own irritability
and envy.

"Why yes, I will, thank you." She thought, I needn't have
sounded so humble. After all, I'm Godfrey's sister, I looked after
him for years, he'll need someone older to restore his sense of
proportion after what happened.

"This is our house," Teena said, turning to Lynley and smiling.

"Is it, Teena?" Lynley replied, overflowing with senseless gratitude. It was a pleasant-looking home, a bungalow, wooden, fancy,
made of wood! with a neat lawn in front and flowerbeds and
a tree with dark rust-colored foliage; and the sea a stone's throw
away, and across the sea the harbor and the hills and houses of
Dunedin City, shining white and green in a luminous light that
stole from behind the gray clouds. And not a sign of people!
Houses, trees, boats, boatsheds, water, clouds, telegraph poles
and wires, television aerials, seagulls. How clean everything appeared! How clean the houses, and the birds and the light, and
the harbor tracked with varying shades of blue and green and
gray. It's beautiful, Lynley thought, but it doesn't really suit me.

Where are the people? For it there were no people where was
adventure to arise, where were the meetings, the partings? En-
counters with trees were too subtle and not desired.

"See the view," Beatrice said, waving her arm in the direction
of the harbor and hills.

"Yes, see our view," Godfrey echoed, with a pride that Lynley

84

could not understand. She understood less when Godfrey began to explain, like a connoisseur, that their view was third-best in the street with some aspects of it the best, though the Widdowsons had most of the sunset; they also had the cold wind.

"So it's six of one and half a dozen of the other. But when we get a crib we go for the best view. I had my eye on a section north of Port Chalmers, around the Bays."

A crib, a section! Oh, he had written of these in letters but their language was strange. He talked, too, as if the whole country belonged to him for him to do what he liked with it. In England it was never like that. You knew your place there and you were respectfully grateful for it and you did not get ambitious above your station. This was something new in Godfrey—to be admitting so freely what he planned to do and acquire, as if he had inherited the whole country like a vast estate; and perhaps he had, for where were the other people?

Here was one. The neighbor. She came to her front gate. A young woman, rosy-cheeked with thick brown hair, no stockings, a cotton dress, cardigan. "Hello, there."

They introduced Lynley.

"I've heard so much about you," Mrs. Baldwin said.

How dare they carry on this easy exchange of information about me! Lynley thought. She could understand now that such carelessness of manner in dealing with the facts of others, the *vital* facts, could be the cause of the ultimate carelessness that had pronounced Godfrey dead. In life, Lynley felt, you had to keep your secrets and your place and be careful what you said and to whom you said it, if you wanted to survive. This easygoing attitude endangered your plans for survival.

The day was chill now. She looked from Beatrice to Godfrey to the neighbor to Teena and Sonny who were hurrying inside to Grandma Muldrew and she saw her feeling of chill transfer itself to their faces. The absence of people began to alarm her. They couldn't all be Mrs. Baldwins! Who will we ask for help? she thought. The view will never help, nor the white houses, nor the trees, nor the boat upturned on the sand and mud of the beach.

"Meet Grandma and Grandad Muldrew."

"So this is Lynley."

How dare they, too, stand silently comparing her with the image they had made from information supplied as if she had been built from an *Identikit* and was now on parade as "the one." There's *the one*.

"Come inside, then," Grandma Muldrew said.

How full of time she is, Lynley thought. She remembered her own mother, how harassed and bustled she had always been, how thin and searching, quick in action, reluctant to rest, how she had not wanted to go to the shelter when the bombs came, and then when raid after raid came in the night how she had eased her fear by going with others to places nearest where the bombs had fallen the night before, thinking, They won't strike twice. It rained that night. She went like a sewer rat to the underground station and there'd been raids in Wandsworth; her magic system failed.

"This is it."

How dark it is, Lynley thought, as she followed the others into the kitchen where a meal was waiting.

14

IT WAS AFTER TEA. EVERYONE EXCEPT GODFREY was at the railway station saying good-bye to Mum and Dad Muldrew. Godfrey walked on the lawn, *his lawn*. He felt his love flowing into it, into the flowering cherry tree, the row of black and red currant bushes at the back of the house, the white hens in the fowl run. Sometimes he wondered what he used to think about before he had a wife, a family, a house and lawn. A home, a workshop at the back, tools, a toolbench; tins of paint in named colors—Enamel Rose, Peacock Gleam, Sand Yellow, Bush Green, Pebble Gray—the colors of the paint taking their names from the natural colors of the land—what a great place it was, a great land!

The light was at the stage of gloaming when for about half an hour it poured into every corner of the city, running down every board of wood and brick and stonewall and every leaf of every tree of every bush-covered slope; a dilution of light like moonlight without the providing moon. It was a twilight Godfrey had not known in England. There his twilight had been neon light making ghosts of human flesh and colors, but more comforting, more human than this gloaming first flush of darkness with the light above, high in the sky, like an overseer. The houses on the hills opposite were already caped in darkness. Soon they would light up, the lights flashing and twinkling across the harbor, and the white streak of light now rimming the top of the hills like

87

a bleached halo of the hills themselves would vanish and it would be night, with a faint glow still visible from beyond the farthest hills as if daylight stayed there. Godfrey and Beatrice in their passion for views had said that one evening at this time they would go with the children to the top of the city rise and look out over the source of this tantalizing remainder of daylight. They had gone, once, in daylight, but had not known the way. They saw Burnside and Green Island, which Godfrey was astonished to find was not an island but a valley of smoking factories. Then, there'd been no privileged distribution of sunset light. And the coveted view to the west showed a valley of new houses, raw, brightly painted, with the clay around them still wet and unhealed as if the skin of the earth had been torn away in a place where it hurt most. The houses forced into these abrasions of clay seemed too brandnew to be touched or lived in. Beyond this valley were higher hills, and beyond those, more hills and Beatrice and Godfrey knew despairingly that if they climbed for years they would never track down the fugitive light. Godfrey had been disappointed and unbelieving when Beatrice said he could not take a busride "to the west" for the day along well-made roads stopping at wayside inns for refreshment. The aloofness and distance of the source of light made him afraid.

Night came. The light and the interest in it were gone. Walking along the path to the front door Godfrey noticed the power lawnmower standing uncovered near the hedge. It will rust, he thought angrily. This is Dad Muldrew's doing. He had no right to interfere with my tools. No doubt he thought he was doing a good job, tidying up the place for the funeral; it was only fair to have the lawn decently mowed for the funeral.

Godfrey stood abruptly to attention as the thought signaled him: it was to have been *his funeral*. If he had died perhaps Mum and Dad Muldrew would have come to live in the house, with Dad Muldrew mowing the lawn until he grew too old to manage the mower—she kicked back if you were not careful; and Mum Muldrew looking after the children while Beatrice worked to supplement her widow's pension. Or would Beatrice have sold the home and gone to live in Matuatangi? And what would Lynley have done? Supervised the funeral, claimed some of Godfrey's possessions for "old times' sake," bought a house or flat, maybe gone home to England only to find she'd lost her footing there?

How important it was to keep your footing, Godfrey thought, planting his feet more firmly on the concrete path (mixed, poured, and set in his own time with his own hands and tools). His own time. His own hands. Thinking this way of the parts of his body, of his share of time, of the necessity to stake a claim in the earth and keep it, he found himself growing more and more alarmed. I must keep my footing, he said to himself, not moving, not daring to move. He was standing upright, he was alive; if he trod carefully he would stay alive but it was important to tread carefully, to make sure no one else usurped his position, to hold fast to his wife and children and house and garden and lawn and tools, to surround himself with life in the hope that life, following the example set before it, would once again flow into him.

He frowned. But wasn't he alive? Officially alive?

He glanced at the lawnmower, uncovered, unprotected, its sweet black oiled parts helpless against the dew and the rain and the salt wind from the sea. Someone had left it outside deliberately. Someone had been determined to witness its decay. Someone had thought, Oh, we won't put it indoors tonight, it will be O.K. to leave it here instead of lugging it through the trellis gate to the back shed; we can cover it up at night or when it rains but it's not really necessary, these motors are tough, they're made tough. Godfrey's dead, anyway. He won't know what we're doing to his pet lawnmower.

Not able to make up his mind whether to rush across the lawn to rescue the lawnmower or to keep his footing on the concrete path, Godfrey swayed to and fro with his eyes shut, seeing against his eyelids in this most extensive private view his grave, the funeral procession, his burial, his body in its coffin surrounded by his rusted lawnmower, his tools, tins of housepaint, his library books, tourist folders—Visit the Enchanting Glaciers— everything but his wife and children who stood upright secure in their treasured footing, gazing down at him while his coffin and his treasures were lowered into the earth. Ah! A thought came to him. Perhaps they would have abandoned him as they abandoned his lawnmower, if they had the chance? He must be extraordinarily careful they did not trap him again for then he might not have such a miraculous escape. He would keep the thought of death. Like the body's functioning it could not be put aside; it would stay, overlooking sex; when the desire had been satisfied it would stay, waiting to be noticed, bargained with, appeased and waiting to provide its own food in return, a meal with an unpleasantly filling capacity like the bright green spring grass that bloats and kills the cattle who still cannot control their longing for it. And one moment it would wear the appearance of life, the next moment of itself, then of love, hate, ranging freely in the mind and body as if there were no wall separating them, nor had there ever been, but the secret, Godfrey told himself, the secret of keeping death out is to build walls, walls everywhere. He thought of the north-country sheepfarmer with his laboriously constructed stone walls and the slanting staked sheep fences to protect the sheep from the blizzard. Godfrey found himself in the cool autumn night putting out his hand to catch an expected first snowflake.

His plans had misled him. No convalescence (though the doctors advised it), an immediate return to work, everything back to normal: all had seemed perfect but did not seem so now when he looked in the sky for snow and struggled to maintain a foothold on his own garden path. His experience was leading him a way

90

he had not known before; certainly it was not this neat domestic path leading up to the front door with its now broken chimes.

> My pigeon house I open wide
> to set my pigeons free.
> They fly o'er the fields to the other side
> and light on the tallest tree.

Nor was it the path out the gate across the Peninsula Road to the Sandhills and the mud and the sea: it was an inward path and direction and it was there that his foothold was now most firmly set, against his will that blew like a headwind in his face as he moved, against all he had been used to in his ten years of living in New Zealand, even in his wartime childhood, his fitful studies at school, his life at the Hostel for Young Men Business and Clerical. He could feel himself standing on this unfamiliar path that had not been poured, set, laid by his own hands in his own time. He could see in the distance his lawnmower, his tools, books, tourist folders, all the material evidence of his life. He could not see Beatrice and the children. He was alone, going to a frightening destination that no other person knew of and that he himself could not name.

"Why Godfrey, you're standing there as if you've been turned to stone!"

I am, he thought. It is safest to be stone when one is in danger of being prised from one's foothold.

He looked carefully about him before he spoke. "Do I? I've been admiring the sunset. We get some good sunsets here," he explained to Lynley who seemed surprised as if to say: Since when have you been interested in sunsets? Views, yes, I'll allow, and the setting sun contained in them, but not the sunset for "itself alone."

"To tell the truth," Godfrey began, anxious to set his lie like a bait where it would be more readily snapped up. "I'm stiff.

91

There's a stiffness come over me. You know what caused it, I suppose?"

"Don't joke about it," Beatrice said sharply.

We'll never be able to talk about it, he thought as they went into the house, with the children, almost asleep, dragging behind and Lynley falling behind too, taking each child by the hand with an admirable auntly pose that impressed Beatrice and Godfrey and drew them together, but when Beatrice tried to enclose his arm in hers he drew it away and leaned, groaning, into a cramped huddle.

"This stiffness," he complained, aware of the appalling truth that two days ago he'd been gripped literally by the final stiffness.

"Would you like something rubbed on it?"

"No, it will be alright. I suppose I caught a chill from being in the damp air."

Again he wished he had not spoken. Everything he said, everything others said to him, had a special meaning that he and they guessed if they stopped to think, but no one could talk about. A chill indeed from being in the damp air! His grave loomed before him. He must censor every word he spoke.

"We'll switch on the fire. I'll get the children to bed, and Lynley fixed up in her room, and we'll get warm by the fire."

Beatrice feared going to bed. How will it feel, she wondered, sleeping with a man who has lain dead in a mortuary, has been measured for his coffin, had his funeral arranged?

"We'll sit by the fire," she said cheerfully.

"Yes," Godfrey said, divining her mood.

With the children in bed Godfrey, Beatrice and Lynley sat by the imitation coal fire in the sitting room. It was the new fire. Godfrey remembered their buying it. He remembered Teena's strange mood and the rain and the pine trees roaring like blood in his ears. He tried to sit comfortably but he could tell with the animal insight of the bears in the story that lately his chair had been occupied by someone who thought to sit in it permanently. He had a wild desire to spring to his feet (carefully retaining his foothold) and accuse, "Someone has been sitting in *my* chair!" He supposed that in the future he might have to deal with many such feelings, for when the body has dropped prone, never again to stand upright, has been pronounced officially dead, it leaves a vacant space of air that is quickly seized by the hungrily prowling living beings starving for space. His chair was not the only furniture of his life where he would sense and know that someone or something had usurped his place. He supposed that even in his bed he would be threatened; for death had lain there, on his side of the bed, and might not be willing to surrender his place.

Too tired to make the effort to go at once to her room, Lynley was remembering with a loneliness how she had planned her first evening in Dunedin, how she and Beatrice would talk about life, the children, and Godfrey; how she would tell stories of Godfrey's younger days in England while Beatrice listened with attentive longing; how she might have withheld deliberately, from Beatrice, something special that Beatrice might crave to know; how she would read in Beatrice the surrendering acknowledgement that these memories belonged to Lynley alone, to dispense as she chose. Godfrey was alive. She had no claim now as sole owner of his early memories. She could tell no tall tales: how could a tourist pretend to know more about a land when the land itself could talk? The fire made a pleasant warmth, flushing their cheeks. Beatrice tried to unfix her attention from the center of the room where Godfrey's coffin would have lain. She kept staring at it with horror.

"Shall we turn on the television?" she asked, hoping to find a new focus.

"Why not?"

"Do you care for television, Lynley?"

Lynley could not answer at once. In her present mood she had absorbed some of Godfrey's caution in speaking. She liked Westerns—cowboys and Indians, covered wagons, pioneer women riding out West with Wagon Trains, but she preferred not to admit this. She felt that her life with Daniel Wandling had placed her above such tastes. He had bequeathed her not only an income but a refinement in manners that she felt she must practice to keep on a level with the income. She liked Westerns because their adventures were past, and neither she nor anyone could encounter them. She would never dip food into bowls from a huge iron pot that swung over the trail campfire with its smoke stinging her eyes and its flames touching and drawing to the surface the too many tiny blood vessels in her cheeks.

"I've viewed from time to time," she said guardedly.

Godfrey looked at her in surprise. He remembered that in the boarding house she sat almost every evening with the young men to watch television. I'll keep her secret, he thought. How much more cheerful she used to be in those days!

Beatrice switched on the set. They sat back waiting for the picture to appear. Beatrice found that to improve her view she had to edge her chair nearer the center of the room where the coffin would have been. She moved her chair back to its original position. I hope Godfrey hasn't noticed, she thought. My fidgeting and staring. I should explain to him.

She decided not to explain because she did not want him to divine with the practiced clairvoyance of marriage that she kept thinking of him as dead, that she could not quite believe he was alive and from moment to moment she feared she would wake from her dream to find that Godfrey was in his clay-piled wreath-covered grave at Andersons Bay Cemetery, and his clothes . . .

His clothes! She had forgotten about any night clothes he might want. He would have to sleep naked. He usually wore either coat or trousers or both. He would be a corpse with yellow skin.

The television picture struggled to appear among graphlines, shadows, clouds. The News. Aid Programs. Embassies. Test Match Results. In Dunedin today Godfrey Rainbird, clerk, of Andersons Bay who had been pronounced dead awakened from a deep coma and was discharged from hospital fit and well. The widow . . .

The newscaster curled his lips in a smile, opened his mouth to speak, then faded from the screen. Lynley had switched off the set. "It's shocking," she said. "Shocking!" Her eyes were bright; she was breathing heavily.

"I'm glad the children didn't hear this," Beatrice said. "They pronounced you *dead*. You might have been *buried alive!*"

"Might I?" Godfrey said coolly. "Indeed!"

"Surely you can't be so *cold* about it! I think we're all tired," Beatrice said.

Godfrey stood up abruptly and went to the bedroom without saying goodnight. Beatrice followed him, calling to Lynley, "We're all tired. See you in the morning. The cat stays in so don't be surprised if you hear him moving around in the night or if he jumps on your bed. Switch the fire off will you please? Goodnight."

"Goodnight." Lynley sat crouched over the fire. She was crying.

Beatrice undressed in silence. Godfrey undressed and opening the accustomed drawer to get his pajamas and finding nothing there he did not ask for them. He said nothing. He climbed naked into bed. They lay side by side, still without speaking. Then Godfrey turned to Beatrice. She could see his long nose at a peculiar angle as he half-turned his face toward her.

He spoke in a whisper. "I'm cold," he said. "Warm me."

15

"TAKING THINGS EASY" WAS A NEW WAY OF LIFE for Godfrey. Thursday set no example to him with its build-up of last-minute activity before the weekend and *its* compulsive home-and-garden laboring. The Fleet Drive neighbors were lining up at the bus stop or rushing off to work in their cars, groups of children wandered by on their way to school; the busy Peninsula Road sent an urgency into the Rainbird household that made Godfrey restless, and Teena and Sonny who had been promised a holiday from school to be with their "new" father, irritable, wanting to go to school, wanting a holiday, not knowing what they wanted; making Lynley after her days of intensive traveling from country to country, feel an emptiness that became loneliness that resulted in her walking aimlessly out to the front gate, staring at the traffic, then returning to her room to "unpack a little."

She had not yet had the courage to mention the six suitcases and a trunk, all her possessions, waiting to be cleared by the Customs at Christchurch. In the bustle of her arrival at the airport when she said, "I'll claim my luggage," and returned with a large case that with her flight bag was her only luggage for the journey, she had noticed the look of alarm in Beatrice's face at the word "luggage" and the change to relief when "luggage" was found to be only one suitcase. No one had thought to ask Lynley about the rest of her luggage. Originally, with Godfrey dead, she had accepted Beatrice's invitation, made over the phone, to "stay several weeks if you wish," but though the invitation had not been withdrawn, the circumstances had been so overturned that all plans and invitations might have been canceled. Lynley had noticed alarm in Beatrice at her words, "I've come to stay too." Delivery of six suitcases and one trunk, Lynley felt, would constitute an invasion. They would take up room. As they could not be unpacked at once, they would stand in the corridor attracting everyone's attention, reminding everyone that Lynley had come from England to attend Godfrey's funeral, but Godfrey was alive. Yet if she unpacked the cases and stored them in the shed it would seem as if she had decided to stay permanently when she'd received no such invitation and if she could thus encroach on a household, though it did belong to her brother and his family, then where else might they think she would invade, perhaps more subtly, with no unpacked suitcases to lead to her detection?

Like most people, Lynley, Godfrey and Beatrice had a daily diet of platitudes picked from a small garden of prejudice and borrowed ideas.

"Give her an inch, she'll take a mile."

This phrase came to Lynley's mind when she thought of the arrival of her luggage. It had come also to Beatrice and Godfrey. They had not been thinking unkindly of Lynley, they were concerned about her plans, but once this phrase so tall and healthy and *right* came to them, it stayed. It was an accepted thought: everyone knew it. Dwelling on it in their anxiety and fear Beatrice, Godfrey, Lynley, found it kept returning to their minds.

"Give her an inch, she'll take a mile."

Therefore Lynley decided not to mention the extra luggage, but she kept walking out to the front gate so often that Beatrice asked, "Are you expecting a letter?"

"Oh no, oh no. Who would be writing to me?"

Who indeed? She wished she had not set herself so in this

97

light. Her remark had risen impulsively. Now she had made herself appear isolated. She knew from experience that others dread and avoid the isolated, for fear the responsibility should fall on them of finding a country for the exiled hearts.

Beatrice watched Lynley uneasily and herself grew restless. If only life would return to "normal"! She had said No to the reporter who phoned for an interview. She said No to a call from DNTV2 which was planning a series, Strange Tales Here and Now. She had also refused a minister who planned to use Godfrey's story as an Easter text. At first she had not told Godfrey of these requests, but when he asked for news, she told him. She wondered if he were so absorbed in his thoughts that he did not hear, for he said nothing. They had put up the canvas chair—the camping chair—on the front lawn, for the day was bright though chilly and the northern sun had moved far enough to shine on the lawn and unless the clouds drifted from their home on Swampy and Flagstaff there would be sun all day and Godfrey could lie in it, in the prescribed pose of "taking things easy."

"Sun is a great healer," Beatrice said.

Since the night before, her feeling for Godfrey had become more maternal. She felt that it now stood in direct rivalry to Lynley's and this gave her a keener sense of what thoughts might be passing in Lynley's mind, and a desire to anticipate them, especially if they were to result in an act that would help or care for Godfrey. It was Beatrice who fetched the rugs and coats when in spite of the growing heat of the sun Godfrey had complained of the cold. His body seemed to have grown impervious to sunlight.

"I've brought your rug and a coat," Beatrice said.

"Thanks. I'll sit up more."

She ran to fetch a pillow. "That's better."

"I hate lying around like this," he began to say, then checked

98

his speech, knowing that he spoke with more truth than he at first realized. Lying down had become a surrender to a nightmare. He understood now the exultant triumph in the opposing forces of war when the enemy is described as "mown down." He remembered his cruel joy in seeing the grass of the front lawn lying flattened. He had not realized before the achievement, the immense satisfaction of being upright; what a conquering pose it was, to so defy the forces of gravity as to balance on the two legs, to raise the arms and drop them at will! He thought of a man's pride in the standing position of his sex and his despair when it refused to "stand to" like a warrior summoned to battle. He looked out at the street at the women going to the shopping center for their groceries, the postman ambling along, one shoulder weighed down by his canvas bag, and it occurred to him that he'd never thought what a marvel it was not only to stand upright but to move along, to change from space to space, ousting air, surviving its beating on every inch of the body surface.

"The balance depends on the inner ear," he said, when Beatrice came with morning tea.

She looked startled. "What depends?"

"I was just thinking. Do you know I've never been idle like this before? I can't wait to get back to the office." And yet—Godfrey believed that he spoke the truth.

"Has Mr. Galbraith been in touch with you?" Beatrice did not say that he'd sent a wreath with his sympathy. "He phoned to ask how you were."

"Say anything about work? It'll be piling up for Easter. All those fools who haven't booked will be wanting seats and hotels at the last minute." (*I've never been idle before. The last minute.* It seemed to Godfrey that his mind had set up a sifting machine that accepted only those words and phrases that referred to his death.)

"They've taken on a temporary worker. He telephoned this

morning to tell you, perhaps to discuss something with you, but you were so peaceful I didn't like to disturb you."

(So peaceful! Others had the sifting machine too!)

"Just as well my office is tidy. The new chap will be able to fit in quite well until I get back to work. The sooner things get back to normal the better."

Beatrice smiled forlornly at the words, "back to normal." "How peaceful the water is today. Would you like the binoculars to look across the harbor?"

Just then Lynley came out of the house. "I've brought my binoculars, to give you some interest while you're out here. I got them duty-free," she said, turning to Beatrice. "They're the *good* kind."

The admiration and respect that Beatrice felt for anything "good" struggled with her annoyance that it was Lynley who had thought to fetch the binoculars.

"They look good," she said. "Ours are old, from Matuatangi." What a shabby provincial place Matuatangi seemed when she spoke of it! It was like the end of the world—which it was. Reared with a respect for the "imported" and a feeling amounting to reverence for the "recently imported" she felt that their own Matuatangi binoculars, a moment ago her inspiration and ally, had betrayed her; indeed, if she had been holding them they might have crumbled to pieces!

"That's thoughtful of you, Lyn. I might be able to spy on the city." Godfrey spoke without enthusiasm. He felt unrelated to the world around him. Areas like wells appeared in his mind. Wandering into them he was immersed, *baptized* in the joyousness of being alive; then, before he could drown the well dried up, and he climbed out and continued his wanderings in a strange inner darkness that had no counterpart in this sunny Dunedin light with the houses across the harbor washed in morning and the bush on the hills ever staunch in its greenness

100

in the face of advancing autumn and winter. This inward world was a place of such desolation that Godfrey found himself surveying the scene around him in the hope or fear of discovering a companion terror that would help to restore the reality, as the shadow of an object may prove that the object is not wholly the world, that the sun and its light are the warm background of both object and shadow.

He felt that his life, formerly a wide stream flowing placidly through a pleasantly dull landscape, its shallow waters warmed and sunned on the stones, lingering by the deeper pools where traces of sunlight still pierced between the narrow willow leaves, had become without warning a torrent that dropped suddenly into a small dark hole in the earth and was destined to flow underground for ever, with the only evidence of its continuing life seen in the unhealthy patches of red swamp that appeared, like the rash of a skin disease, upon the earth above.

Yet in the right season was not such swampland covered with blue flag lilies that people stop to admire and pick and carry away to the warmth of their homes, putting them in vases near the window to receive the full benefit and blessing of the sun?

Godfrey gave his teacup and plate to Beatrice and took the binoculars. "Why didn't you come out to have morning tea with me?" he asked.

Beatrice could not follow the glittering urgency of his question. She did not know what to say. She almost said, Because you looked as if you wanted to be alone and would sleep afterward. The word "sleep" was ill-advised. She knew that Godfrey had seen the death notice in the newspaper—Peacefully sleeping.

"I thought you might be dozing," she amended, her face showing the strain of this need to adapt her vocabulary to Godfrey's mood. She thought, If we'd not had these years of married life, uniting our bodies and our thoughts and dreams until each can almost divine the other's mood, there would be no need for

101

me to change "sleep" to the harmless "doze." Doze. Nap. Catnap. No death notice could read Peacefully Dozing. If we had not been so close I could have said what I liked. This private channel of communication where everything speaks—voice, brow, lips, gestures, manner of sitting, walking, standing, touching, moving, is a human radar I never asked for but cherish: it scans the messages on the screen, it sees the storm and the way to find a clear path through it. The words "sleep," "death," "cold"—no man now will propel us into the storm. Is it not natural we should want to avoid it on such a bright April day?

"Will we have many more days like this before winter starts?" Lynley was gazing, dazzled, at the shimmering whitewashed houses. "And sun?"

The sun was new to her. She was not sure that she liked it. Its publicity was undignified; one felt exposed, unable to rid oneself of flushed cheeks. Also, the sun reminded Lynley of the Trossachs, and the war and Godfrey as a child. Five is so young for a boy to lose his mother. And then to lose his father just when he needed him. Memory of her responsibility in bringing up Godfrey returned to Lynley with distressing vividness as she watched while Godfrey tried to focus the binoculars. Here in this white sunlight where the world seemed pure and clean and favored with the freshest air she wanted suddenly to complain about her life, draw attention to her years of loyal service; but where could she leave her complaints? Like newborn babes on anonymous doorsteps their cries would go unheard, they would perish with the cold.

"Can you see anything of interest?"

"Nothing really. Just an enlarged city and harbor, enlarged houses and trees and roads." Godfrey spoke the word "enlarged" distastefully as if it were part of his diagnosis that pronounced the scene unhealthily in the same category as "enlargement of the liver, the heart."

"I suppose it would be. See any interesting sights?" Lynley, still absorbed in the "purity" of the sunlight thought this national pastime of view-gazing had something of the peeping-tom element made publicly respectable. Though views were also sought after in her own country, there was so little space to share with so many that everyone could not become a connoisseur as New Zealanders could. After all, continually to want to surprise the day in all its moods and behavior—dressing, going to bed; to have a full view from one's favorably placed "section" of the sheet of sea and above it the sun sprawled across a naked sky—Lynley blushed at the unexpected trend of her thoughts.

"You'll find the sun hot," Godfrey said, seeing her flush. He spoke of the sun with indifference as if it were no concern of his. Sensing this, Beatrice felt a premonition of disaster. The sun no longer Godfrey's concern! She remembered as one remembers with painful nostalgia the events of many many years ago, their last Christmas holiday and the rain and Godfrey first up each morning springing to the window of the crib wanting to know if the rain had stopped and the sun would come out. "Any sign of the sun?" he would ask. The memory of the words was dear to Beatrice now. Godfrey no longer cared about the sun and its shining.

On holiday day after day he had asked for the sun, demanded, cursed it. Since he had been living in New Zealand it had been the gift he most cherished. He would lie in the sun in his bathing trunks on a towel "letting the sun get to his back," while Beatrice looking out of the window, feeling happy with the children—babies or infants mauling her or clamoring for her—feeling so suitably *used* in her life, would wave blissfully to Godfrey, noting with a pang of happiness that almost touched an outer darkness of unhappiness the shaft was so swift, that his shoulder-blades had their first summer flush of pink, like the wings of a bird, a flamingo perhaps, or like the nibble-edge of the petals of a daisy. And watching, she would say to herself, It has come true, my dream has come true.

There was no tenderness or gratitude now in his gazing at the sun. That was unlike Godfrey. How could it be otherwise when he had died? He had been pronounced dead.

"Godfrey," she said. "Found an interesting view?"

"Not a thing. Nothing worth looking at." He returned the binoculars to Lynley who thought, He'll have to try harder than this. My Godfrey is not going to let himself be defeated. He'll have to rehabilitate himself.

She put on her coping-costume battle-look. (Hilary has left a yellow stain round the bath. Jack has slopped water everywhere. Henry has . . .)

"You're not going to let yourself be beaten are you Godfrey?"

"It's not a question of being beaten."

"What's it a question of, then?" Lynley asked the question mournfully. Godfrey had "grown away" from her. She no longer knew what he wanted, how he felt, what she should do to help him. And she had taken so much time and care to learn! It was like spending a lifetime's education studying a special subject and then being unable to practice it.

Lynley yearned to care for Godfrey as she had done when he was five; to feed him, warm him in this winter place. If only he were still small, a child, a baby! Then she would feed him when she knew he was hungry and he would accept the food because her judgment was right. She would clothe him when he needed clothes. Now, if he were an infant here on this canvas chair she would bring rug, pillow, place his head on the pillow, tuck the rug neatly about his body almost so that he could not move, smoothing the folds in until there was only the outline of his body (she thought guiltily that if he had stayed dead he would have been thus, in her power, as he lay in his coffin!). And then he would lie in the sun all day without protest, only with gratitude for her care. Perhaps to make his position safe she would use a harness to secure him to the chair, and because he would be

104

too small and helpless only she would have the power to free him from the harness; to free him, and to keep him there! It was not so. She had no power over him, not as she would have had if he had stayed dead! If he had been small the harness would be there *for his own good*; it would not be this terrible constriction that had suddenly grown about him through the fault of others.

She brought across a canvas stool, balanced it carefully, felt the dent in the middle to detect any "damp" and sat astride it. She was wearing a cotton dress with a pleated skirt and a multitude of folds over the bosom that made it impossible to tell if in middle age her breasts had grown to cartwheel size or were mean, tiny volcano-mounds that explode beneath the surface but above it remain apparently dormant. She and Godfrey were alike in features: she "had" Godfrey's nose. Her face was pale, London-pale. The three hairs growing out of a mole on her lower right cheek waved a little like miniature toi-toi plumes as she leaned toward Godfrey. "No don't go indoors, Beatrice. We'll have to rehabilitate our Godfrey."

Our Godfrey!

Beatrice, the teacups and saucers in her hand, returned. Indoors, indoors, indoors her footsteps said softly, foreignly, on the controlled level grass. Indoors. Our Godfrey.

"What is it?"

"I could provide the money if you wanted to bring a charge against those responsible. I'm quite able to keep myself, you know, in this country. They're particular about that when you come here. Why not bring a charge against the doctor who pronounced Godfrey dead? I know they'll try to pass it off as unavoidable human error. I know them." She spoke grimly not fully comprehending her reference. Whom did she know? What had happened to give her special experience in wrongly pronounced death? She knew she had not known this during the war, though she had seen cases of burial alive, yet in a strange way as she spoke, "I know them," she felt that she did know them, that she had proven long experience of *them.*

"You're barking up the wrong tree, Lyn," Godfrey said. Did he mock her? The incongruity of the metaphor filled her with rage and unhappiness. "It's over now, Lyn. Forget it. What's done is done."

"Oh, oh, you sound like . . ."

"Like Lady Macbeth after the murder?" Beatrice smiled, glancing down at her bloodless hands.

"Godfrey?"

"Yes, it's over now. Where are the children, Beatrice?" As he asked the question she had the feeling that he was an old man on his deathbed calling for his family to come to him, asking tenderly for "the children"—his own and his grandchildren who have been brought to the house for the day to say Hello and Good-bye to Grandad.

Godfrey repeated the question. "Yes, where are the children?"

Beatrice was pale. She could feel the sweat on her forehead. "They're playing," she said. "Next door." Then assuming the role of the daughter at the bedside of her dying father she said with restrained sadness, "Would you like to see the children?"

Godfrey was matter-of-fact, neither alive nor dead, about to live or about to die. "No, I just wondered where they were. We don't want publicity, Lyn. It would ruin their lives."

He implied that his own life had been ruined.

"You can at least see there's an inquiry. You can't let them get away with it. Once you let them get away with it . . ."

"Let's forget it all," Beatrice said, faithful to her duties as housewife and comforter. Then she was reminded that "it," the thing that had happened, was stealing Godfrey's sunlight, flourishing directly beneath the sun, drawing all his warmth from him as a vampire sucks a man's lifeblood. Oh what a stupid thought! she told herself. Vampires in Dunedin!

She looked across the harbor to the hills and houses and

106

thought, Nothing could be farther from the scene. How beautiful Dunedin is, how warm and golden the gardens, how unenvious the trees side by side with the houses; and the buses going up and down the city rise; and the clouds and the smoke. Yet ten years ago I was impatient with it. I walked up and down George Street and Princes Street thinking of the fascinating young man.

It surprised her then to remember she was still young. It seemed that she and Godfrey had been living for hundreds of years. She shook herself, trying to discard the extra years from her body but they stayed in her eyes though only those who looked deep in her eyes would discover them. Would Godfrey read her new burden of time? Would she read his?

Godfrey, closing his eyes as if he had divined her thoughts and did not care to reveal his, murmured that he wanted to be alone. Lynley and Beatrice went up the path to the house. As they reached the door Lynley went in first and turning to Beatrice and seeming to emphasize that she had the advantage of the dark blotted corridor from which to study Beatrice against the bright light, she said, "You worked for Dr. Findling, the one who declared Godfrey dead?"

Beatrice flushed. "Why, you speak as if Godfrey's death were a conspiracy between Dr. Findling and myself!"

Lynley did not answer. When she and Beatrice were side by side, both out of the sunlight, she said with accusation in her voice, "Do I?"

Once inside they met the children who had come home from Baldwins and were standing around in the state that befell them at intervals of "not knowing what to do." Their lives, especially in the holidays, often surged forward busily and happily to a certain point where they dropped over the edge into this fretful lake of Not Knowing from where someone was expected to rescue them.

Sonny came up to Beatrice. "They said Daddy's a ghost."

Beatrice spoke brightly. "What nonsense!"

"What nonsense," Lynley echoed.

"Will Daddy take us across to the beach if he's not a ghost?" Teena asked cunningly.

To everyone's surprise Godfrey agreed to take the children to the beach.

16

GODFREY SOON DISCOVERED THAT EVERYONE IN New Zealand was born (or at least conceived) among sandhills and lupins, and from the time children were held naked against Dad's legs while the water flapped over the blue with cold titty-spots to the early morning sneaking on gnarled manuka-stick legs down to the sea for "an old man's dip," the people of New Zealand regarded the sea as they regarded the land: it was a personal possession. *Gift from the Sea*, the title of a popular book, exemplified the national feeling that by some marvelous bounty the land, the mountains, the whole country was an offering (free of course, nothing down and nothing to pay), and what could be more qualified to make the offering than the sea—though on its own terms, something down and much, much to pay.

Godfrey had been impatient with Beatrice when she described Shoal Bay as a "tinpot" beach because it was near the city; it had more rocks than sand; in summer it had too many people; there were too many houses near it—city houses, not holiday homes that were eligible to be in such places; it was easy to get to; it had litter; it was on the inner harbor lacking the horizon view of spectacular tides and surf. Godfrey, to whom from childhood the sea had been a dream that came true once a year or never and when it came true was remembered for unpleasant "real" reasons and not pleasant "dream" reasons, was still an amateur collector of beaches but he was learning—slowly. The prospect of all sea dazzled him; being able to live close to it; to walk down to it; to swim his dogpaddle stroke in it. When he had written to Lynley that his home was beside the sea she had answered, I hope you're not tiring yourself out by commuting. You might just as well be back in London. She had not understood when he tried to explain that he lived ten minutes from the Octagon, his place of work, in the shadow of the town hall, and that their home was a stone's throw from the sea and not therefore in danger of being washed away by the spring tides. Godfrey thought Shoal Bay was "quite a nice little beach"; in his use of the word "quite" and the patronizing adjective "little" one can discern that his beach-appreciation had developed in ten years. The children, however, were divided between their natural delight in so much water that came and went ceaselessly, casting up its treasures and their growing judgment of a "good beach." They had many to compare! All those of the Peninsula on the harbor side, then up the coast from Port Chalmers to Waikouaiti, Hampden, then south of Dunedin. It was a formidable list from which to learn and recognize the qualities of a "good beach." Yet in the end most of their arguments melted with the first fall of foam on the sand as they rediscovered that any beach was wonderful because it had sea flowing and changing, and places to watch it and use it and be threatened by it, and its surprise entertainments of rockpools full of crabs and shells and weeds and serpents. Sometimes when Beatrice suggested they go down to the sea they groaned, "Oh no, Mum!"

Yet when they got there all boredom vanished. The sea was there, it would always be there waiting, coming, going, changing color, glowing in the light of sun and storm. It stayed, offering picnics and sunburn and tiredness.

"Can we have a picnic, Mum?" Teena asked.

"You won't have to be away too long, will you Godfrey?"

"I don't mind. I'll enjoy the walk. We'll take some sandwiches."

"We'll have Daddy to ourselves," Teena said, meaning *herself* and speaking royally, darting a glance of triumph at Beatrice and Lynley.

"I'm not swimming though," Godfrey warned.

"It's quite warm, surprisingly warm." Beatrice cupped her hand in the air as if to catch a sample of warmth. "The water may be cold. No. Paddling only," she said firmly.

"That's decided then," Lynley put in, feeling out of place in the family council but now as self-appointed chairwoman saying her few words, tapping them into the conversation as if she tapped a tiny hammer for order, end of proceedings.

When the sandwiches were made and the grass kit packed with a towel and rug and Sonny's bucket and spade and food, the picnickers set out with the children wanting to walk quickly, showing their impatience with Godfrey who walked slowly while Beatrice and Lynley came to the gate to wave good-bye.

There was an awkward moment. The gate, traditional place of farewells, was wide enough for one person to lean over. Lynley reached the gate first while Beatrice finding herself stranded on the lawn with nowhere to lean walked a few paces along the fence, waving an ineffectual good-bye, feeling rage against Lynley for having commandeered the gate. The ceremony of waving good-bye to Godfrey at the gate, the exit and entrance to the home, seemed so important now that to be denied a rightful place in the ceremony came to Beatrice like the threat of disaster. Disaster brought by Lynley.

Godfrey, walking along the road with a child each side of him, turning for the accustomed wave before going out of sight, had no idea of this struggle for dramatic placing. He waved toward the gate, to Lynley; Beatrice seemed to be bobbing along by the fence. Then with his home lost from view he sighed in a mixture of relief and despair.

They crossed the beer-bottle-strewn sandhills to Shoal Bay. It was a cove more than a bay or beach, with more mud and rocks than sand. The tide was in, covering the small "island" about six square feet of rock dented and pocketed with pools. With sea-wise gaze the children studied the water.

"The tide's going out," Sonny said.

"The island will be uncovered soon," Teena said. "Then we can walk to it and find things."

Teena was more interested in finding, Sonny in doing; already he had taken his bucket and spade from the kit but the sight of the lunch and the bottle of cordial changed his mind. He made a daring suggestion. "Dad, let's have the food now!"

Teena caught the hunger in Sonny's words. It didn't seem like a food-hunger, it was like wanting something else and not knowing what it was.

"Yes, let's, can we eat the sandwiches, *please Dad?*"

Godfrey sensed the urgency. They found three rocks, natural seats, with a fourth for a table, and when Teena had spread the rug over the rocks ("so we won't die of cold," she said glancing directly at her father) and put the sandwiches on the table the three began to eat as if they were all starving. They shared ham, cress, egg sandwiches, bananas. Godfrey raised the plastic cups of cordial to the light to make sure the quantities were level and fair. Then with the children busy eating and drinking he poured himself a cup of thermos tea. Ridiculous, he thought, I've just had tea on the lawn. He looked nervously about him as if he expected someone to shout, Ha! You've just had a cup of tea on the lawn! Trying to keep your strength up, eh? My strength, he thought, twirling the cup. Back to the office next week. Back to my old self. Ha! Even if I went in search of my old self and found it I could not wear it; it would not fit; the rain would have come through in the torn places. The rain. How can I pretend that nothing has happened? Yet others return to a normal life. They told me of a woman who died and came alive and when she realized what had happened she had a heart attack. My heart is sound.

Is it? Is it?

112

He put down his cup on the rock and listened. Is-it, Is-it, Is-it, his heart was saying.

He drank the last of his tea and looked about him at the View. Ah, the View! As soon as he began to think about it he was seized again by the feeling of unreality, of having been deceived. The View had betrayed him. Why had it not changed since he had been dead? Why did the hills and the sky and the harbor continue as if nothing had happened? He felt an impulse to reach his fist across the harbor, seize the city, shake it, shake it, crying, Don't you *know* what happened? Why don't you give a *sign*?

He remembered that soon it would be Easter: the beach, the last supply of sun (but he dreamed; in this country the sun came in all seasons; but what use was it to him now?), Easter eggs, rabbits for the children; Good Friday changed to Dead Friday; death on the roads, in the mountains, the final drownings before summer came again—how well he had learned the ritual of his adopted country! The Easter Show, the cattle and sheep and pigs. Farm Implements, the Wall of Death, the Fijian Fire Walkers, Shoot and Win a Plaster Ornament, Alternate wails and cheers from the churches: He is dead. He is risen. Then Anzac Day most solemn: khaki and poppies.

"Daddy, look *here*, not *there*!"

I must have a faraway look in my eyes, Godfrey thought. Farthest away is the grave, or used to be. He blinked his eyes and stared at the children. They seemed to be made of plaster. They'll break, he thought, falling from that high shelf on to the cold floor, the seafloor. I've been dead, engulfed. I must remember that I'm alive.

"Daddy, the tide has uncovered the island. Come on!" Godfrey looked at the island, pockmarked, wet, necklaced with foul-smelling seaweed. It should have stayed submerged, he thought, but he called, "I'm coming. Yes!" Shivering, exposed to a winter loneliness, "Yes, the tide has uncovered the island."

17

"GODFREY THINKS MORBID THOUGHTS ALL THE time now," Beatrice said to Lynley when they were inside the house and had sharpened their claws and begun what both had been longing for and dreading—the woman-to-woman talk. Beatrice had inherited a vague horror of "morbid thoughts" from her mother whose favorite phrase it had been, "Don't think morbid thoughts."

"He'll be better when he's back at work," Lynley said, standing side by side with Beatrice on neutral ground with not a menacing view in sight though the eyes of both were sharpened like pencils ready to censor unwelcome views over personal territory.

"Perhaps we could emigrate," Beatrice said. "Convicted murderers who have been released often do. And other criminals. Even divorcees. Anyone with a scandal to their name. It would be easier to start life in another country where no one knew you."

Lynley colored. "But Godfrey *has* started life in another country. And I'm starting a life here too." (Godfrey and I are together in this. Surely you're not suggesting we came out here because . . .)

"Oh no, of course not." The thought had not occurred to Beatrice but once it entered her mind it lingered: thoughts are so hard to come by that any borrowed from elsewhere is always welcome. She looked shrewdly at Lynley, sizing her up: late forties, well-dressed, housekeeper to an elderly gentleman who

114

left her an income. It sounds, Beatrice thought, as though she might have performed some services other than housekeeping for the old chap. These women who housekeep for elderly men. I've heard of them.

Glancing again at Lynley she had to admit that here was no old man's darling. The sad irritating fact was that Lynley appeared as she was—Godfrey's sister arrived in New Zealand to attend his funeral and make herself a new home. Beatrice felt new sympathy for Lynley sitting there in all her lack of mystery, her feelings transparent, wanting to own Godfrey and realizing that she couldn't because he belonged now to Beatrice; wanting him to remember his days in England, how she had mothered him, wanting him to revenge himself on those who had declared him dead. It's sad, Beatrice thought, watching her, claws sheathed now she knew there was no danger, that she's not the sort of woman who would be content with cats. Cats are a great standby. She must have Godfrey or some part of him. Why doesn't she join some kind of Union? she thought irritably.

"We're so much at home here though, Lynley. The view is terrific. Be sure you get a place with a view."

There. She had said it. It would do no harm to remind the poor woman that she could not make her life with the Rainbirds.

"That's one of the things I'm thinking of," Lynley said with a touch of pride. "As soon as I get a place of my own I'll move into it. But I feel that while Godfrey is as he is it wouldn't be right to leave him. I mean it would seem as if I were abandoning him."

Beatrice grew impatient. "In what way? How do you mean—*abandoning* him?"

Lynley looked vaguely around the room. She saw the shaft of sunlight that fell through the window illuminating in its path the specks of dust, insects, perhaps germs, not normally seen. When the sun shone, however, they could not escape; they danced or drifted into the trap and were exposed for what they were: their real nature showed. "I wouldn't want to abandon him. He needs our support. He could be threatened."

"He'll not be helped," Beatrice said sternly, "as long as he thinks those morbid thoughts."

Lynley looked wise. "The experience itself," she said wisely, "has been—well, morbid, literally. The thoughts merely suit the experience. Besides, how do you know what he is thinking when he's so deep?"

Her heart sank as Beatrice said simply, "I know."

"Have you tried religion?"

"We weren't brought up to it. Mum and Dad went to church and Bob and I used to go to St. Paul's Sunday School until Bob dropped it for football practice. Then Mum and Dad stopped going when there was a crisis with the wallpaper—the new materials coming in. I won a prize for reciting, The heavens declare the glory of God, the firmament showeth his handiwork, Day unto day uttereth speech and night unto night showeth knowledge. I used to know it by heart."

Beatrice spoke with nostalgic wistfulness of a time she had not really enjoyed. "Why do you ask about religion?"

"We used to pray during the war," Lynley said. "We had never been churchgoers but during the war it was different, there was something important to pray for, to keep your mind occupied. Either your prayer was answered or it wasn't but I always feel the more suffering there is the more miracles you've a right to expect. The hymns helped—Eternal Father strong to Save Whose arm hath bound the Restless Wave.

"Godfrey used to pray as a little boy," she said sharply, waiting tensely for Beatrice to reply.

Beatrice decided not to discuss Godfrey's present habits. Give her an inch, she'll take a mile, she thought.

"I thought it might have helped," Lynley persisted bleakly. "Like during the war."

Would they ever forget the war? Beatrice wondered. "This

116

country," she said, "is more favorable than any other for his recovery. A pleasant climate. Healthy outdoor life. He gets a good wage, we've plenty to eat, we've our own house. What more could we want?"

The list was impressive. Lynley nodded agreement. "What more?" she echoed, glancing out of the window at the bright sunfilled sky. "All the same," she said, "What he's been through doesn't seem to fit in with anything here. I mean the sky is so blue." She spoke in a tone of wonder.

What nonsense, Beatrice thought. Surely she's not trying to say that his sufferings would be more widely understood in a country with gray skies! "We're *people* here, you know," Beatrice cried. "Just as you are *people* over there. It's no use trying to compare your country and mine by weighing the burden of suffering with the verdict that the heavier burden gives superiority!"

"No, I didn't mean that. I *was* thinking of all the tortured and the dead in other countries; I mean that everything here *caters* for you if you live like everyone else, enjoying a healthy outdoor life, getting a good wage, having plenty to eat, owning your own home. But what if you're not like that? What if you don't like scenery?"

Beatrice shuddered at this dismissal of her country's beauty with the word *scenery*. "You'll get to like it," she said. "If you stay long enough."

"But what if you just like it and that's all and decide not to spend your weekends and holidays worshiping it, and what if you don't want a house with a garden, what if you don't mind an apartment on the fifteenth floor of an apartment house with a windowbox to plant flowers in, if you like flowers?"

"Fifteen floors and blot out the sun! Lower the standard of living? You have to fit in here, Lynley, I'll tell you that. Now take Godfrey—"

She could say that, for she had taken him, in body and soul, for life.

"He's fitted in marvelously. He's a real Kiwi and proud of it. Sometimes I have to remind myself that it's only ten years or so since he came out from England. He's popular at work, and the men at work are honest who they like and who they don't like. He's quiet, I know. Sometimes they tease him about being so quiet. But he's deep. He doesn't often go out. There's the Fellowship Society—you raise money to send people to your twin city in other lands; he was coming home from it when he was killed."

Killed?

Had they forgotten, to sit here comparing the merits of their countries? A feeling of guilt came over Beatrice. She believed it was her duty to remember the accident; forgetting seemed a sacrilege, like forgetting a birthday or wedding; at the same time she longed to put it out of her mind for ever. "I'm told that clothes are much cheaper in England," she said wilfully straying.

How can she? Lynley thought. With Godfrey out there on the beach.

"The dear are dearer and the cheap are cheaper. I mean," Beatrice said, "we might just as well talk of clothes."

"If there's anything I can do, anything at all. . . . You know how I feel."

The offered range of "anything" was so wide that Beatrice looked at her with pity. "We'll remember," she said gently, thinking, Why Lynley has come out in gooseflesh on her arm. Godfrey's skin goes that way too. She felt a strong sense of delighted possession at the reminder that she could still move thus, comparing, studying, over the whole of Godfrey's body.

"Are you in a draft, Lynley?" Her voice had the generosity the rich feel when they can spare a fur coat for the poor. There was no cold wind blowing, yet she asked about the draft for she

118

remembered it was an "English" habit to have a peculiarly ob-
sessive relationship with drafts. "Shall I put a sausage against
the door?"

Lynley looked bewildered. Oh, it's not fair, she thought. A
new land, strange customs, a beloved brother whom she'd flown
"all the way from England" to bury and who now was alive but
estranged; and now this coarse foreign language, the absurdity
of putting a *sausage* against the door; a native custom perhaps.
It wasn't fair of Beatrice to so torment her by introducing unfamiliar words and customs into the conversation. Lynley could
feel the pain of longing in her breast. Ponders End. Tooting
Bec. Fulham Broadway. Hatfield the North. Slough the West.
Wapping. Dorking. Horsham St. Faith's.

Then she allowed to happen what she had planned so carefully to avoid—she "demonstrated" herself: she burst into tears.
Apologizing, trying to appear brave, she took out her handkerchief and wiped her nose, then she mopped the tears that rolled
as far as her chin where they were caught and trembling in the
hairs there like "drops on gate-bars hanging in a row."

"I'm sorry," she whispered. "I'm tired."

Beatrice put her arm around her shoulder.

"I'm so tired," Lynley repeated.

Already sensing the mores of her adopted land, she knew that
tiredness was acceptable; it implied that one had been working,
and work was a good and necessary act if one were not to become
a charge upon the state; being tired was acceptable; being homesick was not. Homesickness, any strong feeling, was unproduc-
tive. If you were homesick you had been moping or you would
be, and moping was a crime. The thing to do in this country, to
win approval, was to "get out and about."

Lynley glanced through the window at Out and About. "I
hope Godfrey is alright," she said. Then she wiped her eyes once
more. "I'm sorry, Beatrice. I'm tired."

119

Beatrice patted her shoulder. "I know. We're all tired. It's the reaction. Next week, thank goodness, we'll be back on the road again."

Though Lynley felt grateful for the sympathy, she could not help wincing with distaste at the colonial-sounding phrase Beatrice had used. On the road. As if the Rainbirds were tramps or gypsies. She wished she had never *set foot* (the phrase was so final and personal) in Fleet Drive Andersons Bay Dunedin.

18

AS IF THE YEAR WERE IN REVERSE THE DAYS began to get warm again but the nights stayed cold and the first frosts touched the less hardy plants with a scorch-mark, like that of a branding iron, as if it had been flame rather than ice that struck—always at half-past three in the morning. This insistence on the exact time of frost was a Muldrew habit that Beatrice inherited from her father who inherited it from his grandparents who had "come out in the first ships" and whose every statement was thus a marvel to their small listening grandchild. "Frost comes at half-past three" gave the same sense of mystery as "In the olden days before you were thought of," "When we were three months out, crossing the line," "In the bush where no white foot ever trod, only surveyors." The qualification "only surveyors" was especially mysterious, and for a long time when Beatrice's father was young he wanted to be a surveyor, to get to the heart of this privilege surveyors had in being part of the country's beginnings.

He was haunted by the image of the bush with a giant white foot descending on it, such a *white* foot! "Frost comes at half-past three!" He used to see again a white foot white as a skater's boot, made of ice, descending upon the world. And when he was growing up in Matuatangi and had his first glimpse of the big illuminated sign set above the boot shop he fancied it had some relation to the surveyors and their white feet and to the frost that came at half-past three. This inheritance of family folklore even

121

in apparently causal but often repeated phrases about frost, weather, morbid thoughts, foreigners, Catholics, Protestants, lay under the surface like an earthquake fault that was brought into light and action when disturbances threatened the land. At the time of Godfrey's death and now, when he was astonishingly alive, family tradition and folklore flew about Beatrice like bricks from a collapsing building. Great cracks appeared in the layers of education that had sealed her prejudice; wild hot judgments shot up like lava in the course of every disturbed day. She could sense in herself her new "narrow-mindedness" but she felt she had no control over it. Borrowed thoughts and judgments conserved energy. The application of traditional beliefs gave comfort. During the night now when Beatrice touched Godfrey's skin and felt its chill she said to herself, it is the frost, frost comes at half-past three. Yet even in the hot days that were almost like summer days, his skin stayed cold and often she saw him shivering as if the frost no longer kept to its agreed time but came always. Soon Godfrey stopped complaining of the cold. It stayed with him. He no longer turned to Beatrice for warmth. She scattered everywhere a wild hope that everything would change when he returned to work.

During the past two days she had begun to see with wishful eyes her hope growing and on the Sunday evening when Godfrey's clothes had been made ready with everything replaced or recovered that had been given or taken away, and the routine, even "first in the bathroom" arranged for Monday, and the children's clothes washed and ironed (by Lynley), and the children had cleaned their school shoes and set out their books, Beatrice saw her hope grow tall: it promised to blossom and bear fruit. She could feel the tension in the children: over the past week they seemed to have grown, to have cast away old skin; their faces were new and pale as after a fever. They behaved with an alternating quietness and excitability as though they were starting school for the first time. So much depended on the next day, on

122

"return to normal." When the Manager of Tourist Bureau had suggested Godfrey take a holiday, Godfrey said he preferred to take his usual Christmas holiday, whereupon the Manager (a new man transferred from Wellington to help create "a more attractive tourist image of the South") had seemed agreeable—"I'll expect him when I see him," he told Beatrice on the phone, explaining that the assistant engaged during Godfrey's unfortunate absence was a bright young man who could cope easily with the work. "A bright alive young man," the Manager had said. Beatrice did not repeat the word "alive" to Godfrey. The bright alive young man, Beatrice thought, surprised at her boldness, will have warm skin at half-past three in the morning.

Neither she nor Godfrey talked much of the next day. And when they went to bed that night Beatrice lay with her eyes shut, tending her hope: it had put forth a flower that was slowly opening; a perfect flower that would bear a perfect fruit; unless the chill from Godfrey's body caused it to perish; or some other frost, a half-past three hand or foot descending out of time and season. She opened her eyes.

"I can't sleep for thinking of it," she said.

"I can't either. I should say, Let's forget it, it's over and done with, worse things happen in—well, wherever worse things happen but they don't happen elsewhere."

He turned to her, speaking intensely. "Do you know that? This is the *worst* thing. It didn't happen in Rome or Spain. It happened here, in Dunedin."

"I was just thinking of tomorrow, Godfrey, and everything back to normal. It would be better if we forgot the other."

"I don't feel like an inhabitant of earth anymore. I feel as if I've been blasted back to where they kept telling me to go when I first came here—remember? Go back to your own country. I feel as if I've gone back but it's no use, everywhere's a place I don't recognize."

Other times they would have laughed over this *Go back to*

your own country, made it an excuse for an exchange of memories of their first meeting, what they had thought of each other, what they felt, said, what they had wanted to do, what they did.

Now they lay silent. Then Beatrice, wanting to protect Godfrey, feeling again his strangeness in a new country, said, speaking of the men at work as if they were men on the moon. "They won't like you to keep referring to it. They might tease you." (If a big boy corners you in the playground and starts to pitch into you . . .)

"I can look after myself."

Beatrice shivered. "No one can," she whispered. "No one can. They might kill you, Godfrey. They might be like a pack of wild dogs and set upon you. Set upon you!"

"I can look after myself," Godfrey said again, on the verge of sleep. He was remembering his schooldays, the Bible class, the story of Lazarus, how some had said it was a presumption to resurrect him, how Lazarus might have refused to live again, had he the choice; how some said his life was his greatest gift. They were slick in those Biblical days, Godfrey thought. Perhaps his wife had another husband already, if not in body then in mind. Lazarus had been wrenched by death out of people's lives; he was not going to be accommodated so readily into living. After the miracle and the gaping and staring were over the first thing he'd have to do would be to fork out for his expensive perfumed shroud and the funeral feast. Then he would meet the full force of human fear. Why don't you go back to your own country? Why don't you stay dead? Then there'd be jealousy because Christ had chosen him and not some other mourned relation.

It was simple to think of all this set in a remote time in deserts and streets of dust, poor houses, barefoot people sleeping side by side with goats and sheep. It was almost impossible to relate it to Dunedin here and now with its streets and houses and gardens and beaches; the shop windows full of electric frypans, electric heaters, televisions, three-piece suits, innerspring mattresses; the Marching Girls; the Moana Pool; the band playing in the Botanical Gardens, farting through the full-bodied English roses; the Piping and Dancing in the Burns Hall; the Forbury Night Trots; the pubs; the Railway Station; all the green and white muddle and clearness; the light and shadow over the seven hills. Solid buildings, too, got in the way. The traffic. The plans for Easter, Christmas next year. The children's future. Pension plans, superannuation, insurance. In those old Biblical days living was simple and uncluttered, if you had no desire to survive and no sense of smell; yet plague could seem paradisal viewed from the entanglement of the twentieth century where you tripped over buildings, plans, fences, furniture, policies, the goods inside shop windows; everything priced, glittering, displayed; new yet strangely used like the stones and sand emptied out of some booster-fed fat fowl's gizzard.

Fowls. At Andersons Bay, Godfrey thought sleepily, we have half a dozen pullets: fresh eggs for breakfast.

Breakfast! And you said you'd be first in the bathroom.

19

HE WAS SLEEPY. I MUST HAVE SLEPT ALL NIGHT, he thought, his heart beginning to pound at the realization of the danger he had put himself in by sleeping. The last thing I remember—the last thing I remember was that big moth pressed against the windowpane; its antennae folded over its breast; brasscolored wings with smears of gold; like a brass rubbing of the dead.

So it was Monday. He could hear the children up already as on the first day of a new term, eager for school. He could hear them plodding in their school shoes like little draft horses in the fields around Matuatangi, getting put into the plow after being "fresh" in the long grass. He could hear an argument and Beatrice's Sh-sh-sh.

"I'm sending a note to the headmaster to tell him why."

"Promise you won't put 'love and kisses'?"

Beatrice had threatened once to put "love and kisses" on a note to Sonny's teacher; it was a simple inherited threat that she felt compelled to use as much as she felt compelled to use her inherited way of walking or laughing.

"No, I promise."

Sonny felt worried. He wished his father hadn't died and come alive again. He wished he and Teena hadn't stayed away from school. New games would be in, new rules made for old games, and he would have to stand and watch before he knew what the rules were, and by then they'd be changed again. He'd missed

126

his week as a monitor. The teacher would have a different face as people always do when you are away from them for even a few days. He clomped outside and stood champing at the back door. He was only just beginning to learn how different the world at school was from the world at home. At school you always had to be spotting things, the way you spotted crabs and shells on the beach, and if you missed, you missed them for ever. Though he and Teena had played next door all week with the Baldwin children they hadn't heard of a new game; but you had to be at school to know; at school they might even be walking on stilts now! And he'd never know till he got there!

He stamped his foot on the step.

"Stop clomping," Beatrice called.

He clomped again.

"Mum, Sonny's clomping!"

"Stop clomping, will you," Beatrice called. Her voice was high-pitched. It frightened Sonny. He went down the garden to look at the fowls.

Beatrice went into the bedroom. Godfrey still lay in bed in the trapped state of being unable to retreat from the decision to get up but unable to make the move.

"The bathroom's free, breakfast is waiting, and as you know the Peninsula bus passes at half-past eight," she said, levering him into action.

"Yes, I do know," he said carefully, wondering if she thought he had lost his memory.

"Oh, I'm not saying there's anything wrong with your memory," Beatrice said quickly, thus proving to Godfrey that she *had* thought he had forgotten.

Beatrice was pale. Godfrey, standing, his arms (how thin they had grown!) reaching about like cranes for his clothes, tried to feel that nothing important was happening, that today was the same as any other day. He did not succeed; he knew it was different. He hadn't been among people since it happened. What would the chaps at work say or do or think? They'd joke of course. Already the wag would have thought of some witty remark. And then to get back to the desk among all those folders and bookings; people wanting to book for Easter and getting angry when they were told there was no accommodation at Queenstown or Hawera. Would the clients know about him? What would they say?

I'm getting hysterical, he thought. But after that news and the photo on television they'll all recognize me.

He heard Beatrice shouting at Teena. "Your socks, your best white socks!"

The formal description of her came to his mind. She's raising her voice, he thought, the idea filling him with terror. He called through the open door, "Beatrice, dear, don't raise your voice to the children."

Raising her voice.

Beatrice did not hear him, or pretended not to hear. She had gone outside to look for Sonny.

Godfrey washed, shaved and went to the kitchen, taking his bacon and egg from the warming plate. He was surprised to see Lynley calmly eating her breakfast. He smiled and tried to look cheerful. He was proud, too. "Houseful of kids," he said.

Lynley slit her soft-fried egg with her knife; rich golden yolk bubbled to the surface and spilled over the bacon. She looked startled, then two patches of red showed in her cheeks. "Real country yolks," she said, looking uncertainly at the sudden rich flow as if not sure it should be eaten.

"The eggs are still very pale in England," she said in a singsong tone as if she quoted the words of a poem—Oh the eggs are pale in England, the English eggs are pale—a Houseman poem thriving with lasses and lads.

Beatrice came in panting as if she had been running. "That little devil. In his best shoes on the wet grass." She glanced at Lynley and at Godfrey, then gave them a united glance as a hostess gives her guests at a party when two people she planned to introduce have met of their own accord—Oh so you two have met! She found then that she did not know what to say. She kept beginning in her mind sentences like, Just think, this time last week—. Isn't it strange? Only a few days ago. . . . Who would have thought that last Wednesday. . . .

The clock struck a quarter-past eight. Such a paltry chime, Beatrice thought. Its quarter chime is nothing like that on clocks in other houses where the quarter hour has four notes. "I don't know why we don't scrap that old clock," she said irritably. "It's first-quarter striking is a freak sound. Other clocks—" Other clocks, other people, other husbands. . . .

Godfrey went to the cupboard over the sink, dropped an Alka-Seltzer into a glass of water, watched it fizz, and drank it. Seems as if I'm getting back to the old routine, he thought. He tried to feel that this was a good "sign"; he looked pleadingly at Beatrice in the hope that, divining his thoughts, she would agree it was a good "sign" but her attention was elsewhere. He had the feeling that the line between them had snapped, that some heavy object like a monster under the sea had severed their interisland cable, cut off their communication. He juggled the empty glass in his hand, trying to force her to look across at him, to see what he had been doing, to say brightly in a way that would induce him, nevertheless, to curse her, You're back to your old self again.

She did not look his way. She was talking to Lynley. He could not hear what they were saying. He felt like smashing the glass against the sink, as if the time had come for him to christen something or someone, to set himself free to voyage to a new land. He swilled the glass with water and put it on the bench. He went to fetch his briefcase and hat.

"Do I need a coat?" he called. Surely Beatrice would notice that everything was back to normal again, surely she would come to him full of joy. See, you're asking if you need a coat. It's just like old times!

Instead, she said, "The weather report says fine, dry. You don't need a coat."

He felt disappointed, as if she had reproached him. You don't need a coat. Why did you ask for a coat when you don't need one?

The children came to be kissed good-bye. Teena clung to him. He thought for a moment she was going to cry but she frowned and said, "I made my own playlunch."

He kissed them and they were gone and he was standing at the front door with his briefcase and hat, and then Beatrice was walking with him to the gate while Lynley stayed just inside the front door, in the shadow. He could not see her clearly. He waved. She waved.

Beatrice opened the gate and stood there as if guarding it, as if to say, You can't come back home, get to work, you can't come home—as she used to guard the gate when Sonny started school and used to come running home after going fifty yards. She used to kiss Sonny and calm him and take him by the hand, leading him back to school; and he would go willingly; he had returned for the kiss and the extra share of comfort. Beatrice lay her hands firmly over the gate; her face was stern. Godfrey could see the bus turning into Fleet Drive. It was full, he would have to stand.

Beatrice, watching him, wondering about his thoughts, allowed her hope of happiness to continue blossoming. What a beautiful flower it was here in the morning sunlight with the sea shining blue and the city already drenched with light, its white houses cool, its bush glossy with the gold that brushed over the dark green leaves.

Godfrey kissed her good-bye. His lips were cold. Beatrice shivered. What have I hoped for? she thought.

Then Godfrey was gone along the road, boarding the bus, fumbling for his season ticket, hoping that Beatrice would notice, There, he's giving his ticket to the conductor. The routine has begun again.

130

Beatrice did not appear to see him. She stooped to pick up something from the path, and before she could wave another good-bye the bus had passed with Godfrey clinging to the rail, swaying, feeling ill.

As the bus turned the corner toward the city road past the stretch of reclaimed land Godfrey was flung back against someone he knew by sight, a post office worker who lived near the end of Fleet Drive. He grew dahlias and carnations, had a child in Sonny's class, and a crib round one of the newly fashionable bays: half native bush, half seaview. You knew your neighbor in this country and perhaps this was a step nearer to hating him.

The man looked surprised to see Godfrey. "Don't you live in my street? The house with the view?" (Pommie. Bit uppish. Wife used to be a receptionist for Dr. Findling. Matuatangi girl. A child at school in Peter's class. A good job in the tourist department. Travel concessions and so on.)

The man breathed in slowly as if trying to decide whether he should hold or speak what came into his mind. His voice was unintentionally loud. "Aren't you the bloke who died and came to life? Excuse me for mentioning it. I—sort of had to. I'm terribly sorry. It's good to see you back."

"Oh, that's all right," Godfrey said, as if this dahlia-growing crib-owning neighbor had trodden on his foot. "It could have happened to anyone." He could see the disbelief followed by the intense curiosity in the neighbor's eyes.

Godfrey felt the sweat-drops on his forehead.

"Happen to anyone? You can have it, mate," someone said.

There was uneasy laughter. Some turned to stare at Godfrey as if they meant to prize from him his experience and his feelings about it. He felt at their mercy. They would trample him. Packed in the bus like this they were no more human than a load of sheep on their way to the saleyards. He could sense their panic, their ghoulish hunger and fear, their revulsion, as if they traveled with a corpse.

Godfrey closed his eyes.

Tactfully, the neighbor did not speak to him again. Yet having a child in Sonny's class gave him added power over Godfrey. He could shout suddenly to all the passengers, "I know him, we're almost friends, our children are in the same class at school!"

Godfrey opened his eyes again. He noticed the passengers still glancing covertly at him as if to surprise him thinking about his ordeal.

The bus swerved. Another stop. Crawling traffic now, into the city, around the Exchange corner, the bus emptying at each stop. Out at the Exchange and a brisk walk up to the Octagon. There. The old routine.

Godfrey hurried along, then slowed down. He had a feeling of light-headedness as if his head were floating while he walked, as if a string, a single blood-vessel, perhaps, anchored his body. What if a roving swordfish should appear suddenly swimming toward him and snap the blood vessel?

He darted to the side of the footpath (he had learned not to talk of "pavements") nearer the shop windows and found himself facing a man who threaded wool into a knitting machine. A poster in the window announced, Giant Demonstration of Monster Knitting Machine. Gargantuan Offer!

Godfrey watched the wool being fitted like a brace into the rows of steel teeth. I must get to work, he thought. I must get to work on time.

He hurried up the last block past the shoe store. *Wolverines are here.* Stainless, water-resistant, a quick brush cleans, everyone is wearing Wolverines! Godfrey sighed. How soft they looked, and everyone did seem to be wearing them, even private detectives were wearing them; so slipper-soled a criminal would never know he was being followed.

Godfrey glanced quickly at the shoes of the man behind him. Yes. Wolverines. Suede, water-resistant, stain-repellent, can be cleaned with a quick brush, everyone is wearing them, especially those who wish to creep soft-footed around the world. Godfrey looked intently at the man's face. Lynley has done this, he thought. Lynley is so careful of my safety she has arranged for a private detective to follow me to see that I come to no harm.

"Excuse me."

The man brushed past him and hurried on in his Wolverines. Then he turned briefly to stare at Godfrey and recognition showed in his eyes. Godfrey saw the fleeting horror as the man turned his face away as though he could not bear the sight. That, Godfrey said to himself, translating the glance, is Godfrey Rainbird who was pronounced dead and returned to life.

At last he was in the Octagon. He walked left, three doors up, and stood in front of the Tourist Office. He was surprised to find it still standing, that it hadn't been bombed or burned and wasn't in the process of being demolished. There it stood with last week's speck of dust in the window, and the same old travel folders arranged one inside the other, the same photo of the Kauri Forest, of the autumn colors at Queenstown. Easter Tours. Economy Tours of Australia. About the only new item was a fly-speck on the window, not new in the sense that there had never been one before, but in its own renewal; a curious way of recording time; like the notches on sticks, the shadow on the sundial, the grains of sand dropping through the hour-glass. Nothing has changed, Godfrey said reassuringly to himself as he opened the door and walked in.

20

THE TOURIST OFFICE WAS A LARGE ROOM DIVIDED by a counter with a wooden gate at the end near the door enclosing the desks of the typist, Miss Mander, the junior clerk, Mr. Greenslade, the senior clerk, Godfrey. The office of the manager, Mr. Galbraith, was a small glassed-in room resembling both a lighthouse and the aerie of a crane-driver. No one knew why it had been built or how it had been used before the Tourist Office occupied the building, but it suited Lance Galbraith who, being used to an elaborate private office in Wellington, preferred even a glassed-in compartment to separate him from the clerks beneath him. He could also observe the work being done while retaining his own privacy and share of daylight. While the typist and junior clerk faced the wall of posters and bracketed brochures, the manager shared with the senior clerk, as one of the privileges of service and seniority, a view out to the Octagon and the fountain.

When Godfrey opened the door he found the staff already seated, arranging their papers for the rush of last-minute Easter bookings that would begin as soon as the Town Hall clock struck nine. He stood uncertainly at the door, taking his bearings, also trying to steady the trembling of his hands. He felt as if he had been absent for many years and would find many changes he did not understand, perhaps new methods like pneumatic chutes to the Post Office, tunnels to the Railway Station, a heliport on the roof connecting with Momona Airport. He studied the people he knew: Nelly Mander bent over her typewriter, Peter Greenslade sorting papers on his desk; the new man, the temporary clerk, a Mr. Barber, his name newly painted in gold on a dark strip of wood. And there was Mr. Galbraith who had not been long enough at the office to be known comfortably as Lance, sitting at his desk in his private office.

So. Everything seemed to be in order. Peter Greenslade had moved to Godfrey's desk taking his own name-strip with him. He would, Godfrey thought. He was always envious of my view of the street. He'll know now that all I could see was the back end of Robbie Burns and a few trees and seats and passersby. That was cunning of him to switch desks with Barber. The new chap looks capable enough.

No one had yet noticed Godfrey.

No, nothing has changed. Everything is in order. It must be only ten days since I worked here. Then why are my hands trembling and why do I feel the sweat-drops on the bridge of my nose?

He pushed at the counter door, the blessed barrier between the staff and the booking-hungry clients, and once again he was back at work. Beatrice will be pleased, he thought. It's been frightful for all of us. How crazy of Lynley to come out here at her age, not knowing where to live, torn up from her life in London, so used to seeing crowds that she's never had time to read between the people; time or space; she'll find it here, that's one thing.

"Goodmorning, Godfrey."

"Oh, hello."

Casually.

"Oh, Goodmorning. I'm Donald Barber."

Formal, without sympathy. They have planned it this way, Godfrey thought. They've decided not to refer to what happened. He smiled, timidly. Not ordinarily a timid man he felt now that he should be apologetic as if to say, I'm sorry it happened, Do forgive my sudden reappearance from the dead.

To apologize for being alive!

Peter Greenslade returned to his desk taking his name-plate with him. Godfrey, confident now, marched toward his place but where was the wooden strip with his name in gold, *Mr. Rainbird?*

Just then the door of the manager's office opened and Mr. Galbraith came out. "Mr. Rainbird. Do come in."

He motioned Godfrey to the office and closed the door. "It's good to see you back," he said, smiling slightly at the irony of his understatement, or Godfrey thought that was why he smiled but it was not the reason for Mr. Galbraith was not in the habit of pursuing and studying his phrases after he had spoken them: that was the duty of the person addressed.

"Fair's fair," Mr. Galbraith said quietly.

"Yes, indeed," Godfrey said wonderingly, trying to help Mr. Galbraith.

They said he'd had a high post in Wellington, that he'd come south to "improve the tourist image" of the South Island.

"What I mean to say," Mr. Galbraith went on, "is that you won't think me unfair or victimizing if I explain that the Department is worried. It's like this...."

He has boatbuilder's hands, Godfrey thought. Everyone in this country had boatbuilder's hands and a cattle neck.

"Mr. Rainbird—Godfrey—we've taken advice in this. In the interests of the Tourist business, of the country as a whole, not to mention our Overseas Exchange, we've taken advice."

Godfrey frowned. What was he getting at? There he was with his boatbuilder's hands sailing his ballpoint pen up and down the desk. He doesn't know how to steer, Godfrey thought. He could hear the first Monday morning customers in the outer office, the phone ringing, the tap-tap of Nelly Mander's typewriter, the surprised whine of a trolleybus caught off balance in the traffic.

"In those interests, Godfrey, especially in the wider public interest and that of the Tourist Image."

136

Now. Godfrey prepared himself. He knew what was coming. He felt in advance the bitterness and shock, the helpless anger against persecution.

"Ours is a public service, Mr. Rainbird. If a man disgraces himself, is brought before the Court, goes to prison, we can't continue to employ him—mind you it's not that we don't believe in the rehabilitation of the criminal; it's just that there are other organizations more willing and able to cope with that. We have to remember that our image is a public image."

Resting his elbow on the desk he raised his hand, spread flat, like a keel, turning it slightly back and forth. "Now don't misunderstand me. You're a fine clean-living young man, an Englishman, but you've adapted yourself well to this country—The fact is—."

He put his hand on the desk and steered toward the stranded pen, grasped the pen, and held it like a measuring rule, sideways, between himself and Godfrey. Godfrey was almost sure he was about to say, Now see this pen. This pen is an example of our duty to blah blah blah.

"What happened last week was a terrible thing. I sent a wreath to your wife. I'd like you to know that. I offered my personal help to her. We're not stony-hearted in this place, you know. We were about to take up a collection for your wife and children."

Now.

"We have arranged a month's salary for you and a bonus payment—quite a tidy sum, I've the check here; with free tickets if you'd like to have a holiday with your family—anywhere within the country. Also, I have your formal notice.

"No one, Mr. Rainbird, no one can be sorrier about this than I am. I think it's ridiculous. It's not my decision, it came from higher up."

He waved his hand upward more in the direction of God than of Wellington.

"It can't be helped, Mr. Rainbird. Godfrey."

I knew it all along, Godfrey thought. Why is it that I knew it all along yet did not know? Where have they hidden my nameplate? So Peter Greenslade will keep his view of the backside of Robbie Burns!

"We'll give you the highest references of course for future employment. But you understand that so much publicity has been attracted by the incident."

"Isn't the publicity good?" Godfrey cut in, feeling desperate now that he knew.

Mr. Galbraith looked sharply at him, thinking but not saying, Who wants their annual holiday booked by a former corpse? It's touch and go as it is who does and who doesn't return from the annual holiday. We don't want it thought that we employ corpses to recruit corpses!

"I see what you mean," Godfrey said. His hands felt like flaps of ice. Maybe he hadn't stopped being dead at all. "But I need work. I've done nothing wrong."

"You're a versatile young man. A good education. The highest references. The Want Ads column is full of jobs."

Mr. Galbraith had begun by talking about "employment." When Godfrey stripped away his film of politeness by using the more brutal desperate word "work," Mr. Galbraith, secure in his own niche yet having experienced something of the depression of the thirties, slipped naturally into using the word "job" for he guessed that after what happened to Godfrey few "posts" or "positions" would be open to him. He just might manage to get a "job." It's not my concern, Mr. Galbraith thought, to try to change society and its superstitions and prejudices. It's a crime to do the poor man out of a job simply because he died; but there's more superstition around than there used to be; society is as it is; fair's fair.

Mr. Galbraith's pen came to rest in a peaceful harbor between the In and Out boxes. He dropped the anchor and paddled ashore to the crib built on the water's edge with a marvelous

138

view. The kids were playing by the water, bulky flashes of yellow in their Hutchwilco life-jackets. His wife Edna was stretched out in a canvas chair sunning herself, the first tan of the season: that would be Labor Day; if it didn't rain.

"If there's anything I can do to help."

The interview was over. As Godfrey walked out Mr. Galbraith said, "To save embarrassment I've told the staff you're off for a holiday."

"Have you told them I'm not coming back?"

"They know but we don't discuss it."

Bob McLeod would never have done this, Godfrey thought. This new chap has fancy Wellington ideas. Yet on second thought he felt that perhaps Bob McLeod might have done the same. Surely, though, Peter Greenslade could put in a good word for him!

Mr. Galbraith smiled. "You know how it is," he said.

Godfrey, his hand on the door, stood suddenly still. His blood ran cold. He had read of blood running cold and had supposed that while he was a corpse his blood had been so.

My blood is running cold, he said to himself, aware that Mr. Galbraith was looking at him strangely. Not even Peter Greenslade, Godfrey knew, would be able to help him. He'd worked with him for ten years. The Greenslades and the Rainbirds had exchanged visits. The children had played together once or twice. It was not as if he had committed a murder or any crime. A doctor had pronounced him dead, arrangements had been made for his funeral, he had wakened from a coma and was alive again, and at least he'd still have his old job if someone had the guts to get up and say, Fair's not fair.

But it was deeper than this; it was something that had happened; he had been and returned from where people do not return; the time and the people and their faces were spiked with their fear; the spikes could not be withdrawn.

"If you've any things," Mr. Galbraith called.

Godfrey did not answer. He knew it would be useless to appeal against the decision. In the public interest. Overseas currency. And what was that he'd heard Mr. Galbraith murmur?—Of course it's not as if this were your native land—What did he mean? Go home to your own country? Go home to your grave?

I've no things, he reminded himself, considering Mr. Galbraith's question. There's that woolen scarf, though. Since his awakening he had felt a pathetic concern about his clothes.

He did not speak to Pete or Nelly. He nodded to them in a friendly way keeping up the image of the senior clerk off for a month's tour with free tickets and a bonus.

Once out in the crisp air, recovering a little, he thought, I'm being too melodramatic. I'll take things easy, look over the jobs in the newspapers. I'm a qualified clerk. There have been advertisements for pressure-cooker teacher courses. Teachers get a fair wage, they tell me. And they're readier, in the professions, to take up someone from overseas; even a jumped-up clerk from Camden Town is a foreign novelty. To lose a job is not the disaster it used to be. This country's a prosperous place. I haven't noticed down-and-outs wandering along the Leith Embankment, sleeping in bus shelters; this little southern city is a clean bright place, the sun shines, there's frost on the lawn and the noses, but it melts in time.

Not wanting to take the bus home at once, he walked down to the Exchange into Queen's Gardens and sat under a tree facing the Early Settlers' Hall and the Railway Bus Terminal. A policeman strolling by glanced at him and turned his head for a second glance. He's recognized me, Godfrey thought, but he doesn't remember where he's seen my face. Thinks I'm on the Wanted Files. At least I don't look like a tramp with my briefcase and my neat office suit: I'm wearing acceptable visible uniform.

The first brightness had gone from the day. A gray stillness had overtaken the sky bringing the feeling of emptiness that Godfrey never ceased to be aware of when he looked about

140

him at the few people and the wide space of unoccupied air. So many of the buildings had one or two storys only as if they'd been pressed flat by a big smooth domineering hand that, jealous of its control of the wide upper spaces, lowered from the sky to restrain all usurpers. The sky can do as it likes here, Godfrey thought uneasily, feeling as if the big hand pressed also on his own head, forbidding him to move beyond his allotted share of space, reminding him that he may have been dead and he may or may not be alive but he had to fight to keep his share of space and he must not intrude beyond it. Though it had not been his habit to endow inanimate objects with feeling, he found that since his awakening he had grown more conscious of feeling in the air around him. The buildings, subdued with their one or two storys, had an air of unfriendliness, aloofness, as if they too had discharged all responsibility toward him. He remembered how different the London buildings had been; he thought of them as welcoming, inhabited, generous; if you were overtaken by grief or loneliness you could go to them, almost butt your head against their stone walls and receive comfort, like one of the Peninsula lambs the children loved to watch, butting against the patient ewes.

It's a great country, Godfrey thought, remembering the children and their enjoyment of the animals and the beaches and of the view over the harbor and city.

At least in this country, he thought, puzzling over the meaning and truth of his thought, a man gets a fair go. He had been told that. He did not feel he had any reason to disbelieve it. Fair was certainly fair.

He said it aloud. "Fair's fair."

He thought about his death. He must remember to keep his will up to date, to leave his insurance policies where they could be found, not to accumulate outstanding debts. The television had not yet been paid for; how could they keep up the instalments? Ten days ago his family life had been set, each year divided into orderly payments, each week sprouting banknotes, some of which had to be picked at once and paid away.

What was he worrying about? he asked himself. In a month's time he would have a job as easy as winking.

So he sat in the Gardens thinking of the lost job, the television, the woolen scarf left somewhere in the Tourist Office, of friends who were no longer friends, of aloof buildings and oppressive space, but none of these thoughts could be used as permanent plugs to keep out the sea that flowed day and night in his mind now leaving its flotsam and jetsam on the beach of his every thought and feeling; the sea, the thought that overflowed all other thought and sank through it, finding its deep levels where it made dark pools that stayed at high tide, low tide, dead low water: the thought of his death.

And now since his interview at the office and his realization that no matter how many people saw him, recognized him, knew him for the man who had been dead and who had now lost his job, no one would trust him; all his life now among people who knew him or knew of him speech would be in circles, ripple upon ripple, without the center stone; but the weight of it would be felt; and stones can kill, in brick and wooden bungalows and cribs and glass houses.

He knew that he now saw everything more clearly than he had ever seen it. With a view from the country of the dead how could it be otherwise?

The leaves in the Queen's Gardens were not yet falling. They had changed color, yet they clung as if knotted to the branches. He stared up at their darkness spread like whirling chocolate slices; why? there was no wind blowing. He felt he could no longer look at them; he could see through the spaces like slit-eyes the gray sky peering down at him. I never thought about leaves before, he said to himself. Why shouldn't I think of them now? I almost became one. I shall become a leaf. I shall whirl like this above some poor fool who has died, awakened, is sitting

142

under this tree not wanting to go home because he has lost his job, not knowing where to go, stranded in the country of the living.

But people don't lose their jobs here, people don't die and come alive; and even if they do all this can be *believed* away by avoiding talk or thought of it. There's a chute of human inheritance where the unwanted thoughts go, just as there are institutions for the unwanted people. I can see the alarm, the disbelief. What? In this day and age? In this country? Unwanted people? You're talking through your hat. I simply refuse to believe you.

Yes, I am talking through my hat, up through a hole in my hat, for my hat is the sky and I'm talking past the whirling leaves through the cat's-eye slits of the gray sky to the sky itself and the sky's empty. And what have you to say to that?

He spoke the last thought but no one answered him, though a seagull in a bulky shoulder-wrap tottered past and with her head on one side glittered her eyes at him. Old pro, he thought, past her prime.

He looked across at the railway station at the black-painted fence dividing the city from the life of the station. The Limited from the North was not in yet. Then you could buy a meat pie in the refreshment room and be given a knife and fork to eat it with, if you asked for them, though they preferred you not to ask as knives and forks and spoons were forever disappearing and nothing could be done about it. People were born thieves. Crime paid. Honesty was not the best policy. Fair was not fair.

In the public interest. Overseas Currency.

These phrases kept returning to Godfrey. In the public interest. Far be it from me—how far?

Lance Galbraith had used those words as children use the roughly nailed pieces of wood to make sledges, to make the most of the sudden snowstorm that filled the world; but that was the Trossachs. The Trossachs. The Common. Hampstead Heath. All the same here was Lance Galbraith spreading these makeshift used words under his arse to get him skating away from his responsibility. In the public interest. Overseas Currency. The Tourist Image. Godfrey sighed. He knew he would miss being at the Tourist Office. You couldn't work at something the way he had done for years without enjoying it, cursing but loving the holiday rush. There. Cursing but loving. They had never loved the holiday rush. Fair was never fair.

"Don't you get tired of us bothering you, Mr. Rainbird? Changing our mind and our bookings from one minute to the next?"

"It's our duty to serve the public."

"But when the holiday rush comes don't you wish you weren't in a tourist office?"

"Oh, we curse it all right, but it gets us, we love it. Lies."

Lies and platitudes. Cursing and loving. You curse war but once you get the hang of it you love it, it gets you, killing gets you, you hate it but it's part of the game isn't it? Isn't it? Fair's really fair. Isn't it? And the frightful consequence of creating the platitudes is we fit our life to suit them. You have war but it gets you, in the public interest you love it in the end.

But I was only a child in the war, Godfrey reminded himself. I was in the Trossachs, another country. What could have been safer than the Trossachs? A little Rainbird in the rain: at home.

Oh, but I'll miss the Tourist Office, he told himself again. The seasonal bookings, the tours, the prospective travelers who came in bubbling with Overseas, Overseas rising like a Rotorua geyser from their speech. And when they get to London they'll be smelling a Rotorua geyser, Godfrey would think, but he never told them so, oh no, he never said, one never says; not mentioning the smoke, the fumes, he gave them booklets on Stately Homes, pictures of old churches and thatched cottages, and they'd go out clutching their Overseas Dream. Some would never book, of course. Here as in England Godfrey had advised that the more expensive brochures be kept behind the counter:

144

the travel-hungry dreamers could feed just as satisfyingly on the two to four page summaries instead of the thirty-page tour details meant for serious travelers.

A month's salary, a bonus, free travel. One hundred pounds between the Rainbird family and the wolf at the door. A tidy sum to bribe the wolf with. Certainly there was no immediate worry. Things would look up.

Things would look down. Down. Down into the grave. The topsy-turvy language of lies.

Neat in his suit inviting travelers to visit distant lands. Go to Spain, France. Tour Europe. See Australia. See your own country first.

I'll put out my own brochures, Godfrey thought wildly. Make your tour of silence and ice. See your own personal ultimate country!

Putting his hand in his pocket he fingered his paycheck. He'd have to cash it some time. Why not buy an electric blanket to keep out the cold spell and its ice-embroidered letters? He had to protect himself, didn't he?

He was not used to spending money rashly. Spare money went into the fund for the upkeep of the house—painting, papering, the garden; the children's future, too; holidays. And this paycheck was not spare money!

But who would deny him a change to get warm again and stay warm? He retraced his steps toward the Exchange, walked up Princes Street and into the music shop where he bought an electric blanket, handing over his check for one hundred pounds, waiting while the assistant said, "Excuse me while I make a phone call."

The assistant returned. "Mondays," he said, "we don't have this much money but the bank next door has okayed your check. If you wait a few minutes we'll have your change. Do you want to carry all this *cash* about with you? It's not wise. The other day, up in Auckland . . ."

"That was in Auckland," Godfrey said sharply. "This is Dunedin."

"It could happen here too," the assistant said smugly, not really believing what he said.

Suddenly he leaned toward Godfrey, staring. "You *are* Godfrey Rainbird, aren't you?" (Will the *real* Godfrey Rainbird please stand up?) "I mean the Godfrey Rainbird who . . ."

Godfrey was used to the question. He was beginning to wonder if he *were* the notorious Rainbird. He did not answer the assistant who looked at him curiously, frowning as he walked from the shop.

Once on the bus Godfrey planned what he would say to Beatrice. To pay nearly a quarter of his salary for an electric blanket was extravagant yet so, too, had been his dying and his revival and the loss of his job. He could feel the fingering authorities of the grave upon him: the attempt to keep warm was an extravagance also not approved by death.

With the blanket on his knee and the motion of the bus soothing him gently to a nodding slumber he began to feel that after all fair was probably fair or as close to fair as it would ever be.

21

HE GOT OFF THE BUS. HE WISHED HE HAD STAYED on, for he would have to walk a hundred yards along Fleet Drive where the women giving final touchings and pattings to the candlewick bedspreads in their front bedrooms or sweeping their paths or dusting their front gates would notice him and wonder why he was home so early from work. They'd be curious, too, about the bulky parcel under his arm. Women in front bedrooms fondle the candlewick bedspreads with gentle hands but have less gentle flights of fancy. What was his parcel? Why had he bought it? Why was he home when it was not eleven o'clock and that was a housewife's time, a woman's time, no time for a man to be home. And after what had happened in the Rainbird family could they afford to splash their money about? Funerals were expensive and had to be paid for whether or not the coffin was used and the corpse buried.

He saw no one at the window or in the front garden of the houses. Only, through the bars of a front gate a small child watched him, her glance penetrating, almost chemical in quality as if it might have the power to dissolve or change something within him. He looked hurriedly away and walked on until he came to his own front gate, remembering as he pushed it open that Beatrice had seemed to guard it to prevent him from returning home. There was no one in sight. The sitting room blinds were down, black, rectangular, with faint light showing through like displayed film that had failed to trap its photograph.

147

They appeared like the blinds drawn in the house of someone who has died, yet the night before they had not seemed so, from within, with the light on and the family gathered around the fire.

Beatrice had craved, once, for venetian blinds. "I'd love to have venetians," she said in one of her periodical moods when certain domestic objects became part of an unbearable yearning that had to be satisfied or the world would end. She'd bought venetians for the side rooms, meaning to fit them throughout the house but had discovered they suited neither her method nor her patience. Godfrey found her one morning acting as if she were fighting with the blinds—one cord in each hand, pulling, wrenching, one side of the blind pleated against the top of the window the other lopsidedly against the sill. Godfrey felt envious of her, that women should have furniture, household goods to struggle with, to strike, arrange, discard, destroy. At least the men too, in this country, had objects to attack: on a Sunday morning at eleven o'clock a lawnmower could be obstinate, could fight back if it were in the mood.

Godfrey looked down at his hands. How powerful they have grown, he thought, since I came to this country and had a house and garden to care for. What did I fight with and try to control in Camden Town and Clapham Common North Side? I used to read, dream about women, and that was an arduous and battling a time when I kept ideas and dreams, instead of grass, down to size. My hands were pale then. Now, I can row a boat. He smiled in bliss at the thought of rowing. He could steer around the rocks, drop a line overboard in the bay, haul up cod, dogfish, an eel, a skate, though people here didn't eat skate and dogfish. *Frying tonight.* Rock cod. Rock salmon. Rock and chips. Peer murdered at riverside, duke's son arrested, famous singer in accident, Green light says Government; Rock and chips and the eveing paper!

He opened the front door and walked in. He heard a household orchestration in the kitchen, a snake hiss of a cistern, water running, vacuum cleaner whining, its nose in the corners, percussion of china from steel sink to formica bench; murmur of voices; Beatrice and Lynley sharing the housework. He listened. The efficiency and absorption frightened him. He had a feeling of loneliness for though he could hear water, steel, china touching, moving, working, he could not hear human hands. He was suddenly aware of the almost habitual silence of hands. But of course Beatrice and Lynley possess hands, he told himself reassuringly; it is their hands that carry the dishes, guide the machines.

Suddenly he shivered with horror. A huge hand in a dark red rubber glove was thrust through the opening door and a voice sounded harshly in his ears.

"I'll do up the passage and down the front."

The long-nosed moustached vacuum cleaner swept toward him.

"Oh. Godfrey."

Lynley called over her shoulder. "Here's Godfrey!"

He saw that both Lynley and Beatrice wore these outsize rubber gloves. He could not see their hands. He longed to seize Beatrice's hands, to confirm her possession of them; he longed to touch them. The exuberance of Lynley set free for the first time in weeks amid physical effort jarred his nerves. With the brief introduction, Here's Godfrey, she bulldozed her way down the passage while Godfrey had the impression she had forgotten everything in her lively play with the chromium-suited dark-moustached vacuum cleaner. Her behavior reminded him of her flirtings with Jack, Henry, Hilary; indeed the cleaner could have been Jack, Henry or Hilary the way she skylarked with it.

Poor Lyn. She looked almost beautiful last night, he thought; When after her crying she came to dinner in her pearls.

He went into the kitchen and shut the door, pinching as he did so the fat black flex of the cleaner. He put down his parcel and walked quickly up and down the small kitchen, wanting to embrace Beatrice but repelled by her huge wet gloves. She knew, he thought. She would know about the office. Peeling off her gloves she put them down on the bench where they retained the shape of her hands, their fingers making empty dark tunnels with a bowl-shape, like that of a flower, where the wrists had been.

"I always use barrier cream now," she said, trying to speak calmly.

He felt confused. Barrier cream? A barrier, a wall, a gate. How she had guarded the gate to prevent him from returning home!

"You've lost your job, Godfrey?"

He felt that she wanted to kiss him and would have done so had she not been imprisoned by having four hands. The rubber gloves poised on the bench were not going to be set aside so easily. Their shape stayed, waiting. He thought, wildly, that they looked like organ pipes, then, if he had five penises he could fit one in each hole, and then he realized the spectacular plurality of his image, that a man has one only and ever, that its singleness made him regard it with special care and affection. He was attracted, fascinated by the gloves, and now that Beatrice had washed the barrier cream from her hands he looked in wonder at their whiteness, their seeming innocence, in strange contrast to the dark hooded alleys where they had lurked. He and Beatrice sat then each on a hard kitchen chair as at an interview.

"I suppose I should have expected it," Godfrey said. "The public interest. The good name of the firm. Corpses are bad for business."

"The undertakers don't think so," Beatrice said brutally. "Oh, Godfrey, I'll make tea," she said, springing up as if she had been wound by a key to do so. "We've only just finished the breakfast dishes. Lynley and I were going to have a cup anyway."

He bent over her and grasped her hands. How her wrists blossomed!

"You feel cold," she said, withdrawing. She measured the tea

150

into the warmed pot. He heard the pitter-patter whisper as it fell. She looked at him and smiled.

"You'll have no difficulty getting a job, Godfrey. You're qualified, intelligent, you know a lot, and you're from overseas, with experience."

He struggled to keep upright in the sand beneath his feet.

"But I *know* I'll not be able to get work. Not anywhere."

"Oh, Godfrey, don't be so pessimistic. What's to stop you?" Beatrice looked on the verge of tears.

Today was going to be so wonderful wasn't it? Let's look on the bright side. Look on the bright side. Every cloud has a silver lining. How comforting they were, she thought, the autograph book verses where you felt it was your duty to cheer people up; they were not so far from the In Memoriam verses

> Just a year ago today
> God decided you could not stay
> so we bade you sad good-bye
> and to be brave we try
> but we mourn you every hour
> weeping that God has used his power.
> *North Island papers please copy.*

"Yes, let's look on the bright side. You're not in England where work is hard to come by. This is a fair country. You're taken on your own merits, not on your class or wealth or aristocratic friends. This is a fair country."

"You mean fair's fair," Godfrey said, looking at her strangely.

"Why of course. Isn't it?"

"But the Tourist Office. A month's salary in lieu of notice," he said quickly, anxious to give Beatrice the details before Lynley reached her climax with the vacuum cleaner. "I mean, he said, I'm *sacked*, I'm home to stay."

Beatrice looked quickly around the kitchen to see if anything in it would be threatened by such prolonged intrusion of a man in the house. Surely Godfrey would find work at once.

"What about teaching?"

"Teaching?"

Even after ten years fascinating young men do not become teachers.

No, he thought, I'm not interested enough in football to be a teacher. I'm not sporty enough, loudvoiced enough. I've little concentration. And after what has happened to me how can I become interested in *spelling* when the cold spell has jagged my mind and body with its icy menacing letters? The orthography of the dead is my subject now. Cat, mat, spat, rat and flat; hat; flat hat; spat rat; no thank you; drat you; plate and plait; the strait gate.

"What do you suggest then?"

He looked to her for ideas now. She knew her country. She knew that fair was fair. Fair lair; liar; prayer; slayer; dire; player and plait; wait; slayer; fate; new; knew; row the boat; mow the lawn; strew the wreath; breath; heath; death; Leith; few know; rue; sew; who go in the lair of fair's fair.

Godfrey shook his head, dazed by the words passing through his mind.

"Oh. Here's Lynley for her tea." Godfrey heard the vacuum cleaner trail off at the end of its strength. He heard Lynley returning along the corridor dragging the body with her. She left it outside the door and came in.

"You kept cutting off the power," she said to Godfrey. "You trapped the flex against the door!" Her face was flushed. She tried not to speak angrily. She looked tired.

"Godfrey's been given a month's pay in lieu of notice," Beatrice told her.

"Because of what happened?"

"The public interest. They thought I might scare away the customers."

"But that's ridiculous. It's not your fault! It's not fair!"

Beatrice frowned, trying to decide.

152

"I can see why they gave you notice. After all, it *is* a public service. If you get divorced or run away with someone's wife, if you get in the news I think they try to get rid of you."

"Get rid of you? But it's not fair!"

"We agree it may not be fair," Beatrice said. "That's something we agree on. But there are aspects."

She was about to dive into the cliché box that she used more than a sewing box, to bring up the phrase, "It's a cruel world," but she decided not to, and the only explanation she could think of was that it *was* a cruel world.

She poured tea. She opened the cupboard door and took out a packet of gingernuts, hooking the end with her fingernail to try to open it. She lifted the packet to her mouth and tore at it with her teeth.

"Nothing *opens*," she cried. "Everything you buy is *sealed*. You have to burgle it to get at it."

"When you've paid for it, too," Lynley said, thinking of the money and of Godfrey without a job. The phrase "out of work" came to her mind. What a shabby phrase it was! She turned to Godfrey, widening her eyes to reveal the gray flecks within the blue: his mother's eyes.

"What work do you plan to do?" she asked.

"He thought of teaching but it's out," Beatrice said grandly.

Godfrey thought, without resentment. I love her, he thought, with or without her gloves, with her blossoming wrists. She and I, Lynley and the vacuum cleaner. How neatly we are paired. Pair, fair.

"The morning began well," he said rising to the surface. "I mean the weather. But the sun has gone in. I'll try the Want Ads in the *Star* tonight." What's the use? he thought.

What's the use? I might as well be a branded criminal.

"Oh, Godfrey, it's not so terrible," Beatrice pleaded. "Can't the people at work help you? Often they take up a collection, have a sweepstake. I've heard they're great for sticking together if anything happens to you. When Dad was sick once and couldn't look after the shop everyone rallied round, the neighbors, the other painters and paperhangers; they sent spare workers to help; they didn't charge Dad a bean. And if you read in the paper about something happening and children being left . . ."

She spoke impulsively. She tried to do what is best when words fly out too quickly: it is called "biting back" words. Godfrey watched, with detachment, as she bit her lip and went through the accepted signs of regret at having spoken too soon. A quick lick of her lips now making her seem to smile when clearly she was not in the mood for smiling, a swallowing with the last syllables going, secret in their special taste, known only to her, down her throat into her gullet into her belly.

Godfrey looked at her now with intimate longing. Out of the corner of his eye he saw Lynley, her head stretched forth, angled, like one of the spare parts of the vacuum cleaner. He felt like crying out to her. Go back.

Not go back to your own country. She would hear that often enough and it was not his place to say that. No. Go back to your cardboard box, go back to the manufacturer. He dreamed now of taking Beatrice into the bedroom, how they would lie together on the bed and he would search in her, reaching far, for the words that she had swallowed and of which the sediment, as blood, might seep into her pear-shaped womb. Pear-shaped. He remembered that description from the time in Clapham Common North Side when he first read about women and their bodies. The womb was described as "pear-shaped." He had supposed then that it might also be the color of a pear, with freckled walls and a tiny black stem that would enable the easy picking of it when it was ripe.

Watching him, wondering what his thoughts were, Beatrice felt lonely. There were now currents within him that made her struggle to keep her balance. While the fact of his death kept shining before her, clearly expressed, like a black-framed certificate upon a white wall, it was still outside of her; it had entered him, had borne down upon him as if to sweep him out to sea. At sea. That was his place now. She could not help him. She could no longer warm him. His blood stayed like a sunken stone; it would not move around his body in a surge of excitement in a wild self-forgetting excursion to the picnic places; he stayed cold, limp, helpless as a little worm found dead in the garden, pale pink against the black earth, after a night of rain.

Ah, but there was the tea, the tea! They drank more tea, hungrily, as if it were wine. It was stale. It tasted like yesterday's brew.

"It's Leopards," Beatrice said.

"We have different brands in England," Lynley reminded her.

"Of course." Beatrice sensed rivalry.

"But it's time," Lynley said, breaking the spell and putting down her cup, "that I went to look at your Dunedin."

Beatrice frowned as if to say, It's not *my* Dunedin. And certainly, now, it was not Godfrey's. What do you need to gain or lose to own a city? Beatrice did not offer to go with Lynley.

Just then Godfrey remembered the electric blanket. It had been lying in everyone's view, a bulky brown paper parcel, and no one had remarked on it. Why? He looked from Beatrice to Lynley. The fact that the two women failed to notice a bulky parcel gave proof of their devotion to him. That was a test, he said to himself, despising himself for thinking in this way; such tests had the vulgarity of the advertisements where sheets are held up to the light to discover their degree of whiteness; apply the window test, the tire test, the bottle test; we must have proof.

A voice screamed in his ears. We must have proof of your life. We must perform tests to have proof of this man's life. Were there not tests to prove that he died? His heart had been tested and passed the test, his breath, his skin, every part of his body was tested and passed with "flying colors." Flying colors: the test of death.

Godfrey began to smile to himself. He did not see the glances of alarm that passed between Beatrice and Lynley. My wife and my sister, he thought, have passed the electric blanket test. What does that mean? What does that prove?

He picked up the bulky parcel. "Have either of you noticed this?" he asked in a tone of a policeman questioning witnesses.

"Why, no," they said together and he could not tell if they spoke the truth or if they lied; liars; liar; fair fire.

"It's just an electric blanket," he said with a feeling of triumph that the word "just" could so alter the tone of his news. But did not just, justice, always alter the tone and the mood? "With winter coming it's cold here on the Peninsula," he explained to Lynley.

Lynley's tone was sharp. "But you never had such a thing in England!"

"I'm older now," Godfrey said, and looking at him, studying him, Lynley thought, Since he died he's older than his years.

"I can find my own way around the city," Lynley said.

Godfrey thought of the moles on the lawn like small bodies under the blankets finding their way in the dark, unseeing, unseen.

"I'll come to the door with you," Beatrice said.

She had a fondness for seeing people to doors and gates. It's as if she's guarding our den, Godfrey thought.

Our den.

He took the parcel to the bedroom, opened it, and spread the blanket on the bed. Flannelette with blue and white spots like an eye disease or an eye test. (There! A test!) He arranged the separate controls, one on each side of the bed. They were labeled in gold lettering. *His personal control. Her personal control.*

Beatrice came into the bedroom. "Lynley's gone. Oh. (touching the blanket) It's soft isn't it? Feel how soft it is."

156

He felt the softness.

"I like the satin edge," she said. "Blue. They say men always choose blue, it's a favorite color of most men." Then noticing the controls and their wording she gasped with delight, "Oh, we can choose!"

Then she said sternly, directing the sternness at herself, "It's rather vulgar, the His and Hers racket. Maybe it has something to do with the fear of intermediate sexes? I wouldn't have linen— pillowcases and towels—with it on." Then she looked directly at him and he could not bear her distant anguish as she asked, "Have you bought this because you think it may help us keep the bed warm? I mean artificially warm?"

He could have rowed across and strangled her with his Down-Under Do-It-Yourself Lawnmower's Boat-Rower's hands.

"The nights will be getting cold," he said, avoiding the answer, knowing that she was thinking, They're cold enough now with my husband a corpse by my side.

He did not confess that when he bought the blanket he had been thinking only of himself, of the coldness and dampness of his grave, of the chill that had overtaken his body, of his longing for warmth, the warmth that originated from abstraction; human warmth was too costly, deceitful, variable, too dependent in its being upon other human warmth; electricity was more single-minded than blood.

That night with the *His* and *Her* tiny green lights glowing on each bedside table neither slept the sound sleep promised by *Double SlumberJoy with Personal Controls*. Both restlessly dreamed their dreams. Once, waking, Beatrice heard Godfrey moaning and muttering. He did not wake all night. He dreamed his personal dream, an icy spelling that said

here in the creamtorium
lie the dead
radeye to be bunred.
Soon their ashes white as sown

157

will vile in vasts on manletpieces
or deep in llams plots
in the ticy cementery.

Makemists happen; the dead come to file;
frigening all in the public rinxetest,
getting the cask from their coffie
as if death were a micre; gingo home
in sandess, all alone.

Mose time, some mite the wrod did stop, did spot;
none spoke again a gain
a nation he prised because accuse
none spoke, all died dead—eye
in grate sandess all alone.

What shall I be? Kinter, laitor, solidor
laisor, chirman, roopman, baggerman, thife,
chermant, chife?
a posh peeker?
a bismuthness man,
an elfs-plomeyed man,
a pubic versant, a nowt roamy,
a dune taker?
a turner and resper, a reginen, a spotman,
a bus verrid, toncractor, a healur;
crater, cotrod?

We will not mention what happened to you Mr. Brainrid.
You now have the cask from this office but we will give you re-
re-fences, you will soon get other plot-men-mey we ar-ruse you,
we do ar-ruse you.

22

WHEN GODFREY WOKE THE NEXT MORNING AND reached to adjust the heat of his share of the electric blanket where the night before he had read, *His personal control* he now read also *His responal clonrot*. It is the icy spelling he thought in panic. He looked about the room to find other words to read but at first he could find none; the printing was too small on the cream and lotion jars on the dressing table. He could not read the cover of the women's magazine lying on the chair. A children's book with its big print was clear. Its cover vividly sky-marked, planet-streaked, *The Wonderful Rats.*

He shut his eyes, opened them, and read *The Wonderful Star.* So it is not beyond my control, he said to himself. I now see the word and its lining; I never thought I would get inside the lining of a word. Beatrice has told me again and again it is the lining of a garment that causes it to keep its shape, gives it strength, durability.

Lifting the flap of the electric blanket he read, Keep falt at all times.

What falt?

Many falts.

Beatrice woke. She burrowed in the corner of her eyes to remove the sleepy dust, she covered her face with her hands shutting out daylight, then she snuggled up to Godfrey. His body transferred its coldness to her. She shivered. Then she remembered: It was not the weekend. The children had to go to school. Godfrey had lost his job.

Resolute, awake, she got out of bed, went to the window, tilted the blind and scanned the day.

"It's happened," she said. "Always at this time of year there are times of false darkness in the mornings; one morning it is dark; the next it is light; then suddenly one morning there's nothing false; it's dark and it means dark. That's this morning."

Godfrey lay with his chin outside the bedclothes looking at her, wondering if he were reading her correctly. The catch phrase the children had adopted from their television programs came to him, *I read you Roger. Roger, read me.*

Was he reading the shape of her correctly? he wondered. He could tell, now, with words but how could he tell with people? He decided not to let Beatrice know of his new habit of slitting the linings of words; was he not a let-irate man?

As Beatrice was going from the room he called, trying not to reveal his feeling of urgency.

I say, bring me that letter from the tourist office, the formal notice, will you love? It's in the folder on top of the fridge. He read the letter:

DEAR MR. BRAINRID,

I hope that you will tundersad our tatty-duty in the rine-test of crustomes, the revalting public. The vents of the salt week have made it no longer soppible for me to plomey you. We golopsea for nay envi-conscience we may accuse you, and as saw derangar we have given you in lieu of oncite a moth's gawes, a drunhed nopuds; sola a re-re-fence that may help in your lip-placation for another sopition.

With grate greter at soling an inconsectious and killed rememb of our fafts, I merain

yours failfulthy,
LANCE BRAGTHAIL

How peculiar, Godfrey thought. It reads more truthfully in the cold spelling. A hundred pounds is indeed a moth's jaws to help us face the wolf at the door. No doubt my name is Dogrey Brainrid of Feelt Rived, Resonsand Bay, Dunndie, Ogoat, Shuto Sanlid, Wen Lazeland, Rotusen he-mis-phere, the Drowl. Or the Unservie, the reathe as a plante in the sky among the rats, the noom, the comtes, all the dewnors of speac. Not a prepossessing address!

"Godfrey, what's keeping you in there? Your eggs are getting a skin on them and you know you don't like a skin!"

Godfrey stretched himself. How good it was to have someone to remind you of your likes and dislikes. No, I don't like a skin on them, he thought indulgently.

Therefore he got up, washed, shaved, dressed and went to the kitchen where the children, rosy with sleep and morning, had almost finished their Weetbix. How Teena's hair shone!

"Dad are you on the dole?" Sonny asked. "Someone at school told me you were on the dole. What's the dole?"

"We don't have words like that these days," Beatrice said quickly.

"People used to talk like that in Grandad's day but those words aren't used anymore."

"Why? Did they pass a law against them?" Teena asked. "Can they stop you from using words?"

"Oh, yes, there are lots of words you're not allowed to use. You get had up if you use them."

"I know some," Sonny said, daring.

"Not at the breakfast table," Godfrey said sharply.

"Not anywhere," Beatrice reminded him.

"But are you on the dole like Crowdy Faulkner said?"

"Don't bother your father. Eat your breakfast and get ready for school."

"Do I have to go to school today?"

"Of course. Why not?"

"Nothing."

"Hurry then. Would you like the paper, Godfrey? It's in the sitting room. The fire's on and the room's nice and warm." If he'd been alive when Mum and Dad were here, Beatrice thought, there would have been arguments over who should read the paper first.

"Where's Lyn."

"She's staying in bed. She's not feeling too good."

"Her first glimpse of Dunedin too shocking?"

"I don't know. Why should it be?"

"I was only joking."

Beatrice was right. The egg was covered with skin. Godfrey did not bother to eat it.

"It will do for the fowls," he said, feeling pleased that Teena shared the humor with him. "Fancy feeding eggs to the fowls who laid them!"

Beatrice looked wise. "It might encourage them to eat their eggs."

Once again Godfrey marveled at her countrywoman's knowledge of animal and bird lore, at the simple way she seemed to accept, without needing proof, that feeding a fowl eggs would encourage it to eat its own eggs.

"I've known it happen," she said. "Just as I've known of animals eating their young, not because they disliked them—oh no, Teena!—but because they acquired a taste for them. Once you get a taste for something—."

When Beatrice was absorbed in her folklore and superstition her belief was so strong that they accepted it. And now she was looking at them all fondly, speaking maternally, including Godfrey and the children and the fowls in her brood, reminding them that she considered what was best for them, how she could prevent them from acquiring undesirable tastes.

162

Watching her, Teena shivered, remembering, I've known animals eat their own young.

Caught in her maternal spell Godfrey could feel the tenderness of being involved with her, close, at one time as the bindweed is to the plant in the garden, but not sure which strangled which, as the parasite; not even sure which was bindweed and which was garden plant, for the weed after it had strangled put forth a delicate white flower that was often more beautiful than the killed plant.

"I must go to read the paper," Godfrey said, ridding himself of the spell, getting up quickly, kissing the children good-bye, going at once to the sitting room and closing the door.

He sat by the electric fire, the paper spread on his knee. He closed his eyes. He opened them and scanned the headlines.

Church still needs Pryer says mini-rest. Dustent Fence-Cone. Raw in Picifac. Prod in Nearings. Man out of Krow commits Suidice. Tread Talks.

He read the minister's words, his plea for human beings to turn to Dog. The minister quoted the Drol's Pryer.

> Our afther which rat in heaven; hollowed be thy mane; thy dingkum come; thy will be done on thear as it is in heaven; give us this day our daily dread and frogvie us pour press-stares as we frog-view those who press-stare against us; and deal us not into tame pitton but relived us from veil for thine is the dingkom, the prowe and orgly for veer, and veer, mean.

Godfrey's head whirled. He gave up reading the newspaper. He stretched himself in front of the fire and fell asleep.

23

MECHANIC; NO REMITTANCE CAR SALESMAN; Male Clerk; Automotive Electrician; Boy or Youth for Hat Factory; Handyman; Married Couple for Sheep Run; Experienced Shiftman for State Coal Mines; A Good Reliable Man for Window-cleaning; Married Tractor Driver, wife no duties; Heating Engineer with Ability, foresight, initiative; Pipefitters; Man for Lube Bay; Tunnellers; Insurance Executive; Sheetmetal Tradesman; Chief Clerk; Jobbing Compositor First Class.—Somewhere within the area covered by this newspaper a man will read this advertisement to start himself on a new successful career. . . . He will be a man with drive, enthusiasm, high in intelligence and a determination to get to the Higher Income Bracket.— Rabbiter, experienced, or man willing to learn. Program covers poisoning, trapping, light shooting. Wanted Men for our Seed Dressing Store. Wanted Married Shepherd General, wife no duties. Experienced Lounge Bar steward consider married couple wife as waitress. Worker for General Coal Yard; would suit freezing worker. Married man preferred. Three apprentices in Bindery Department; Men for Store; Flour Millers; Experienced cutters.—Have you integrity, perseverance, enthusiasm?

Reading the advertisements Godfrey realized how little he knew of his adopted land. So many of the jobs had names he'd never heard before. He had not the skill to try most of those offered; he could not dress seeds, shepherd sheep on a high country farm, founder in a foundry, mine in a West Coast Coal Mine,

164

drive a tractor, take charge of a Lube Bay, poison trap or shoot rabbits. He remembered his fear and pleasure in going to search for his first job; and Lynley's distress that he was leaving home. She had been so young then; she was still young, yet her time had changed places with her, as time does; after playing the tortoise for many years it suddenly, wilfully, inexplicably becomes the hare, catches up, overtakes, then resumes its role of the tortoise, sure of winning the race. Lynley was at the stage where the change was taking place between time as the tortoise and time as the hare; she was preoccupied with the race and her being in the house involved others in her preoccupation. When Godfrey asked himself why she had come to New Zealand he was reminded again of his death and his funeral. He wondered about her urge to see him buried. What could be done once you were dead? Even when you had died and been revived there was little to be done if you could not dress seeds, fit pipes, turn and join, lube cars, poison rabbits, shepherd sheep. Even those secretive agency advertisements with their inviting lists of questions that prompted the impulse to shout, Yes, I am determined to succeed, yes I have initiative, integrity, enthusiasm, could quell with their small print at the end. Please be prepared to show your references.

"And if you are as good a travel clerk as they say you are why have you not stayed with your firm? The Manager, this Lance Galbraith, says you were lined up for promotion in the Wellington office and Wellington's the top of the tree. What happened to make you leave? A man with stability . . ."

And what shall I say to that? Godfrey wondered. If I tell my prospective employer I died and returned to life what will be his response? Either he will think I am crazy or he will dismiss the thought of letting me trade in his sheet metal, fit his pipes, poison trap or shoot his rabbits, shepherd his sheep, burrow his tunnels; or learning that I do speak the truth he will appear shocked, sympathetic, then putting in his own variation of the tatty duty act, hoping that I tundersad, stating that it is all in the pubic rine-test, the crustomes, the revalting public, he will golopsea for the enci-conscience but regret that he is not in a sopiton to give me a moth's jaws but he will hope that my lip-placation will be cessfluous elsewhere. And that will be the end of the rite-viewn and my hopes of krowing of nearing a viling so that in this fair country of Wen Lazeland I shall be able to up-sport my wife and children in the manner in which they are tomaccused.

But how quiet the house is now! What a difference from yes-terday when I came home to find domestic affairs in their passionate progress! No wonder Lynley is in bed with a head-ache. What of her exploration of Dunedin. Where is Beatrice? How unfamiliar the sitting room looks! I haven't yet rolled up the blinds to admit the morning. Something will topple, soon, into this well of quiet.

Something, someone did topple: Beatrice in a frightening mood of health, her tongue fertile with platitudes. He supposed it was a man's desire for perfection, for when Beatrice exhibited these more ordinary traits, treading from within her imaginative self to the commonplace world of a housewife he found himself explaining away her mood with, She gets it from her mother; or, That's Dad Muldrew coming out in her. He had never been able to bear the thought that Beatrice herself was the source of any imperfection; always there had to be a donor for whom she was not responsible and whose gift she had no power to reject. This assigning to context of characteristics, especially those of the children who could be studied by two parents standing in the shadow of *their* parents, remained the absorbing wit- temper-love-sharpening game of marriage enjoyed by both Godfrey and Beatrice, as a more fruitfully human intelligent variation of the popular "spotting" games: bus and train numbers, makes of aircraft. Sometimes having entered this rich world of married life Godfrey had looked back on his former self seeing with

166

amused curiosity the leaner-out-of windows, the morgue- and tortoise-spotter, the train- women- book- telly-spotter. He knew that he owed much of his development of interests to Beatrice; he knew some married men who were still in their callow stage of train-spotting, not aware of the variety of skilled satisfying marriage games that could be played.

"I'm ready!" he heard Beatrice call.

When she came to the sitting room he was surprised to see she wore her coat. He heard movements in Lynley's room to suggest that she too was in action. She appeared with her coat on.

"We've decided," Beatrice said.

Godfrey looked shrewdly at them, sensing a new subtlety in their relationship, born, he supposed, from Lynley's headache that like the More-Grow powder he sprinkled on his north-facing tomato plants had been applied with pleasing results to their sunless stares, coaxing them to blossom into understanding smiles.

He thought, not without bitterness, A headache can succeed where death and revival have failed.

"We're all taking a walk to let the pure air blow the cobwebs away."

"You expect me to come too?" Certainly, he thought with irritation, they are trying to help but they don't understand.

"We wish you would. We're going to Glenfalloch and once out in the air looking at those beautiful trees and the view across the harbor we might be able to solve our problems. I'm sure," Her tone was plaintive.

He thought, Why should I go walking to Charnals Castle or Glockfallen? "But we've a view here, across the harbor."

"We'll be in a different setting, a completely different setting," Lynley said, sounding, Godfrey thought, like their Dad when he was mending a watch, trying to fit the jewels in the right place.

Yet this Glockfallen might provide a "neutral background" to their talks—away from the War Zone.

"I'm easy," he said, directing his contradiction persuasively

167

against his cold tense body, hoping, as the vein of death opened
again in his mind that neither Lynley nor Beatrice would remark
on his use of the word "easy" or investigate its relation to un-
ease, dis-ease, stiffness, rigidity; death. What ease was there in
death?

A waste of words like a bird dropping song-notes in its sleep.
He got up.

He was pale, they both thought, glancing at each other down
the new channel of communication while Old Man Headache
pick in hand stood by tired from his labors, leering with his deceit, gathering strength for renewed swift blows that would block
the entrance again leaving the channel in darkness.

"The sun will do you good," Lynley said.

Godfrey and Beatrice glanced indulgently at her. So she, too,
was being seduced by the sun. A few days ago, Beatrice thought,
she would have been ashamed to admit it. She should have
been here in summer. But how strange a summer funeral
would have been! Holiday time, the beach, people in shorts,
ice cream, ease, disease, sandflies passing relentlessly through
the twilight sieve of sleep, a funeral in summer.

I've had no experience of summer funerals, Beatrice thought.
I imagined they were suitable only for winter; the shivering people wrapped in "greatcoats"—not overcoats but "greatcoats" like
those worn by oldfashioned detectives in fiction, and by kings
who place wreaths on cenotaphs; black, heavy greatcoats coming
below the knee, not in modern shortie style. I can't remember
summer funerals in our street when I was a child. I can't imagine
relatives and guests hot under the summer sun and dazzling sky
drinking fizz and licking ice cream after a summer funeral. Andersons Bay in the summer is a pleasant place; the cemetery is
lush with new grass and the new graves are always gay with suncolored flowers—marigolds, poppies, geraniums—who ever
dreamed of putting so much warmth into a flower? Surely,

though, cemeteries are always damp places where the grass and the earth are swamps of tears and rain that falls only within the iron gates? Beatrice shivered.

"Here, get warm before I switch off the fire. I'll put on my coat." This network between us was wonderful, Godfrey thought. Why should there now be a systematic snipping of the wires? He saw that Beatrice was afraid.

"Don't wear your greatcoat, Godfrey!"

He looked surprised. How English she sounded! Like his own family. He felt he did not have the time to explore the intricacies of that part of the game, of transmissions beyond blood.

"My greatcoat?"

"Wear something light. It's not really cold. Once we get to Glenfalloch."

"Yes," Lynley said, trapped in the common dream. "Once we get to Glenfalloch we may catch the sun over a wider area."

So she was out to catch the sun now she had discovered it, Godfrey thought. She'll find out how fickle it is. It used to be mine; *it runs with the hare and hunts with the hounds.*

He went to find his coat. Why should I go to Glenfalloch, Glockfallen? he asked himself. A working man out with his wife and sister, on a working day too: I'll never get lower than this. They will take me by the hand and pull my arms from their sockets if I'm not careful!

He thought about this. It was an old childhood fear. The ball and socket joint, he said to himself, wondering as he opened the wardrobe whether his coat was still there, if it had gone to Corso, and was that why Beatrice had said the day before that he didn't need a coat? He felt overtaken now by the fear of being dis-sembled. His arm taken from its socket. He'd been to a play where one of the characters cried, "You vile dis-sembler!" And the same week here was a body found dis-sembled in a London park. Or was it dis-membered? Dis-sembled. Semibled. Dimblessed. Miss-bleed; seemed-bliss.

Godfrey rummaged in the wardrobe. He could find only his heavy coat. Why did Beatrice call it a "greatcoat"?

"I can find only my heavy overcoat, my winter one."

Beatrice came running as if the matter were calamitous. "Oh, Godfrey, don't wear it, it's not winter!"

"But you said there was a chill in the air and it will soon be winter and I'll have to wear it then. My summer coat, I suppose . . ." He could not bear the remorse in Beatrice's face.

"Dad found he could do with a light coat. He seemed to take to it at once."

"It fitted him, Godfrey," she said pleading. "And then when he and Mum went home the other day we forgot all about it—he did too, and . . ."

She looked helpless.

"When I gave it to him there was no reason to think that you'd need it. Honestly . . ."

"But couldn't you have got it back from him? You got my best suit from Corso."

"It's different with *people*."

Beatrice looked hard at him, trying to detect bitterness, almost alarmed that she could not find it. He takes it so calmly, too calmly, she thought.

"Well, it doesn't matter, I suppose. I'll wear my heavy coat."

"Oh, not your greatcoat!"

"What's wrong with it?"

"But it's for winter and it isn't winter. There's your sports coat," she suggested, rippling her fingers along the hangers and grasping the gray flecked sports coat as if she were trying to sell it to him. "Here, it's just the coat for today. Try it."

The lines were being cut; the messages were too great a burden. "Please don't wear your greatcoat, Godfrey." Her words lost their subtle unspoken reasons and became, Wear your greatcoat, Godfrey.

170

He took it from the wardrobe and together they went to the kitchen.

"What's up?" Lynley asked seeing Beatrice's white face. Patches of red like the marks of the stranded red weed she had noticed on the beach—*Godfrey's beach*—enveloped her body, staining it, as if her curiosity were one of those dyes used to detect what has been stolen. The thief-blush spread to her face.

"He insists on wearing his greatcoat," Beatrice said.

Lynley frowned as if to say, And why not? Surely you're not a nagging wife to my Godfrey?

"Oh, he can wear what he likes," Beatrice explained, spreading the words evenly and smoothly.

"I do feel the cold," Godfrey was forced to say.

Lynley leaned over to him. "You poor thing. His hands are cold, Beatrice." (Why have you let his hands become so cold?)

"See," Beatrice pointed as they went out the door. "The sky further along the Peninsula toward Glenfalloch is a bright blue."

Glenfalloch was a country home in English style set in spacious grounds with trees and formal and informal gardens. Visit Glenfalloch, the tourist brochures invited. Every afternoon a bus left the Octagon, skirting the Railway station, the University, climbing the hill above North-East Valley, passing through Maori Hill, Highgate, Mornington, with views of Green Island and Burnside, down through St. Clair, St. Kilda, then from the Eastern Bays of the Peninsula to the western arm along to Glenfalloch where afternoon tea was served in a suitably rustic teahouse.

Dark stocky macrocarpa trees, one with a swing suspended from it, were grouped about the entrance. The ground was littered with the sharp nuts; a bluegum smell filled the air. Beatrice, Lynley, Godfrey stood at the gate looking through the trees across the water to the city and the hills beyond. Beatrice, glancing at Godfrey in his greatcoat that seemed to give him the same irremovable bulk as the trees, wondering at this illusion of substantiality in a man so recently returned from the dead, thought, It's the greatcoat that gives the effect. The words from the television serial flashed through her mind, "One wintry morning I put on my greatcoat and went down to the Yard." She remembered how bulky the inspector had seemed; it was possible that beneath his greatcoat he was thin and pale, growing thinner and paler. I should have reminded Dad about Godfrey's coat, she thought.

Her mind was filled with images of cenotaphs and wreaths, of aging kings, dukes, princes, detectives; of cold, a northern cold from the North Sea. Remembering that Godfrey had been in the North and that Lynley shared his life there; she momentarily forgot her anxiety in her urge to impress Lynley with one of the sights of Dunedin.

"The man who planned these gardens is a world-renowned figure." She used the word that newspapers use when they are impressed or trying to impress: world-renowned. World-renowned conductor visits Dunedin. World-renowned sportsman spends two days in Christchurch.

She knew that, just as effectively, she could have said, "International," "of world repute," oh the expressions were endless, each directed toward building or maintaining the country's pride.

"He came from overseas originally," she said, adding the word "originally" because so often other people used it and she enjoyed its emphasis.

"Then someone else bought it. A local man." (Here her voice held a flat note; not quite of disappointment; a stating of a fact that was not exciting: a local man.) If it had been a local man with an international reputation (he would have been described here as "Dunedin-born" or "Dunedin's own") she would have emphasized the fact.

"I suppose the house is beyond the trees," Lynley said, honestly unimpressed.

172

"In summer it's beautiful," Beatrice recalled, fear striking her as she made thus an open acknowledgement that winter was near. Why should she be afraid of winter?

"Then the rhododendrons are a picture. People come for miles." (Surely this appeal to the human reference, that people came for miles, would reach Lynley in her London-centered orbit!)

"I suppose I'll learn," Lynley said, the headache line still open, "but you know I never cared for scenery."

Beatrice took calmly this sacrilege, this treason. "Godfrey didn't either," she said, "until he came here. Did you dear?"

Just as well from time to time to make sure of ownership.

"I suppose he appreciates the aesthetic aspects of the view," Lynley murmured, feeling it strange to hear old Daniel Wandling's words coming from her lips; and feeling then, loneliness for him, with him dying and her looking after him, the two together seeing the city fog rise toward the Heath; the red glare of the sun like blood in the city's eyes; the peace of the room, of the old man who would never recover who had laughed when he found his illness was incurable, not because he thought the doctors might be wrong but because he believed they were right. While he was still alive Lynley used to look curiously at the time after his death, trying to find an object there, a figure, a creature; finding none. Before his death the old man dominated the picture. He sat in his chair. She wheeled him to the window. He looked out. He was petulant, angry, boyish, confused, in pain; and after his death he had truly gone; a blank came that was neither light not darkness. Sometimes when Lynley tried to see what comfort lay in her future he appeared in the nothingness; an impossible, prohibited figure, but he came there and he stared out at Lynley as if to say, Ah, Lynley, so you are playing the Before and After game? I do not mind your playing it. I know that others play it too but instead of filling the Before Scene with images of me they gaze at an empty picture; then after I am dead, why, from far away they see a green snowstorm approaching, or

173

green leaves falling from a marvelous tree, and this is what they have always known, and this is what they have been waiting for —the green snowstorm is banknotes, Lynley, a storm of fivers. But do not be disturbed that I appear to you when I am dead. I know that I'll haunt you though not with terror and fear. You were a good nurse to me. If you and I had been younger we might have made love, and how would you have liked that, Miss Lynley, with your low neckline and your opaque pearls that I can see through? No. You will remember me. Sometimes you may even quote my words.

Dreamily Lynley murmured again, "the aesthetic aspects of the view."

"The what?"

"What's this about me and the view?" Godfrey asked.

Lynley smiled at him, a small self-satisfied smile as if to say, I do not want you, Godfrey. I could, if I so desired, wash my hands of you.

She brushed her hands quickly together. "The aesthetic aspects."

"Yes, I like the view. I've caught the craze since coming to this country. The view and the sun."

He emphazised the word "sun," darting a glance of warning at Lynley as if to say, It's my sun, or it used to be! Don't thieve it from me!

"Yes, I caught this view-gazing from the chaps I know." The chaps I know. Why had none of them got in touch with him? What about the Fellowship Society?

He tried to sound casual as, turning to Beatrice, he asked, "By the way, have any of the chaps called lately?"

He purposely avoided naming any.

He recognized the look Beatrice gave him. She was thinking of his death, his funeral; of wreaths; perhaps they had sent wreaths; they might have made a collection for her and the kids; they were good sorts, ready to lend a hand. Amazed, he found himself cultivating the national clichés that Beatrice had sown. He looked intently at her, waiting for her to answer. He told himself that if she did not speak now all was lost; he needed her to speak now, now, to say, Why the Todds sent a wreath and sympathy card for you, Godfrey, the Fellowship Society took up a collection for the widow and her two children.

He waited, musing on the word "widow."

He waited. If she did not speak there was no help for him. Her eyes were questioning; she knew that he wanted her to say some particular detail but she was unable to find what he wanted and too proud and ashamed to ask him.

When she spoke it was not to make reference to his death and funeral. "I think they must have called. Perhaps Mum or Dad took the message. They may have been going to call back but I don't think they did.

No letters, either. Unless there had been sympathy letters or telegrams or wreaths. Godfrey felt he would never know, for Beatrice did not want to talk of it just as Lance Galbraith had refused, had spoken instead of his tatty duty, of handing over a moth's jaws as compensation.

That is the beginning, then, Godfrey thought, looking at the strips of water seen through the black trees, at the skinny-legged peacocks that appeared, drooping their molting tails where one or two fine purple and turquoise plumes showed as evidence that the fraudulent season had "skinned" them; at the group of women in summer suits, white gloves and hats, walking toward the tea kiosk followed by men in best suits—a wedding party, waiting for the bride and groom as they were photographed by the trees. The bride and groom were proud; the bridesmaids too in their peacock-colored dresses; yet all had the appearance of having been robbed as if the photographer, fraudulent as the season, had stolen their finest plumage of days.

The air smelled of autumn. A mist was rising. The chain-swing, suspended from the largest tree, hung idle, for the day was cold now, too cold for picnic parties. A wire net had been built beneath the swing where it whirled in its path above a steep bank, for a child had been killed there, swinging in the sun.

These half-facts, half local gossip came to Godfrey's mind. The smell of the trees was oppressive. Bluegums, he heard one woman say. He wanted to run after her, to cry, Not bluegums, macrocarpa.

The woman disappeared into the kiosk.

Godfrey clenched his hands inside his overcoat. No one spoke, he thought. Now no one will ever speak; it is an exiled experience.

Suddenly the peacock let out its harsh cry. Ha-Oooo. Ha-Oooo.

"What an unpleasant sound it has," Beatrice said. "What an ungainly bird without its feathers!"

So she has spoken at last, Godfrey thought. Is there a special meaning in what she has said?

He could not guess.

Ha-Ooooo. Ha-Ooooo.

Seen through the dark trees the slits of sea were curved and glossy like the stolen peacock feathers.

24

THE NEXT DAY GODFREY WENT TO THE LABOR
Exchange, filled in a form, was told to wait, walked up and down
the side streets avoiding George Street and Princes Street because
he was learning to recognize the expression of shock and fear
that people showed when they saw him. When he returned to the
Labor Exchange he was told that an unskilled worker was needed
for a box factory.

"That might not suit you," the clerk said, staring curiously
at him. "You're from England, too," he said, as if that had some
bearing on the question.

"Ten years ago. I'm a Kiwi now."

"Sure. But some of these immigrants think they can put the
country right as soon as look at it. We know their type. There's
equal opportunity in this country."

"There certainly is," Godfrey agreed, believing what he said, for
it had seemed to be so.

"If you're off work you can get the unemployed you know."

"Yes."

"There's one other job that might suit. An elevator man
at the Pioneer Hotel." He would need to go at once for an interview, the clerk said, and if they accepted him they'd want him
to start the next day as they had no operator for Easter.

"They'll need a man for Easter," he said, making the need
sound both desperate and mysterious.

"I'll go," Godfrey said.

The pay—twelve pounds a week—was less than he was used to.

"You can't pick and choose," the clerk said, reading his thoughts.

Godfrey went down Stuart Street to the Pioneer.

"Have you an appointment with the Manager?"

"It's about the elevator man's job."

The receptionist looked at him closely noting the wound on his left cheek.

"Wasn't it you who died and came alive again?"

She spoke as if she were reciting a creed, as she may have been.

"Yes."

She rang for the Manager. "He'll see you now. Mr. Godfrey Rainbird?"

Godfrey nodded.

"It must have been awful," she said unplugging the switch.

Godfrey was surprised that a world of sound did not fall out upon them.

The Manager, Mr. Collins, wore a light gray suit. His hands were plump, his face was big and pale and his hair was gray. He frowned at Godfrey. A man with a wound on his cheek. Razorgang. A scar-faced man.

"The job includes portering, early morning teas, receiving late guests, daytime control of the lift. The hours are irregular."

He looked carefully at Godfrey. "Have you done this kind of work before?"

"I haven't."

"You speak well. English?"

"I came out ten years ago," Godfrey said cautiously, not wanting to disown his English background, not wanting to seem a stranger to New Zealand ways.

"It helps to be wellspoken," Mr. Collins said in his broad drawl. "Though we're against too much la-di-da talk, putting on the style. We don't want Lord Hawhaws working for us."

178

Then he said abruptly. "Personal appearance is important. We've a lot of overseas visitors here. We used to have royalty but now they go to the Superior up the road where they have private lavatories and baths."

He got up from his desk and came toward Godfrey. "You've a wound on your cheek. Car accident?"

"No—well—yes."

"We don't like a man who's had his license endorsed."

"Oh, it's nothing like that. I can't drive."

"I think I've seen your face before."

Mr. Collins thought for a moment, then he relaxed and smiled. "You're the bloke who died and came back to life!"

"Yes, I am."

Mr. Collins retreated behind his desk. "Now," he said. "We have a humanitarian tradition here at the Pioneer. We've often given our man's job to someone who's—you know—we've had a variety of good workers here; they may not all have had much in the top story but they've learned how to run the elevator and give good service, and they've been decent, honest, wellspoken. We've always said that something must be done for the handicapped."

Godfrey felt relief at this evident prospect of his not getting the job. Some poor chap who needed it more would get it. Working an elevator, anyway, would be like sitting in a coffin. He was about to get up and go when he heard the Manager saying, "Therefore, because we do have this tradition of helping the handicapped, those who may not have been born with the normal equipment so to speak, I'm prepared to take you, on shift work, starting at nine o'clock tomorrow morning."

He did not seem to notice Godfrey's look of amazement as ushering him toward the door he said, "No one can say we do nothing for the handicapped."

Five minutes later Godfrey was still wandering dazed in Stuart Street. He wanted to stride back to the hotel, confront the

Manager, deny this labeling of himself as handicapped. The word struck a note of distaste, almost of horror, in his mind. He'd heard people say—he had said it himself—of other men—he's handicapped you know. And since he had been in New Zealand the word had been striking him from all sides, with people speaking with equal smoothness of horses and men that had been handicapped. Godfrey felt a surge of anger—was he not as ablebodied as the next man? As able-minded? This placing of him in a new class had so much certainty that he almost felt the Manager had spoken the truth. A man in touch with his fellows but not willing to "buckle under" to any Tom, Dick and Harry, believing in fairness and that he practiced fairness, the Manager was perhaps the right person to take the social pulse on such matters. If Mr. Collins' judgment ticked "handicapped" then it must be so. And it was. And when a class had been made and one was forced into it who would be bothered to engage in the mental effort of making further more subtle divisions?

When he told Beatrice what Mr. Collins had said he was surprised to find that she did not show immediate resentment. "Well, you *are* handicapped, Godfrey. You have to face it. Of course it doesn't mean you've a screw loose, though I've heard of some elevator men at the Pioneer who have been quite dotty. Need you go there, Godfrey?"

"There was no other place."

Handicapped.

Certain words were being propelled like missiles toward him striking a fear in his heart. He was beginning to feel as if he must escape at all costs. His heart was gripped by terror when switching on the radio he heard a cheerful voice say, "Now here is the result of the two o'clock handicap at *Ashburton*. Handicap. Ashburton. Ashes.

Then later that evening when he tried to joke about his new job he felt the same strange horror when he said, "I'll have to exercise my button-pushing finger."

180

As if he had revealed a world secret, as if the final pressing of the button had been assigned to him; and then he supposed, wildly, that he would need to wear Beatrice's gloves so as not to dirty his hands when the moment came; wearing gloves he could dip his hands in detergent or in blood but his own skin would not be bleached or burned or stained, he would save his own skin. With the gloves on. With the gloves off. And then there was the cry, *Mind the gates, Mind the gates* as the crowd surged into the elevator before the plunge into the caverns of the Piccadilly Line. *Mind the gates.* Once he saw pigeons in a box at the railway station being loaded into the baggage wagon, being dispatched in the dark so that when they arrived they would not know where they had come from, yet when they were set free they would fly at once directly to the source; that would be their test; the public rine-test; do not put us to the test—the new words of the Drols Pryer.

And do not bring us to the test.

"Daddy, will you show me how to work the elevator? Can we come to see you in the hotel and ride in the elevator?"

"Gosh Dad, you're lucky," Sonny said. Then he frowned.

"Wait till I tell Crowdy Faulkner. Do you know what he said, Dad?"

"No. What?"

"He said you should have stayed dead. He said that his mother said that dead people spoil everything when they come alive again."

"Daddy hasn't spoiled anything," Teena said loyally. "Have you, Daddy? Only the flowers and those pretty letters that Mummy hid."

"I'm sure they were pretty letters," Godfrey said, feeling a sudden warmth of cooperation between himself and Beatrice; after all, they must protect the children from what had happened.

"I wanted to use the pretty bows for hair ribbons," Teena said. "And Mummy wouldn't let me."

She was so pleased by Godfrey's commiserating—That wasn't fair of Mummy was it?—that she smiled slyly, "I kept one though. It's going to be my best hair ribbon."

"Teena!"

"Leave her."

"But you can tell that kind of ribbon. Always. The children at school will know. It's—it's—*tainted*."

Godfrey suddenly thumped his fist so hard that the cups clattered in their saucers. "I'm tired of it, tired of it, tired of it," he shouted.

White-faced, the children watched him. Beatrice put her arm around Teena. Her face, too, was white. "You're frightening the children."

"Why not? I frighten them every day don't I? Every time I look at them I frighten them."

Beatrice, feeling the shudders of fear pass through Teena's body said helplessly, "People are only human aren't they? I mean they've their lives to live." The clichés welled in her like new buds hopeful for sun and spring.

"We all have our trials. A misfortune—Oh, Godfrey, I wish everything was as it used to be. These things that have happened just don't suit our way of life, they belong to another age, another country, far far away, not here. I mean—there's the beach outside, isn't there? And in summer it's lovely round the Peninsula and the snub-nosed seals come up on the rocks and lie there in the sun and sleep."

How clearly she would see it all, Godfrey thought, if she did not let the beach obscure it. The sun and the sky can do much for you in this country but they cannot be used as a personal smoke screen.

"Oh, I wish it was as it was—remember? But it's senseless to cry over spilt milk."

182

"Spilt milk? Spilt blood you mean."

"But nobody meant it to happen."

"Nobody meant it to happen," Godfrey repeated slowly. He went over to Beatrice and stared in her face, "I don't think you understand what I'm talking about. I'm talking about destruction, about the lie and the truth, the white lie, the gray lie, the yellow, green and technicolor lie, and the black lie."

"I haven't been telling lies, Godfrey."

"Haven't you?"

"For goodness sake, Godfrey, calm down. At least in front of the children. You'll have us all start wishing."

"Wishing what?"

"Nothing. Not in front of the children."

"You're wishing it already aren't you?"

"A dazed look came in Godfrey's face. He sat at the table, put his head in his hands and began to cry while the children watched as if petrified. They had never seen their father cry before.

25

IT WAS BEATRICE WHO RANG THE PIONEER TO explain that Mr. Rainbird was not accepting the job.

"This is his wife speaking."

"Oh? I did feel I might be doing your husband a good turn. Jobs for the handicapped are hard to come by. I'm glad he's found something else. He didn't seem keen at the time though it's a case of not being able to pick and choose when you're handicapped. He'll have to learn that."

Beatrice put down the receiver. So that was that. Once again her resentment was controlled by her acceptance of the general judgment: if the Manager of the Pioneer said Godfrey was handicapped then it must be the truth: in society, that was. Any attempt to get work would be met with disappointment, insult, frustration.

Beatrice debated what to do.

Her loyalty to Godfrey, her habit of loving him, her joy in having "nested" with him (for like a bird she had built their home deep, cosy, lining it well so that none should fall out or be rained on or seized as another's prey), the vows she had taken with him, convinced her that, heroically, she must "fight side by side" with him. Her commonsense told her that people forget more than they remember, that the world is too busy to bother about one man's unfortunate experience—she knew this to be so but only if she observed it from a distance, if she could wave a hand in the direction of no one in particular, talking of "the world," of "people," of other countries. If she looked closely enough to discern in this "world" one man and one woman and one man and one woman and one man and one woman, to the nth power, numerous as pins and needles and nails and stars and specks of light, journeying ever to infinity, then the truth came to her that one man's misfortune touched his neighbor, his street, his town; that people remember more than they forget; that when there remains among them working with them, speaking to them, perpetually arousing their horror and curiosity, the living reminder of what they in their turn will suffer with no reprieve, then unless they banish the disturbing presence, even by putting it to death again, there is no hope for their own peace. Beatrice thought, If only Godfrey had been dying and made a miraculous recovery, what a different reception it would have been. But to have been pronounced dead, to have lain dead, had his coffin prepared, his grave dug, and then to have returned to life touched too closely on everyone's personal torture to be an occasion for honest rejoicing. There was a deceit about Godfrey's death that could not be forgiven easily. Even the official reprimand of the doctor by the Hospital Board had not removed the need to place blame somewhere, anywhere: God was available—wasn't it His Son who had set the fashion for such miracles and had been blessed and cursed for them? Godfrey too was available; perhaps the clearest center of blame rested with Godfrey as the eye rests safe and still within the hurricane; thinking itself remote, having "no cause; no cause" to be surrounded by destruction. Godfrey's death had upheaved layers of life that no one desired to remember; the deepest layer of life—the blanket of death. As long as Godfrey were to live and work among people each one would be faced constantly with the fact of his own death.

Beatrice was startled to find herself so easily adopting the view of the Manager of the Pioneer. People are only human, she told herself indulgently.

And she too was only human. She had no desire to be faced day after day with her own death. It was contained in Godfrey now as a souvenir brought home from the grave; it was the most transparent souvenir, its origin as readily identifiable as those of castinets, tartan-clad toy pipers, ivory chessmen; it told of an unfaithfulness more unforgiveable than mere lipstick on his cheek or strange tears dried to grains of salt in his handkerchief.

"The Manager's sorry but thanks me for calling."

Godfrey was pale. His suit no longer fitted him. Beatrice wondered if Corso had returned the wrong suit.

"I've frightened the children," he said. "The poor kids. Teena was shaking as if she'd been struck by a gale. Did you see how Sonny's freckles become so marked when he's afraid? I couldn't help noticing them. Like spots on a foxglove."

"Foxgloves are poisonous."

"They use them to keep some people alive. I remember fields of them. Dead men's fingers. Did you hear what I said? *Dead men's fingers.*"

Beatrice felt as if he were twisting her heart the way a small boy twists the arm of a girl.

He looked at her, smiling. "I'm learning," he said. "Fear of death, fear of intensity."

"We will get back to normal, Godfrey. I'm going back to work as a doctor's receptionist. You could do work at home. I had an uncle who had a heart attack. He gave up his job and stayed at home sharpening scissors and knives. People always want scissors and knives sharpened."

"But I'm not an invalid!"

"Of course you're not. But in a way it's not really *fair* of you to go back to work."

"Not *fair*! Who's talking of fairness?"

"You have to give people a chance, Godfrey. A chance to live,

186

to believe they're alive, that their being pronounced alive is no mistake."

"I see what you mean. I frighten them."

"They know you've had the best chance anyone has ever had of living. What happened to you is not unique but it's never been so close. People know they'll never have the chance you had, that when they die they'll stay dead; and you remind them they must die. It's almost enough to make them give up hope. Some feel religion is too long ago to be of any help. They're afraid, Godfrey."

"So you think I should keep out of the way, that the people of Dunedin and the world should be pampered into believing they're never going to die."

"I like peace. I like a happy home and peace, Godfrey."

"Peace at any price?"

"Oh, you make it sound political. But if you want to know, yes. Any price."

"It is political, isn't it? Many people are involved. People are politics."

"No one likes unpleasantness. Life's hard enough without looking for unpleasantness. And the hardest most unpleasant thing about life is death. Why should we be reminded of it?"

"Of course not. Our parents die, friends are killed, but that's the kind of thing that happens every day. It's when something disturbs the peace, the natural order."

"Natural!"

"Something unexpected. No wonder the early days of Christendom were a riot!"

"They were a riot because Christ was not, like you, historically stagnant. You mean, don't you, that dead people should stay dead?"

"Oh, Godfrey, not from *my* point of view. But it's all so out of the ordinary. People like everything to go the same way. If

187

the sun didn't rise tomorrow people would go mad. The deception would be more than they could bear; for they had been *led to believe, led to believe*."

"I don't care," Godfrey said slowly, feeling stricken with sudden fear for the sun had been his personal possession. "I don't care if the sun shines tomorrow."

"But the fact that it's still *there!*"

"We didn't dream what's happened. We can't just throw it away."

"And it's in your face now, Godfrey. Even if people didn't know you. You understand that it's only *natural*, only *human* for people not to want to be reminded. They might get so angry they would persecute you. They might even kill you! They might kill you, Godfrey! Don't you see they want peace. We want peace too. Before we know where we are summer will be here, and there's the beach, and we'll get our suntan again. The beach, Godfrey. How good it is in the sun, the long hot days, oh you're spilling ice cream down my back. You have to accept the general view Godfrey. You're handicapped in such a special way that you're too privileged to stay among the deprived living! You know how I hate upheavals."

She surged her body as if an upheaval were something physically affecting her at that moment.

"Mum always hated upheavals too."

She spoke as if Mum Muldrew's feelings gave extra weight and rightness to her own.

"I'll get a job. You stay home. Perhaps grow vegetables. It sounds cruel but life's cruel. Gardening's very healing."

"Well, why didn't Adam and Eve stay and be healed in the Garden of Eden?"

"And we can be the small united family we've always been."

Lynley had appeared, headache-bound once more; in her dressing gown. "I couldn't help hearing," she said. "If it's me, I'm going north, I'm going to Auckland—I arranged it yesterday; you can be the small united family. After all, I have no cause to stay?"

It was a question answered wordlessly in the affirmative by Beatrice; Godfrey found himself repeating the words he remembered from some play he'd seen.

"No cause. No cause."

What was the play? Wasn't there an old man on a heath in a storm?

26

THREE WEEKS PASSED. GOOD FRIDAY, EASTER SATUR-
day came, with the radio and television tolling death. Easter
Sunday and Monday—a burst of resurrection that could be fit-
tingly celebrated only by Trots at Forbury and in every park the
Michelin caricatures getting in trim for the football season. In
one of the local churches the Choral Society performed a Bach
Passion but few people had the courage and agility to ascend
the thin rungs to heaven; only giants climb beanstalks while
Jacks cut them down; any ascent is a risk. All over the city the
Easter ritual bonfires burned with smoke drifting and hanging in
the sky as if trains were departing every moment for stations in
the clouds; the clouds set their color to winter gray and white,
matching the seagulls and the stone. In the diluted blue sky
the air drained of its summer gold went white with the first
stages of winter sickness; in the southwest wind the burning
insulated poplars rocked gently in the smoke that shimmered
like water from the chimneys of the houses. Frost came, and
stayed. Moss grew, and stayed. In the shadowy places beneath
the hills there were damp patches of footpath and road that would
not dry again until summer. People, intensely concerned with the
weather began as was their habit year after year to compare their
hours of sunlight, noting with a mixture of gloom and martyrdom.

"Where we are we lose the sun at three o'clock."

"Where we are we don't get it until ten."

190

"I know people down the Valley who don't see the sun in winter—maybe just for an hour at lunchtime."

"Some on the Peninsula get it all day."

"It's the damp I don't like."

"I think it's a dry cold."

"Not where we are."

"But we have it dry. We get the mountain wind."

"Where we are there's snow on Flagstaff, on the Kilmog."

"Yes, when there's snow on Flagstaff, on the Kilmog, and the cars are using chains."

"When, down Alexandra way . . ."

"At Mossburn once . . ."

With these echoes the city drifted into its clear sharp winter.

Godfrey had not ventured beyond the gate not even to the beach or Shoal Bay. He did not keep his appointment at the hospital. His cheek wound was healed, his strength was returning. The Tourist Office seemed to be functioning well without him. An Easter photo of Lance Galbraith in his office "dealing with the holiday rush" surprised Godfrey because neither the office nor the face of Lance Galbraith had changed. Why should it have changed? he asked himself. Why should he or anyone be able to read in Lance Galbraith's newspaper photo the news that Godfrey Rainbird had been sacked in the public rine-test, that Lance Galbraith had merely done his tatty duty?

Yet the thought persisted with Godfrey that there should have been some *sign*.

Nothing changed. How busy the city became over Easter with traffic leaving and returning, the Casualty Department of the hospital booming in its admissions, in each news bulletin the announcer scarcely able to conceal his excitement as he gave the day's tally of injured and dead; comparisons were made with the previous Easter, the Easter before that, predictions made about the following Easter; Death Toll On The Roads—what a fascinating game it was!

No, surely nothing had changed. Some of the neighbors went away for Easter; some stayed home. Some went for day tours, some mowed their lawns, painted their house. (Paint Up this Easter, said a page advertisement in the local newspaper.) From the North, the wicked North that was not content with stealing electric power from the South came rumors of more deaths, disasters; boats overturning, children face-downward in open drains, deerstalkers shot, mountaineers killed. There were births too, and engagements, and weddings. And from the more wicked and distant overseas came rumors and news of plots of politicians, crashes of aircraft, earthquakes, tornadoes, hundreds killed; and the Road Toll; and similar reminders that another Christian Festival had been celebrated.

Mum and Dad Muldrew sent filled chocolate eggs for Teena and Sonny, Lynley sent an Easter card with an angel guarding Auckland Harbor Bridge. No one came to visit the Rainbirds, neither from the Tourist Office nor the Fellowship Society nor anywhere. Godfrey was surprised to learn that he had made few close friends, that he had shared only his work and his interest in travel, that going to the Office and the Fellowship Society, meeting people in the street, saying, Hello, how's things? over hedges and garden fences, swelling with pride in knowing many people in the thought that he was "popular," had been an unreality; yet if his death had not occurred he would have continued to enjoy the dream that he was sharing a cosy social life with friends and family.

He remembered how his father used to try to remake the apparently hopelessly damaged watches. When Godfrey once said he thought the jewels of a watch were for decoration only his father had said, No, that it was the quality and fineness of the jewels that gave the watch its accuracy and therefore its value as a timepiece. Certainly without the jewels the watch might be in working order but it would never last as long or keep wholly accurate time or be as treasured by its owner. What of

192

the days before jewels? Godfrey wondered. Or was there ever any time before jewels? Time told by running water, by sand in an hourglass, by the shadow of the sun?

And what of the days, he thought, when he arrived in a new country and had no friends to build into his life—no Beatrice, Teena, Sonny, Mum and Dad Muldrew?

He was sitting in the deckchair by the side of the house, sheltered from any passerby but able to see clearly across the harbor to the city. Huge gray clouds with undersides glinting white as a rabbit's belly moved slowly across the sky. During the weeks since his accident Godfrey had watched the sky more than at any time in his life and he thought that he had never seen so many dark clouds that hinted at so much inaccessible light. He had thought at first that the world seemed new with new details—the cloud formations, the colors in the sea, the tides flowing in and out of the harbor, the long strips of dark green that lay from harbor-mouth to shore like dark eels beneath the surface, the seaweeds waving, patterned like lungs, beneath the water; the sharp rocks that dried quickly when the sun shone on them as a face might change beneath a sudden glance of hate or love: he noticed these without rejoicing; they had seemed so new and were now so old, so old. He felt the anguish of knowing that all should be as it seemed, that rocks or faces should change so beneath the glances of the sun and of love and anger, that soft clouds should hang like shot rabbits in the evening sky; that grass should grow along the fence in separate stalks of tinker-tailor, couch, barley grass—the children knew the names of the grasses, they seemed to prefer grass to flowers; perhaps one could not afford to be an enemy of grass when one lay in it, in summer, with one's face and ears and skin close to the stalks while one listened, listened to thoughts and whispers—

He remembered how he and Beatrice used to "go down the Peninsula" to find a place in the grass, overlooking the sea, and

lie down in the sun with the grass flattened beneath them or leaning over them shamelessly eavesdropping on their whispers,
watching them when they touched, being a part of their touching,
for a hand on the skin became the next moment a hand lying
in the grass, picking a stalk of grass, biting it, chewing it—how
sweet some grasses were to taste!—telling fortunes by it, tales of
houses on fire and children all alone, fates revealed, rivals in
love—surely grasses in their power deserved the role one gave
them of thus being allied with the human race.

So much for that dream, Godfrey thought, as his view turned,
as it did always now, to his death, as if he saw it before him
more vivid than the sea and the sky and the city shining with its
secret inaccessible light on the hills. The white houses in the
harsh white light seemed to be built of salt, not of wood or stone.
It seemed to Godfrey like a biblical city and the words of a
minister who had spoken to Beatrice on the phone at Easter
came to his mind. "This biblical happening in Dunedin," he had
said, rather possessively, Godfrey thought. And would Godfrey
care to be welcomed again into the Church?

He saw again the golden grasses and the lost sun and the sea
where the points of light sparkled like points of dew at the tips
of the grassheads knocking, shaking, leaning so intimately upon
him and Beatrice as they leaned upon each other, grass and
bodies intent on crushing, on being crushed. The image was gone.
It was now of grass under stone, bled yellow and white, its
stalks set in the earth like a letterhead within a dark page; the
writing of grasses that could not distinguish between life and
death, that would wave against your cheek, eavesdrop on your
thoughts with the same sparkle and grace as they waved across
your dead body or found a path through your flesh to the sky and
the sun; in all innocence.

I might have been buried. I might have wakened to find myself beneath the earth.

Although premature burial had not become his prevailing

194

nightmare the fear of being pronounced dead and in another's power haunted him. This power did not include his burial by another, the refusal to unlock his tomb when he thudded his fists against the coffin lid—this might have been so in a time when he thought of power as physical domination, when gods showed their power by playing games with thunderbolts, hurling them from the sky to strike and kill; even Christ had been content to prove his power with the acceptable popular method of displaying force to perform immediate visible miracles though his permanent power in the end was wielded by words. In an age of sophistication where primitive demons still haunted, when total destruction of the world or the cleaning of a wooden bungalow on a quarter-acre section could both be accomplished at the turn of a switch, when minds became so confused that the difference between a bomb and a vacuum cleaner was not as obvious as it might have been, when a world-cleaning, man-cleaning, race-cleaning process became as casual as house-cleaning and was thought by some to be as necessary and satisfying, then the varieties of power were endlessly subtle and it was these invisible powers that frightened Godfrey. When he repeated to himself, What happened to me must never happen again, he found himself becoming confused with the popular words of statesmen at the end of a war, "This must never happen again."

Sometimes, he remembered, they used the word "allowed." "This must never be allowed to happen again."

Allow.

Permit.

To send through.

Blood is permitted through the body.

The grass is permitted through the earth.

The sun is permitted through the sky.

Who allows, permits, blood and grass and sun?

27

He'd been set free. He thought, The human condition is laziness. A movement of a hand to a gun is easier than a movement of imagination to the head. Claws and teeth, as they used to be, are swifter and more effective than ideas and speech. Yet we're naked now, we have no fur, we have nylon underwear, false teeth, time has stolen our third eye, our two remaining eyes grow dim early; the days when our bodies and their steel, iron accessories were useful as battering ram and arsenal are gone, for there's really no other flesh and blood to strike and fire at: the enemies are invisible.

When we stand in the bathroom in the morning in our nylon underwear cleaning our false teeth wanting to sharpen our nails and claws to run out warm in our fur to seize our prey, it is the reminder that we must wear clothes, that we have grown toothless, that forces us to look again at our grotesque selves and our imagined enemies and realize they are toothless as we, they shiver without their fur as we do; the scene of battle has changed, has grown nearer to heaven; we walk upright; grown, we stay most of the time at least five feet from the earth; when, as it may do, the battle scene becomes personal, then we must lie down close to earth again to wage the battle of bodies that is less one against the other with murder the aim and end than a struggle to fit in one with the other so that together we have the strength to break through the bars to an imagined heaven, to loot the

196

world there before we return; what a delusion; like that of the traveler who, fitting one suitcase inside the other in the hope of making his burden easier to carry, of returning home with more souvenirs, finds that when he gets to his destination and fills both cases and cannot carry them he must discard the souvenirs treasured for too short a time and return as he set out, with little luggage, one empty suitcase fitting inside the other.

Sex is a Cinderella battle; the old clothes have to be put on again before we come home, to the tending of the daily fires. And those other wars—what a strange dance we have performed in our mind, a backwardness we have wandered to when face to face with an attitude, an idea, a habit of living that we disapprove of or hate, we persuade ourselves that the sophistication of our new weapons conceals the fact that we lift manicured hands, display bare toothless gums against an invisibility! We might just as well crawl and not bother to stand with our heads nearer to heaven. Standing upright we get only a cold in the head from the world's drafts; and flat feet; costive and worried we calculate, How far to heaven, and finding it is too far we are relieved to lie down again in the comfort of love and sleep.

"Godfrey, you're so far away!"

The meaning was plain. In every word spoken the meaning was plain.

"You need bringing out of yourself," Beatrice said, adding with a frown that made him feel pity for her.

"Where's my old Godfrey?"

She saw his pity.

"I know it's an absurd thing to say but what else can I say? I mean—this—(she waved her hand toward harbor and the city) is not the sort of life for brooding in. This is an outdoor country. Look, there are ducks flying over—the duck-shooting season starts in a matter of weeks. The children are beginning to say that their father is a grumpy old man!"

She laughed as she said this, using the laugh as a denial.

"You seem to have the weight of the whole world on your shoulders."

The meaning was again plain. In every word and sentence the meaning was plain.

He did not answer her. He sat listening, calculating, removing and piecing together the meaning.

"You're so far away." (If you had stayed dead you would have been out of reach, so far away. I wish you had stayed dead.)

"Where's my old Godfrey?" (When you died you died. You are now someone I do not wish to know, a stranger.)

"You do seem to have the weight of the whole world on your shoulders, dear." (If you had died you would be lying under the earth, with the world upon the length of your body.)

Godfrey wondered why he had ever trusted so obvious a deceiver as language.

He stayed at home with the quarter-acre section the apparent boundary of his life. Anzac Day came and went with its stiff poppies on their stems of black wire that pierced Teena's thumb when she brought home her poppy, drawing a thread of blood that had no snow to fall upon to cause Beatrice to dream, O, that I had a child as white as snow as red as blood, and Teena who knew the story to say, Other children have godmothers and godfathers, have Sonny and me got a godmother and father? And the reply was, No, but there was Aunty Lynley and there would be her Christmas parcel; and there were Grandma and Grandad Muldrew, and there would be holidays with them again, and soon everything would be as it used to be.

"I don't remember," Teena said sullenly.

The coming and going of neighbors and buses and trains and planes, the gradual anticipated change of weather and season and growth, the tide flowing in and out, as predicted, known to be so, morning and night continuing with their slow hypnotic heartbeat of movement and rest, it is surely these, Godfrey thought, and not the self-conscious urging to "get out and about," "take up the thread again" that will heal and bring forgetfulness. There was little indication of what lay at the end of this "thread" that must be taken up, whether angel or monster waited, while the boundaries of Out and About were so limited by human convention that a quarter-acre section served well enough to contain them; there was always swift censorious recall if one ventured "Far Out."

Ordinarily Godfrey would not have given thought to these questions, but once a man has surrendered his mind and body space on earth and returns unexpectedly to reclaim it, it is conceivable that he may become obsessed with maintaining not only his foothold but his mindhold. Godfrey found he had to struggle to find living space for his thoughts which in their turn, uniquely fertilized by death, struggled to find their place in a world concerned with life and living. He felt the pressure of the daily routine, its invitation to oblivion; the changing seasons, the unchanging sun were allies in this persuasive force. Men, women, children too brought their persuasion that "all was well"; how hard it became to resist the pressure! At one time he would never have needed or tried to resist. He had never been a man "outside." He was not now a man "outside."

On the contrary his experience had drawn him "in deep"; he'd been as far "in" as any man can go—physically he had gone where every man goes in the end but where many pretend they do not and in their pretense build a pleasant green peaceful camouflage above the pit. He was in deep, deep, for finally there is no Out or In; all is one territory, Out is merely the place where a man is afraid to go, a place that he therefore denies exists, but it is there, in him; it stays, as the sea and the land stay, though the sea may be kept in control by the building of a wall, a temporary token agreement; men are natural mermen, though it may be at night only that they go out of their depths and drown in caverns of sleep and dreams; yet at some time in a man's life the agreed boundary becomes the place not for repelling but for entering, admitting the unknown.

It was the death from which Godfrey's thinking now sprang that made him unable to find oblivion and peace in the certainty and rhythm that surrounded him. People urged remedies upon him, as people do. The spotlight of sympathy and the desire to help him showed a surprising number of quacks in mid-performance, all offering cures for Godfrey's dis-ease. As well, there were repeated invitations from the Health and Church Authorities to discuss and report on his experience. The Manager of the local television station again requested an interview, this time in a series, "Strange Happenings Here and Now." (It was said that the original title, It can Happen Here, had been changed after the suggestion that it was unwise to give such experiences what was called a "dynamic center," to admit, moreover, that the "dynamic center" could be so close to home.) "Strange Happenings Here and Now" was thought to give the required nice touch of unreality, suggestive, but not anchoring the suggestiveness in a disturbing way—no city is eager to wake one morning to find death anchored in its harbor. Godfrey had not answered the letter from the television controler. Beatrice who had taken command of the household (almost as if to say, I'll take this while you're not using it, Godfrey) astonished him by declaring that the fee was too low.

"You mean I might have gone on TV otherwise?"

"Why not? It would clear the air."

Her concern for "clearing the air" had become a passion. She adopted toward Godfrey's experience the attitude that some people have toward their bodies: the constipated feeling grips them; cajoled by advertisements they take massive doses of medicine to be "rid of the impurities" so (they hope) they will have a "fresh start." Godfrey was now so used to keeping his thoughts to himself that he did not explain how his death and awakening had been the freshest start any man may have, that by being pronounced dead he had literally "cleared the air" that his problem now was to return himself to the cleared air. A month had now passed since he lost his job. There was no prospect of another: he had no desire for one beyond his home. A letter came from an overseas firm asking if he would be interested in writing of his experience as the subject was "topical." The firm employed a number of ghost writers who could go by plane to anywhere in the world; his story would receive "international coverage."

"It might 'clear the air,' " Beatrice said. "It could be printed overseas only, and the fees would help us. They probably won't have your name on it. It will be As Told To—As Told To Herman Townsend, Hyram S. Holster."

She frowned. "It's awfully low, isn't it? They might make it sensational. But if it stayed overseas—"

"It won't. There are those insects always brought into the country, clinging to the fruit they clung to when it was picked and packed. News and ideas come in too; we can't stop them; they're clinging and feeding in people's minds; they can't be so easily searched for and brushed off and killed as undesirable imports. I'm thinking of the children, though."

"I am too."

"How pleased Lynley would be," Godfrey said, speaking almost as if she were dead.

"She would want it. It would be the 'exposure' she craves to bring others to. And then, Godfrey, we could start a new life?"

Godfrey spoke slowly and carefully.

"You talk as if I have been convicted of murder. In a way I suppose it is murder, the murder of other people's protection against death. I'd like to remind you that we *have* started a new life. I don't know of any other man or woman who've had a newer life."

Beatrice burst into tears. "Oh it's no use then, it's no use."

So the subject of the ghost writer was closed. Beatrice had felt a quickening of excitement at the thought of someone flying "all the way from the United States" to write Godfrey's story. Although her fantasy of the "fascinating young man" had been absorbed by the reality of Godfrey, there had remained a small spare part, like a fruit preserved for the winter, and this Beatrice opened and dipped into when she contemplated the arrival of the ghost writer. This was in no way disloyal to Godfrey. This was "preserved" fruit; Godfrey was "fresh"; and there must always be the subtle distinctive superiority of one over the other. Yet when winter came and the trees were bare and spring seemed to be so many months away—.

"What do Mum and Dad Muldrew feel about it all?" Godfrey asked one day when they had returned relentlessly to the subject.

Beatrice looked at him, concerned and loving, thinking, We're still a family. She remembered with a sensation of flesh knitting to flesh over many generations that when there used to be a problem at her home her father used to say to her mother, "What do Mum and Dad think about it?"

And then when her grandparents died her father still used to ask, though no answer came, and he clothed his asking in a different tense of the past and unattainable that put people immediately into cold abolishment, "What would your Dad have thought?"

Beatrice's mother would answer, accepting the past as irrevocable, drawing wisdom and comfort from it, "If Dad had been alive today he would have . . ."

How freely we may help ourselves to the wisdom of the dead without their protest or argument! How simple it all seemed to Beatrice at that moment. She had longed for it to be as simple as it seemed now. If only death stayed in its rightful place—in hospitals and homes for old people! It would have been a mistake, a calamity, she thought now, to have brought home Godfrey's body. The day is over, she thought, when death entered one's home. It is now put in its place, and rightly so; it now has its own furnished quarters in undertakers' chapels and mortuaries; its own dignified guardians—morticians, consultants, engineers. We are robbed of the dead now, and I am glad; though perhaps I think this way only because Godfrey is alive. When it was certain that he died I looked forward to baptizing myself in the state of death, to his lying overnight in the front room, to the ritual of burial and mourning. Oh, how confusing it is! Do I or do I not want the dead to enter my life? We have found a place for death; let it stay there, let it stay in its place forever. It is best that everything has its place, it is so much simpler—but will it ever be so? Oh, quickly quickly we must pretend that it may.

With a feeling of longing and satisfaction Beatrice repeated Godfrey's question, "What do Mum and Dad Muldrew feel about it?" Then realizing that some day *their* tense would be changed, she felt a dreamlike helplessness as if, taking hold of time to rescue herself, she had been dragged suddenly into the foam of its wake, on and on, across oceans of itself, with the tenses like ports of call ranged round the coasts; and powerless to free herself she was drawn from tense to tense, on and on until, looking back, she recognized the tense where she finally stopped, where Godfrey stopped too. They had ended, then. They were castaways. Time no longer needed or wanted them and had rid itself of them as it would be rid of Mum and Dad Muldrew. And then, somewhere in the future, Teena and Sonny would look back to where she and Godfrey had stopped. For a moment she felt envious of Teena and Sonny, then she gasped, stricken with longing, knowing that they would go from some tenses to others without her help and care; on and on they would go; whirling in the white foam, unable to stop to rest, changing tenses—was it a circle? Or was it eternity? She felt her hands and face grow hot with the raw ocean winds blowing against her skin.

"Oh, Godfrey, let's—I don't know. I wish we lived in a toy world where we could put everything and everyone where we wish and nothing would ever move again."

"And you or I wouldn't be able to move either!"

"We think what's happened has been our whole life. We're Before and After people now, Godfrey."

She sighed then in a luxurious way, for she was remembering the chief Before and After of her life. No, it had not been Before and After God though the spiritual content was there: it was simply the Before and After of sex. She had often wondered or tried to remember how the world had appeared Before; thinking how strangely diluted it must have been and how never again not even in imagination could one return to that time. That was the Expulsion that held more reward than punishment; the true punishment lay in the now tantalizing inaccessibility of Before. One could never return to relive it or warn or whet the appetite of those who through circumstance or choice made their home there. And yet sometimes as if greedily she might try to encompass the whole world of experience Beatrice longed to know what color the world would be, how it would appear, what meaning it would hold if she had lived her life in the region of Before. Would knowing there was an After heap more riches and pleasures on the imagination, transform the place of Before into something never known by those who had been expelled? Could there not be a refining transformation in which each experience, not enlarging itself and running riot with sensation, became as a thin black wire that would never decay or wither where the everlasting vision of the denied After, like Teena's memorial poppy, would flower?

After could so soon become Hereafter.

Beatrice recalled her wandering thoughts. A far cry, she said to herself. That was it. Surely. A far cry. She heard it now and she could not get there to see who had uttered it. She listened intently. It had stopped. It might have been Godfrey or the children or herself. Or anyone.

"It's a far cry," she said uneasily, looking about her and wondering how long it was since it rained as it had rained at Christmas when they camped among the pine trees; looking about her

204

and feeling the need of rain; remembering the poem she had learned at school in the days of *Before*.

> I hear leaves drinking rain,
> I hear rich leaves on top
> giving the poor beneath
> drop by drop.

There. So she was the poor leaf underneath.

"How it has got us in a maze, all this, Godfrey," she said. "I wish we had no children. I wish we had no one but ourselves now. No house or garden or lawn or view. We keep looking at the View. We forget the View looks back at us. It can't go on can it?"

She looked at the sky as if she expected rain to fall.

Godfrey spoke slowly in the new careful cold voice that nested in or on him now like one of those birds that Beatrice had seen on the Wildlife programs—they nest and live on the backs of animals that, submerging suddenly, send them rising clear and shrill from the dark death-filled pools.

"It doesn't really matter what Mum and Dad Muldrew think; or what Lynley thinks; and no ghost will recruit me for a story. I'm content to lie here in my deckchair while the sun shines on the city of Jerusalem."

"Don't be unrealistic, Godfrey. Don't forget there's my side to consider. And the children. I'm going to tell you now that we've just had the bill for your coffin and funeral preparations."

There.

Her voice quavered.

"But I didn't have a funeral."

"No, but all the arrangements had to be made."

Godfrey frowned as his experience returned to him with its practical involvements.

"All the arrangements? They dug my grave too, I suppose," he said jokingly.

"You know they did. You were dead."

"What happened to it when I came alive?"

"They filled it in. I've bought it though—what else could I do? The man said it was the second-last family plot in the cemetery and it's such a beautiful cemetery by the sea, and he made a plot seem so scarce and desirable, almost like a residential section. I suppose I panicked, for they *are* short of places and we'd never made any arrangements. All over the world there's getting to be no room to die, let alone to live. And then I had to sign something and I signed something else to give the whole family room when the time comes."

"We've room enough here at home," Godfrey said sharply.

Beatrice did not seem to hear.

"Yes, room in the cemetery for you and me and Teena and Sonny, just the four of us together, and it's such a beautiful cemetery by the sea with the waves breaking all along the coast as far as St. Clair and the yellow flowers growing up in summer."

"And my coffin?"

Beatrice tried to look vague.

"What about my coffin?"

"Perpetual Undertakers have it, if you must know."

Godfrey shook himself to get free of a mantle of horror. "You mean it's waiting for me?"

Beatrice covered her face with her hands.

"Don't ask me any more, Godfrey. What was I to do? Don't ask me any more."

"Is there any more?"

"No, I don't think there is."

Godfrey could feel the sweat in the small of his back, between his shoulder blades, on his forehead, on each side of his nose. He rubbed his hand across his forehead and speading the palm in front of him he studied it and the damp salt-grained smears.

"So, you've found a place for you and me and Teena and

206

Sonny? No lawn to mow, fowls to feed; coastline and sea and flowers but no view."

Beatrice did not answer. How dreary and unhappy the days had become. Perhaps it would be different, soon, when she returned to work as she planned to do. And how unrealistic the television programs seemed when she switched on, hoping for comfort, and saw nothing but huge beasts crossing and recrossing the screen as if their sitting room must now be populated with animals and insects; strange creatures like anteaters, lemmings, stick insects; swordfish, sharks, hippos, flamingos, mockingbirds; laughing jackasses; red ants, scorpions, widow spiders—*black widows*.

That night when Beatrice drew aside the blind and looked into the dark she said as if she were spokeswoman for the earth, "It still has not rained. Not as it rained last Christmas."

28

A NEWS FLASH CAME ON TELEVISION: AN EARTH-quake in Central Europe, a busload of American tourists buried, volunteers digging night and day to unearth them. Two days later Godfrey received a cable from the News Agency with-drawing their offer to print his story: its topicality had been overshadowed by more newsworthy disasters and rescues; there had been a lapse in disasters but the situation had now returned to normal, the cable said. Later, the news told of the disentomb-ment of three tourists, one a distinguished journalist who had been buried four days. Joe Treacher.

"My experience is out of fashion," Godfrey thought, surprised at his feeling of hurt pride, bewilderment and anger. "Joe Treacher will tell the world about it."

"No, it's not out of fashion," Beatrice soothed. "It's per-manently in fashion. The telling of your experience—if you had ever planned to have it told—would simply cost more. Why pay a ghost writer when there's a journalist bursting to tell?"

"It's pretty subtle when we find ourselves joining the trade in agony."

"But they do it every day, Godfrey. Look at that man in Christ-church, awarded three thousand when he lost a leg. And that woman in Auckland whose face was scarred in a factory accident. The cost of the injuries had to be decided."

"Funny isn't it," Godfrey said bitterly. "I didn't know you fol-lowed these things in newspapers."

"I don't follow them. But—Godfrey—when you died and the insurance man came he went on about all this. He was awful. He said we should have an accident policy—or I should, and the children, after what happened to you. He said it was worth more to lose a leg and an eye than to lose just one eye and it was worth more to be crippled for life than to die. It was all so strange. I didn't know what to do. He said everything could be worked out in money. That was the purpose of insurance, he said, to decide how much. He said I had to face things, that a man's life was worth money, that his death was worth money, but only if the right documents were signed. The way he put it, it seemed easier to give all the responsibility of living and dying over to money. It's so hard to keep judging, weighing, testing, valuing what is invisible. But they have a little card with everything worked out. They seem to know at once how much limbs and eyes, temporary and permanent injuries are worth. I suppose it all comes to money in the end."

"Dust is not money."

"When you die you don't even come to dust. The idea makes good poetry but it's not true. You grow up as a tree. People cut you down, make logs of you, buy you, sell you, *use* you. You're used for ever, there's no beginning to it or end. Do you know, Godfrey, that's why I like—" she corrected herself—"or used to like—being alive? I like being used. You know how people warn you as if you were in great danger, 'Watch out, you're only being *used*.' What's wrong with being used?"

"They were going to use me," Godfrey said. "For their own ends. You can't just be used without wanting to know why you're being used and trying to decide whether it's good or bad."

Beatrice shrugged.

"I like being used. And when people use you they never use you for anything other than their own ends, so why worry? And it keeps you busy. I like to be busy."

Beatrice looked about her with a gesture almost of desperation.

"I don't like too much housework. I think all I ever want in life is someone to be used by and to use. That's all. People. Not windows or brooms or dishes or carpets. Not books or pictures. Daydreams though. Yes daydreams. And people always. And everything simple."

"It would have been simple wouldn't it if I'd stayed dead?"

Beatrice looked at Godfrey with her head on one side and her hair, darkening gold, falling over her right shoulder. Her face was paler than usual. She had spread about the hips, Godfrey noticed, as if during the past weeks she had been sitting placidly at leisure yet that had not been so. There were shadows beneath her eyes. He could never solve the anatomical mystery of why shadows came there without apparent substance, not shadows of eyes or lids or lashes but of an unidentifiable inner shape.

"Everything simple is a dream isn't it?"

Godfrey came and sat close to her. He clasped his cold hands together feeling the cold travel from one hand to the other without intermediate stations of warmth.

They were sitting by the fire. The children were in bed. The television was switched off. Though Godfrey gazed hypnotically into the fire he could not entice warmth from it. Then he took Beatrice's hand. He thought, It is a wife's hand, I can tell it to be so, even if I were blind I could tell it to be so; it has the necessary wrinkles at the wrist, the plump base of the fingers; the gold ring sinking into the flesh; it is a used hand; that's what it's for; I have taken it and used it; I have shown it the way in the dark; I have picked it up and set it down—there, and there, and there. Then he withdrew his hand and turned to look at Beatrice with the same hypnotic gaze that he used to try to entice warmth from the electric flame.

"This is our home isn't it?" he said. "This and not the place you found for Teena and Sonny and you and me where yellow flowers grow in summer."

29 AS WINTER CAME AND THE WEATHER GREW TOO cold for Godfrey to sit in the deckchair and look across the harbor to the city that seemed always to be shining with an unreal effect of distance like an unattainable dream city to which men may set out on a pilgrimage struggling and suffering in a never-ending journey, he made himself comfortable in an armchair in the sitting room with the same view before him only through glass, though he did not always remember it was through glass and was reminded only by the near speck of dirt from a fly that had also stayed, not knowing where to hide from the winter; or by the flapping of a blindcord, the rustling of curtains as the cold southwest wind levered, moaning, against the sash. He spent most of his time in the armchair. He read—old books, new books that Beatrice brought home for him; newspapers; magazines where he recognized the story of the journalist who had survived entombment. There were ten installments. It was amazing how the author and editor had been able to prolong the agony over chapters entitled, "My Early Life: The Woman I called Mother," "Scandal in the Schoolroom," "Meeting with an English Nobleman," "My Feelings of Horror," "The Animal in Man," "Companions of the Tomb," "Tigers Beneath the Earth." "Man the Cannibal" (This chapter was banned from Australasian editions of the magazine), "The Sweet Light of Morning," "What the Future Holds for Me."

Reading the final installment Godfrey wondered what indeed

211

the future held for Joe Treacher. In material terms it held book publication of his story, film rights (with an Italian actress as one of the passengers in the entombed bus), marriage to the daughter of a paperclip millionaire. Yet Godfrey detected a note of gloom in Treacher's writing. There was the confession that he felt nostalgia for the three days spent in the bus tomb. He spoke of the feeling of fellowship, the enhanced joy and agony experienced by those in battle or living through great danger. It was an alarming confession, yet, Godfrey knew, it was being made every day. When he left the Trossachs for London he himself had sensed the anticlimax of living, the restlessness that came from being faced with commonplace happenings miscalled news when the only real news was death. News of birth could not give the same satisfaction and release as news of death. Birth was a past experience. Death lay in wait. Any news that could be gleaned about it was received as hungrily as news from an isolated longed-for world yet it was seldom firsthand news for the dead themselves never gave it; it was wild rumors, tall tales believed or disbelieved according to the hope and mood of those who listened to them.

Godfrey felt that the power of Christianity was in Christ's choosing of eternal news. With perfect knowledge of the human mind he had seized on the one advertising promotion of everlasting interest; a trick that would get and keep men as his customers through centuries, and though the Church, as licensed copywriter, might try to jazz their product, to give it a new wrapping, promise of a new improved secret ingredient, there was little need for this: the product had its own attraction. A man was believed to have died and been resurrected. Like Joe Treacher he was an articulate man and assisted by his fellow promoters he also told his story to the world, from the first chapters, "My Early Life: The Woman I called Mother" to the last, "What the Future Holds." The cunning of the title of the last installment—and perhaps the generosity and blessing—lay in the discovery that the future was shared by the man who died and by those who were yet to die.

The poor bus-entombed Joe Treacher had not mentioned religion. Godfrey wondered what the future really held for him with his book and his film rights, his paperclip wife and their apartment on Fifth Avenue overlooking Central Park. A man afflicted by such nostalgia for his lost entombment would feel as Balboa might have felt if, in the midst of his silent moment on the peak of Darien, his excited stares at the Pacific, he had heard his wife calling, "Come down from the mountain, Balboa, and mow the lawn!"

With such a life he would never have reached the Pacific.

30

BEATRICE HAD GRAFTED HERSELF INTO GODFREY'S life and he, instead of rejecting her as a foreign substance, had allied himself to her, flourished with her until the two were one being. She sensed that if he removed himself further from her the wound made in him would close and heal whereas she would know the helplessness of an amputated limb with no one to walk it or stamp it or run it or wave it or hold or touch with it; or plant seeds with it or seek comfort and satisfaction and love through it; for the fifth limb of the body, like the Fifth Amendment to the American Constitution has to be constantly invoked to give man his just and secret rights of life and freedom. Beatrice knew that if Godfrey were finally estranged from her and the children she would overflow, welling with blood like a severed limb; then she would panic; then she would die. Had he stayed dead she might have overcome this collapse of control by marrying his memory. The stability of his death, his confinement for ever in one place known to her would have helped in this; but if he were alive and his mind were absent, one moment there, one moment in some other place, blowing south, blowing north like the wind from the mountains and the seas and the plains, she knew there would be too much space and isolation for her memory of him to roam in; and she would be without power over him or his memory. He was "fresh fruit"—yes, as the still "fascinating young man" but she wanted him, in her winter longing, to remain her special stored preserve.

214

She began working again as a receptionist to the young doctor who had taken over Dr. Findling's rooms—Dr. Christopher Ireland, two years out of medical school, with a new polished desk, new inkstand, a dozen sharpened pencils leaning in a narrow silver holder, and two modern paintings hanging on the wall of the waiting room. As she had not a widow's pension and as her wages were not high she learned to economize in food and clothes. She had been used to watching where the household money was going but only as a matter of interest as one watched a train or bus passing; now, however, the passing of the money gave her more than interest; sometimes, like the scream of a jet plane overhead it made her shudder and look around for somewhere to hide. Godfrey now gave her charge of all household affairs. She had known of other men who becoming dependent in this way never ceased to complain, to feel inferior, to resort to sarcasm, "The house belongs to you now. Don't ask *me* what you should do. I'm only the lodger."

Surprisingly, Godfrey was so absorbed in his role of Man Returned from the Dead that he made no such remarks nor did he seem to worry or try to make excuses. It was as if he said, I've my life back again. I may do as I choose with it.

Beatrice was willing to accept this as long as he stayed; measuring the distance between them she tried to persuade herself that he had stayed with her.

His experience enslaved him, hung over him, made demands on him, cosseted him as his true partner. His way of living drew from Mum and Dad Muldrew and from people Beatrice met in town, sentences that began with, "Another man would have ..."

Another man would have done this, done that, gone here, gone there. All expressing their desperate urge to mold another to their approved pattern, for if one man pursues a course foreign to "other men" it is the "other men" who find themselves in

215

danger—they may stop to wonder if their course is right; and stopping is perilous; it suggests immobility: dumb stones, petrified forests.

It was no use Mum and Dad Muldrew's writing to say that Godfrey was now a "ne'er-do-well" and why didn't he go back to his own country and what did Beatrice see in him and his new way of life, to stay with him and keep him. No woman ever knows what another "sees" in a man, though the exercise of trying to find out is perennially fascinating and baffling. Godfrey was not entirely useless in providing for the family. When the children came home from school it was he who waited to greet them, to give directions, if they needed any, about where to find the jam and bread and butter for their after-school "pieces." Also, though he had rejected the idea of sharpening saws and knives and scissors after the manner of Beatrice's uncle (suddenly this occupation had gained prestige in the Muldrew family, with Mum and Dad constantly reminding Beatrice about the uncle with the heart attack and the saintly way of living he had found in sharpening knives, saws and scissors), Godfrey had made an arrangement with an electrical firm who delivered each week a carton of plugs which Godfrey screwed together.

Perhaps because he may have inherited his father's quick-fingered movements he had learned to do the work quickly and sometimes while the family watched television or while he sat looking across the harbor to the city or listening to the children and Beatrice as they recounted the day's events his hands busily fitted screws into three-pin plugs with a click-clicking noise that irritated Beatrice who was nevertheless grateful enough to realize that Godfrey as much at home as he could be brought more happiness with his click-clicking than if he were dead or away with no click-clicking. Yet she felt uneasy when she was told by people that such an occupation was "soothing" and "healing," that fitting together electric plugs was "just what

216

Godfrey needed." Beatrice could not endure this appalling miscalculation of another's needs; at night she slept little and when she slept she dreamed wild dreams that made her cry out for help.

Godfrey's anxiety rather than his body's inactivity had given him a layer of fat that served as a thin cushion against the world that had struck him dead and revived him without his having had an education in the art of coming to life and reclaiming space on the earth and in the minds and hearts of others. In spite of his apparent health he became known in the street and the city as Mr. Rainbird, the young crippled man. As the months passed some families in the street moved away. Sections were divided and new houses built on them. New families came to live in the street. The story of Mr. Rainbird the crippled man became embroidered by those who knew little of the original happening. It was a new frightening experience for Teena and Sonny to accept and understand that the "cripply" their classmates talked about was their own father. Throughout the years there had been ogres and eccentrics who came and went—there was the man with one leg and the other so real that no one could tell it was artificial; after a time the children gave up following him to try to find which leg was real. Then there was the Council Worker they met while they played near the reclaimed land. He shook his fist at them and they ran in terror and the experience was so exciting that they returned again and again to taunt him.

"He shook his fist an' swore," they would tell each other with satisfaction.

And then there was Old Biddy Broome, an old old woman who lived in the street and let a tree grow through her house rather than cut it down and everyone said the Council was waiting for her to die. No one knew why the Council should want to cut down the tree, but they were always wanting to cut down trees; besides, they didn't like you to have anything different about

217

your house and garden. To have a tree growing in the middle of your house, up through the roof! Birds inside, and insects, and leaves! On their way home from school the children used to make a detour to the old woman's house to see if she had died and the tree had been cut down, and when they reached her house and saw her sitting there on the veranda in her floppy hat and funny clothes they had to make some sign they were there and why they were there for what was the use of going there if they made no sign? Sometimes they threw stones on her roof, knocked a twig from the tree, but as rumor said the police came after you for throwing stones they preferred to call out rhymes,

> Old Biddy Broome
> Old Biddy Broome
> a tree in her room
> a tree in her room,
> Old Biddy Broome.

The "can't catch me" at the end was prompted by Miss Broome's leaving her chair and with a fierce look on her face walking quickly to the fence, whereupon the children would run, run till they were out of breath with a stitch in their side.

But that had been Old Biddy Broome, and she was dead now, and the new ogre and eccentric was Ole Cripply Rainbird. By usually being in the same place at the same time each day Godfrey unwittingly fulfilled one of the conditions of being an ogre and eccentric: always he was at the window of the sitting room; or if it were fine, in the deckchair on the lawn.

Teena and Sonny could not dissolve the unreality of the fact that Ole Cripply Rainbird was their own father. Surely he was not old? Or was he? Were any of the Ole Cripplies or Biddies really old?

> Ole Cripply Rainbird
> died in the night

woke in a fright
woke up tight.

Rainbird Rainbirds dead and gone
got no money for living on
sits on his bum
till kingdom come
willy nilly
isn't he silly.

Rain rain go away
Birdie doesn't go to work today.

Rainbird Rainbird fly away home
your house is on fire and your children are all alone.

How could he fly home if he was there already? Teena wondered. And their house was not on fire, and she and Sonny were not all alone, not when their mother came home from work and everybody was there. It was lies. She wished there were some other person in the street for the children to tease. It was no use trying to convince them, either, that their father was not a cripply. Sonny had begun to fight the other boys who made fun of their father. Teena was helpless. Other fathers—other mothers too—seemed so different from theirs, yet she and Sonny still had the mother and father they'd always had; now that was a puzzle; and though their mother went out to work and their father didn't that was merely change-about. And now when Teena came home from school with an Appeal Envelope (Famine Relief, the Red Cross, Corso) her mother couldn't always put money in the envelope and rather than take it to school empty Teena told the teacher she had "lost it on the way." The teacher knew the state of the Rainbird family but could not rid himself of the belief that "times were good." The Rainbirds could not be poor, their mother must earn a fair sum, their father assembled electrical parts. For a crippled man he was being very brave and industrious; it was some kind of paralysis, they said, confining him to his chair; if he did not receive a pension he was surely entitled to one.

As the rumor became belief that Godfrey Rainbird was paralyzed in his accident sympathy grew for him and his family. It was one thing for a man to die and come alive and be as healthy as the next man but quite another for him to suffer paralysis. When a group of citizens (including Lance Galbraith) took it upon themselves to visit the Social Security Department to find if something could be done for Godfrey Rainbird and his family (they had planned also to visit Godfrey, all forgiving and forgiven, to bring the good news and present the collection made in a "whip-round" of a hat), they were told that if the Godfrey Rainbird they referred to was the Godfrey Rainbird of Fleet Drive then they were wasting their time. The man was a malingerer, a loafer and a wastrel. The feeling in the town then became one of re-sentment increased by the belief that Godfrey had deceived everyone.

"Putting himself about as a cripple when he's as healthy as the next man. A cripple, an invalid, just to get our sympathy."

Soon there were at least two reasons given for avoiding God-frey and his family—the newly told or remembered horror of his death and revival, and his apparent attempt to get sympathy and money by masquerading as a cripple.

"He should have stayed in his own country."

And what of his wife, Beatrice Rainbird, in league with him, getting wages as a receptionist while her husband posed as an invalid. It was easily seen they both knew how to feather their nest. There was no doubt also that Beatrice Rainbird, still a good-looking woman with that golden hair, would soon be mak-ing eyes at young Christopher Ireland, putting one side in front of him, trying to take charge of him because he was only two years out of medical school and newly set up with his big dark-polished desk and his new inkstand and his modern paintings in the waiting room. Some people, including Beatrice Rainbird, would go to no end of trouble to get what they wanted. Surely the Rainbird home was not a decent environment for their two innocent children!

31

SONNY AND CROWDY FAULKNER WERE COMING home from school together. They were passing the beach where the workmen had heaped stones to prepare for the widening of the road and the building of a hard shoulder. Every few moments the boys picked up a stone and clattered it down again. Crowdy began to chant, looking sideways with a friendly grin at Sonny,

> Ole Cripply Rainbird's dead an' gone
> 's got no money for living on
> sits on his bum
> till kingdom come
> willy nilly
> isn't he silly.

Sonny stood still, jerking his mop of black hair that sprang back on his forehead as if called to attention. He felt every limb in his body urging him to action if only so that he could be busy, whirling around like a windmill, using the chanted rhyme as the windmill uses the wind in its sails. Then darting to a pile of stones, seizing the biggest he could find in such a frenzied swift search, he rushed at Crowdy Faulkner and before Crowdy had time to dodge Sonny sent the stone crashing against his head. It struck him on the forehead, above his eye. He made a squeaking yelping sound and turned his head and blood spurted from the wound. Then he fell, striking his head on the hard road. He lay still.

222

Sonny gave a big gasp as if to suck in all the air he would ever need again, then he made a stamping movement with his feet (his "clomp") like a horse getting ready for a race, and then he ran, ran ran home.

White-faced he opened the kitchen door and went as he did every afternoon to get his piece of bread and jam.

Teena saw him first. "What's up?"

A guilty look came on Sonny's face. "Crowdy Faulkner was after me."

"What did he do?"

"He called me names," Sonny said. And somehow it seemed then to Sonny as if he and not his father were Ole Cripply Rainbird.

"What did you do?"

"I bashed him good and hard."

Teena looked frightened. "You're not allowed to bash. You'll have the Pleece." (She spoke the word "Pleece" in a high-pitched tone like a whistle.)

They heard their father calling from the front room.

"It's Dad. He wants to know what's up."

"Nothing's up."

Then Sonny, unable to keep his awful fear to himself, said, "Don't tell anyone, cross your heart and hope to die, promise, promise?"

"I promise."

"Spit for good measure."

Teena spat.

"There was blood everywhere," Sonny said, sounding half proud and half scared. "I bashed him good and hard."

"Dad's calling. He wants us."

Sonny was embarrassed by his father. He couldn't understand why he should stay all the time in a chair; last year, when he had died, was years and years ago, and Sonny was in a new class at school and had had nearly two birthdays. Why didn't his father get up and walk around and go to places like other fathers? When they came home from school now they had to find their own pieces of bread and jam and their glass of milk. It was cheating to stay in a chair and pretend you were a cripple; but then his father had never pretended; people only said it and then believed what they said; it was all made up.

The two children went to the front room where Godfrey sat with books and papers on one side and a carton of half-assembled electrical plugs on the other.

"What's up in the kitchen?" he asked.

He sounded more eager than alarmed as if he hadn't had news from anywhere for months and months. He sounded proud, too, like a king who might ask his subjects returned from distant lands, "What's the news from the Northern Hemisphere?"

Practical as ever Sonny answered. "It's not in the kitchen. It's Crowdy Faulkner."

"What about Crowdy Faulkner?"

Sonny looked guilty. "Nothing. He called me names and I bashed him."

"Well, what's the fuss about? No bashing in future, remember. Go and change your clothes, don't forget your shoes, and be good until Mum comes home. She won't be long. It's her early afternoon."

There was a look of eagerness on Godfrey's face as he spoke of Beatrice as if, were he the king, he would feel that the last dearest messenger to return from the farthest country would be Beatrice, his queen. Yet he knew this was not so. When Beatrice came home she brought little news. She seldom talked of her work. Nor did they talk of Mum and Dad Muldrew who still tried to persuade Beatrice to persuade Godfrey to sharpen knives and saws and scissors as if then he would have a more effective armory, a sharpened sense to excise the numbing loss of his death and his life. Nor did they talk of Lynley who had bought a house in Auckland and was letting two flats attached to it. From time

224

to time she sent checks to Godfrey who gave them to Beatrice to cash; but neither spoke of them; Beatrice had begun to feel rising hate for their benefactress.

Sometimes now before Beatrice came home she would go to the lounge bar of the Pioneer for a glass of sherry. This afternoon she dispelled her usual feeling of tiredness with two glasses of sherry and she was looking forward to being at home with Godfrey and the children and she was sure that at last summer had come and they would have their first share of it for two years and it did not matter how much it rained or the pine trees moaned or how the sea on the ocean side pounded against the rocks and sent its spray flying as far as the graves in the cemetery. The yellow flowers would be out, the warm flowers—they flared softly inside her as she waited in line for the bus. She remembered there was a good program on television that evening, with people, as a change from lions and tigers and pumas inhabiting the sitting room. And looking dreamily out of the bus window at the summer-blue sea she felt the mingled warmth of the sherry and the marigold-fires put forth her almost forgotten blossom of hope.

When she saw the police car outside their gate with the light in the roof throbbing and beating like blood inside a transparent circular official punishing heart she stared.

"What on earth?"

Dazed, she walked up the path and in through the front door and a young man who seemed to be occupied and equipped like someone with a tennis racket in his hand for a season not yet begun, almost leapt up to her.

"Mrs. Rainbird? I'm Constable Rogers."

Before Beatrice had time to think or grow afraid the constable smiled at her ("your serve, my set, love three"), then frowned. "Mrs. Rainbird, it's about your son. He's assaulted another child who is dangerously ill."

Beatrice looked sternly at Constable Rogers. It is all so strange, she thought. Last time it was I who was inside the house and the chimes played:

> —My pigeon house I open wide
> to set my pigeons free.
> They fly o'er the fields to the other side
> and light on the tallest tree.

She heard in her mind the remainder of the song,

> And when they return from their merry merry flight
> they shut their wings and say goodnight.

and she saw herself as a child in the infant room at school resting her hands together and her head against her hands and her eyes shut and her body rocking gently: a pigeon asleep.

"Did you hear me Mrs. Rainbird?"

And last time I came to the door and there was the policewoman to tell me about Godfrey.

Beatrice smiled. "The only son I have, Constable, is a harmless little boy of nine."

"That's the boy."

"Don't be ridiculous."

"He's with his father."

"Godfrey!"

Beatrice almost ran to the sitting room where Teena and Sonny, white-faced, were standing one on each side of their father as if it were he who had been accused.

"He's The Pleece, Mum," Teena said, again with her voice rising to a whistle as she pronounced the word "Pleece."

Then Constable Rogers explained what had happened and that there had been witnesses.

"A truculent little boy," he said.

Sonny's face was flushed and his eyes were bright with a starry Christmas look in them. Beatrice leaned toward him and put her hand over his forehead in one of the intimate motherly gestures

226

that always filled her with reverence for herself and love for her children. His skin was burning with the sunless warmth that comes from the body. How simple it might be, she thought, remembering her longing for things to be simple: to say firmly, Sunstroke; put the child to bed in a darkened room; give cool drinks.

"The boy, of course, is not culpable in law but the incident has to be investigated and your child's environment looked into. I'm sorry to say there's been talk. Talk."

Then his eyes tried them all. "The Faulkner boy might die; or his brain might be injured for life."

Beatrice was not listening. Her arm encircled Sonny while Teena clung to Godfrey and all made a melodramatic picture of a family about to be evicted or imprisoned; the naturally dramatic grouping of disaster; but not so melodramatic; not so Victorian. With detachment Godfrey studied this detail from a worldwide crowd scene: he, Sonny, Beatrice, Teena, Constable Rogers, were a corner of the picture, perhaps a faded few square inches that someone some day might want to clean, retouch, restore the life and color of the scene, put back the original patch of bright blue in their dull corner of sky. Eviction, imprisonment, death. A white-hot sword touched Godfrey's senses. He smiled. It began there, he whispered.

That's not the right environment for children to be brought up, Constable Rogers was thinking as he left the Rainbird home and climbed behind the wheel of the big black Chrysler. There was drink on that woman's breath. That type are all alike. And this Rainbird chap pretending to be a cripple when he's as healthy as the next man. It's no place to bring up a family. I've heard others say the same. It's time the Rainbirds learned to live as decent citizens. We don't want delinquents in this country. A crime wave might be alright in London or New York but we don't want it here, not in a decent city like Dunedin.

That night before Beatrice slept she heard again and again Sonny's protesting cry, "But Crowdy Faulkner and me were friends!"

And her stern correction as if good grammar were evidence of good behavior.

"Crowdy Faulkner and I."

"But Crowdy Faulkner and me makes it sound like friends. I's only for writing in school."

"We don't hurt our friends like that."

And Teena's words, "The Pleece always get you for throwing stones."

"But he pitched into me, calling me names."

"We have to learn not to throw stones at our friends, not at anybody."

"But he said Dad was a cripply and he's not a cripply!"

"The Pleece always get you!"

The last sounds Beatrice heard before she slept were Teena's high-pitched cries, and a whirring of wings, like a scattering of precious pet pigeons flying away, away into the tallest tree.

And the chimes like an alarm in her head,

> My pigeon house I open wide
> to set my pigeons free.
> They fly o'er the fields to the other side
> and light on the tallest tree.

32

TWO WEEKS LATER GODFREY, BEATRICE AND
Sonny set out in a taxi for the Children's Court. The day that
promised to be fine brought rain and Teena watching from the
neighbor's window and not paddling on the beach in picnic
weather as she had been promised, sat mournfully nursing a
teen-age doll, Gloria, glamourous in scarlet shift and high white
boots; but her nursing of it had no intimacy: it was not her
doll; and though she had been given permission to try the permanent wave on the blonde everlasting hair she was not interested. She tucked Gloria into her wooden bed and she felt the
doll's forehead and frowned.

"You're sick. Perhaps you'll die and you won't come alive
again because you're not allowed to."

Then she leaned and whispered to the pouting lips, "But you
can really come alive if you sneak and visit us and tell no one."

She covered the doll's face as she had seen it done on television when people were dead. Then she looked out of the window at the rain raining on the wallflowers and the roses and
the front lawn where the glossy blackbirds big as chickens were
prodding for worms. She saw the taxi with her mother and father
and Sonny, the doors closed, the windows wet, and the three inside warm in the back seat, Sonny between. She wished then
that she was at school in the large room with the hard-cor-
nered desks and the six-sided hard yellow pencils, and the chairs
and shoes clattering and scraping on the floor; and the sun

shining in with wide yellow rays full of whirling dustbeams. And then she wished she were home in somewhere soft and warm, somewhere with no corners and sides and scraping and clattering floors.

She uncovered Gloria's face.

She took her from the bed and bowed her again and again so that she made her built-in Ma-Ma-Ma, Ma-Ma-Ma, the infant cry, by some quirk of mechanism sounding from deep in the teen-age belly while the long-lashed eyelids made a desperate flirting motion. The cry stopped and the eyes closed as Teena lay Gloria on the floor. Then she decided to wave Gloria's hair. She reached out and carefully opened the top of the permanent wave set and slid the contents from the packet: little bottles with tiny stoppers and star-shapes printed on the glass; a blue hairnet like a spiderweb it was so soft; a pink drier with petal spokes like a flower that Gloria could sit under; and a tiny make-believe switch to get the correct temperature.

Teena's eyes were shining. "How hot it is outside isn't it, Madam? Just the day for a picnic on the beach. And so you want a special hair-do for your party? The sun ruins your hair you know."

Taking the little pink comb she began to comb Gloria's ever-lasting hair, speaking sharply when each vigorous tug pulled Gloria forward and she began her infant wailing, Ma-Ma-Ma, Ma-Ma-Ma.

"The way you're crying you'd think the Pleece were after you," Teena said, each time turning the doll upside down and smacking her on her pink plastic cottageloaf bottom.

"There, you're behaving like a child. You're lucky to be alive and not dead, dead, dead!"

"The school," Sonny said in alarm as they passed the school. Godfrey turned and had a glimpse of huge windows milkwhite and wet with rain and light; and a gray playground where no one

230

was playing. There seemed to be no children at school as if they had all become animals who instinctively desert the area where one of them has suffered. There was a formal appearance of desolation as if "thistle and darnel and dock" waited to burst overnight through the playground and moss would creep along the wooden fence and gate and the windows crack under the sad pressure of their unused windowness.

"Those are the stones," Sonny said as they passed the reclaimed land.

Godfrey and Beatrice turned urgently to look but the stones did not move or speak: plump, sharp; smooth; they should not have been left lying there; the land was a swamp; who said they could reclaim the land? The tide was in, the tide would always flow in, and high. In my country, Godfrey thought, surprised that he was separating himself and returning to his first home, We have respect for the sea and what it wants to do, and we control it just so much, a little pressure here, a little pressure there, and fenland stays fenland because the marsh birds like it that way. And wasn't he a marsh bird then with the land reclaimed under his feet and nowhere to nest and live and breed? Which were the marsh birds? Peewit, heron, pied oystercatcher, tern? The birds with long beaks and legs and the habit of standing lonely without moving for hours while the sea washed about their feet.

"That was the stones, Godfrey," Beatrice said, bewildered and angry at his absorption. She had thought that on his first visit to the city since his interview at the Pioneer he might have shown a flicker in his darkness of "the old Godfrey."

"Yes, the stones."

And it was there too that *it* had happened, almost at the same place. Had Beatrice forgotten? The land should never have been reclaimed. It began among the stones; a stone on your shoulder, blocking the sun, for worship; and in your hand for murder; and at your feet to stumble over and to speak your name into the grave; and a stone in your heart for you to know the depths of the well-spring and the lonely splashing echo.

"I don't know what they think they're trying to do with the city." Godfrey burst out possessively.

"It's not the city I'm caring about," Beatrice said. "You know what I'm caring about."

Sonny flicked the crackly paper from a black-and-gold-striped sweet out of the bag of Winter Mixture that had been sold two for the price of one because it was no longer winter, it was summer—sun, beach and, soon, holidays again.

"Will the Welfare get me, Mum?"

Beatrice enacted a joyous laugh. "Sonny, why should you think that?"

"The Welfare gets lots of kids."

"Of course it doesn't. They're kind people anyway. They want to do only . . ."

A feeling of horror at her poisonous cliché comforts made her unable to complete the "what's best for you." She leaned toward the window as if trying to identify another landmark. The stones, the stones—ah, the railway bridge, black and red, the stifling steam and soot like the dirt that cleanses; traveling under it they would be obscured in smoke and emerge with the past fallen from them after a kind of railway baptism; and there was a garden—right in the city—geraniums, snapdragons, wallflowers, marigolds. Marigolds!

She smiled at both Godfrey and Sonny. "No," she said, "the Welfare won't get you, Sonny. You and Teena and Daddy and I will go to another place to live, away from Dunedin."

"By the beach?"

"Yes, by the beach."

"Near enough to go straight into the water?"

"Near enough to go straight into the water."

"With islands?"

232

"Islands and shells and seaweed and crabs and pipis and everything."

"And Daddy won't be Ole Cripply anymore?"

"No."

"True?"

"True."

"And they won't say what they say about him, dying and that?"

"No, Sonny."

A cunning look came into Sonny's eyes. If good things were being given in such abundance it might be just as well to claim all he could think of for there might never be another chance.

"And I'll have a bike with turned-down handlebars and a transistor? And a skateboard?"

He thought guiltily of Teena. He had been taught to share. He supposed she would ask for girls' things, dolls and teasets and party dresses.

"And can I have a leather belt with bullets all the way round?" Beatrice smiled dreamily. In her desire for peace she sensed that Godfrey too was listening with the eagerness of a small boy, waiting his turn to plead.

"And can I have a job and forget that I died and people were afraid of me? And everyone will forget what happened and I'll be in the Tourist Office again because I like the work and I like this country with its craze for talking about hotel beds and its pampered sheep wiggling their fat rumps against the View; and Centennial or War Memorials that are public lavatories or tea kiosks; and I like arranging tours to the West Coast and Mount Cook and Milford; and seeing the strange jobs advertised in the newspapers in the strange way my brain reads them, reads and retranslates, for in a sense I've been translated myself."

Beatrice smiled. "Are you listening, Godfrey? It sounds like paradise doesn't it?"

But Godfrey was still thinking of the marshbirds and a bird of paradise was not one of them, it was a tropical bird privileged with sun and color.

"Do you know the bird of paradise, Beatrice?"

Beatrice gave a cry. "Oh, yes, I remember, there was a bird of paradise with ruby-red body and blue wings and the children loved it and the grownups wanted it dead—remember? It was killed and as soon as it died the colors faded. That was the bird of paradise. Did you know about it, Godfrey?"

"But I was talking of our paradise, now."

"Where is it? North or South?"

"South is ice."

"Is it south then?"

They came to the city.

33

"WHAT KIND OF GENTLENESS DOES THIS MAN think he wants? Why can't he go out and rough it like the rest? The experience he's had might have ennobled another man, made him stand ten feet tall in charity but it's shrunken him until he's exchanged a life, a wife and family for pieces of electric plugs. A man who's had this experience could be of use to others, in church work, in social work; his reprieve has been miraculous; he's had a second chance to walk on earth, a return to life that all would envy and long for but few are granted; and what does he do with his precious life but sit all day like a crippled man, a poor victim, looking out of the window at the sun shining on some unreal city. It's a crime that he can't go out and get a job and produce, do something for his adopted country. Who does he think he is, his family crumbling about him, his wife so distracted she has taken to drink, his children sly stone-throwers who have set out on the path of murder?"

Beatrice looked about her at the group of men and women who made up the informal Children's Court, at the motherly and fatherly concern and rage showing in their faces: these were the guardians of the city and its people whom she'd seen only fixed in smiles and handshakes on the front page of the newspaper, and once or twice during the lunch hour again smiling and handshaking outside the Savoy or the town hall.

The young lawyer dispatched by Lynley from up north was passionate and had dark shadows under his eyes as if he too had returned from the dead yet why should that be a sign? Beatrice glanced quickly at Godfrey; his entire face was in shadow. Is that us? she wondered. The people that other man over there spoke of? She defined the speaker and his position vaguely in an attempt to diminish his power and she turned to gaze at the young lawyer, wondering where Lynley had found him and why he should be so eager to speak up for the dead.

"Do you not think a man returned from the dead may carry his kinship with those who stayed dead, may be overwhelmed by compassion in the contemplation of the millions of others dead, some of whom he and we by our silence or our speech sentenced to death? Do you not think that as a price for his new life they may have demanded from him promises, vigilance, ambassadorial cunning?"

The young lawyer frowned and gritted his teeth, "It makes me laugh, he said, "that the Tourist Office has no further use for such a distinguished traveler."

He's straying, Godfrey thought. What an interesting young man. From the north. I wonder where Lynley found him and if she is really going to marry that retired director of a Cinema Chain. A Cinema Chain.

Sonny wriggled between them. He had tried by every means to make himself smaller and smaller and disappear. The faces of the important people were so big, bigger than moons and footballs and dry hills without trees, and the Moeraki Boulders outside the Museum.

"Compassion is not usually expressed in the neglect of wife and family and the day-long assembling of electrical parts." The important Welfare Man said "electrical parts" as if they were something rude. "—in sponging on rich relatives who have fled north rather than remain in the company of this degraded man. And what is to become of the little girl in this environment? And the boy with no father to take him fishing, deer stalking, to show him how to play football and cricket, to be a man? Isn't the child's

236

mind warped enough already in a home that revolves around death?"

The sun has warped the boards of the house, Godfrey remembered. Paint up, paint up for Easter!

He looked at Beatrice and the tears on her face. *North Island papers please copy!*

They came to the city. Three hours later they were home again and Godfrey was in his chair by the window sorting the electrical plugs that he'd not had time to assemble during the morning; and Teena was asleep on the sofa still clutching the teen-age doll that she'd refused with tears to give up when they came to take it from her; and Beatrice was packing a suitcase of boy's clothes; and Sonny was sitting in the corner watching with a new quietness, a mixture of care and calm showing on his already alien Welfare face.

34

BEATRICE KNEW IT WAS THE BEGINNING OR THE end of the robbery, the surrender of hostages to the living. There seemed to be no objection or defense when a month later the Baldwins complained to the Child Welfare Department. "What kind of a home and upbringing," they asked, "can be expected for little Teena Rainbird who spends all her spare time sitting beside her father rocking and cradling her teen-age doll?"

The Baldwins had bought and paid for the doll. They were glad it was able to comfort Teena, but Mrs. Baldwin who originally gave the doll to her daughter and, through her daughter, to herself as she'd never had one that said Ma-Ma-Ma, Ma-Ma-Ma, and shut its eyes when it lay down and had everlasting golden hair, was overcome with rage and a sense of loss whenever she saw Teena with Gloria. The doll had no cry left, absolutely no cry! Its mouth moved and no sound came out. And something had obviously happened to its eyes because it wouldn't sleep anymore with its beautiful long lashes lying against its now scarred cheeks! The child could not be trusted with such a valuable possession!

"Is there a relative, someone close and capable with time and energy to devote?" The little boy needed help to correct his antisocial ways but the girl had shown no aggression and her teachers reported her wellbehaved, polite, serious with a tendency to withdraw; they recommended a change of environment, a totally new home background.

238

"Is there a close relative?"

"Lynley?"

"Don't be afraid, Teena," Beatrice whispered as Teena, alone, with her name-ticket around her neck, boarded the plane to Auckland. "Look down over the country and you'll see everything made small, just a fistful of snow for the mountains and the sea in a silver sugarbasin."

Teena did not answer at first. She lay Gloria down in her arms and the now ever-open startlingly blue eyes stared up at her.

"But I don't remember Aunty Lynley! She was here a long long time ago before Biddy Broome died and Sonny threw the stone."

Beatrice frowned. "Biddy Broome?"

"Old Biddy Broome, a tree in her room. I wish Daddy had come to say good-bye too. He said he knew what it was like because when he was a little boy he had something around his neck like this."

She fingered her name-ticket. "And he went a long way in the train because he lost his mother in the bombs. Why is it *lost* and not *dead*?"

She looked wonderingly, with a new alarm, at her mother.

"It's time to go," Beatrice whispered. "Kiss? Cold face to cold face."

Before Teena followed the hostess up the steps to the plane she looked herself up and down respectfully and then she looked at Beatrice as if at a stranger. She knew the truth.

"I'm going to be adopted, aren't I?" she said, smiling shyly with a joy that Beatrice resented and could not understand. Then the overpowering summer sun seemed to suck the plane up into the sky and it drove forward shining like a sharpened silver knifeblade and was gone.

Godfrey pursuing his constant electrical rhythm heard but did not see the plane in the sky. Now they have carried off our children perhaps they will be content, he thought bitterly. They must exact payment for miracles. They? Or is it I?

Autumn came with its diminishing boundaries between dark and light, ripeness and decay. There were floods and the reclaimed land surrendered itself for three days to the sea that flowed greedily over it, its waves exploring and relearning long-lost territory and, departing, leaving renewed promises slipped between the layers of silt and clay. The children still passed the Rainbirds' home but they were new children arriving as if from nowhere like a wandering tribe. They were Godfrey's chief interest now that Sonny was being buckled into politeness and strangeness by the hot concern of the welfare world and Teena was being remade with an identity disk and a cinema chain hanging around her neck. The understanding between Godfrey and the new children was like that between the persecutor and the persecuted, so close to a feeling of love that it filled the need that Godfrey left out under his personal night-sky as a bowl set out overnight is filled with soft rainwater and dew.

"Hello, Ole Cripply."

"Hello."

"Ole Cripply. Ole Cripply."

"What's your name?"

The child would tell his name. "We live near here. We've a television. My father's on the Council. Are you really Ole Cripply? Why do you go behind the window in winter?"

It happened of course as it does happen. A child went home.

"I was talking to Ole Cripply today."

Mother's question was sharp. "What did he say?"

"He gave me a lolly."

"I've told you about sweets from strangers!" She used the word "sweets" only in this context.

"What else did he say—" she was hesitant—"and do?"

"Nothing. I like him. I like Old Cripply."

240

She wanted to say, But you mustn't like him, nobody likes him. She wanted to say, I forbid you to go near him.

I'll discuss it with the child's father, she thought.

And that night she discussed it.

The boy's father was stern. "The mother drinks, the children are under the Welfare, the husband's a crank. They're not fit for decent folks to have anything to do with."

"Still," he said goodnaturedly, "I don't suppose harm can come from saying Hello to anyone."

"But it's the first step, saying hello—the first step to—fraternizing," his wife argued.

"But it's not war. The war's over. The Rainbird chap's harmless. He's had a raw deal. I used to chat with him myself in the old days. He booked our Waitangi tour—remember? The old days! How old? One, two, three years."

"Yes," he repeated unbelievingly, "I used to chat with him in the old days."

What was time doing to bring so much distress and disturbance just by passing while people went about their principled wellappointed lives?

"There's some injustice here," the father said, thinking, It's not up to me to mend it.

"It might be wise to tell the child to keep away. You never know."

"That's what I've been trying to tell you all along. You never know. Especially when they seem so harmless."

They spoke the truth. They never knew. Perhaps it was only and forever the children who knew and they weren't telling.

"Hello Ole Cripply."

"Hello."

"Ole Cripply."

It seemed no longer a term of abuse: it was one of endearment. Sometimes Beatrice, warm with sherry and the still-blossoming red, yellow or gold flower, geranium, marigold, inside her, coming home and seeing Godfrey with his chosen tribe, watched in rage. What about his own flesh and blood? What about Teena, Sonny? Even Lynley with her cinema chains, identity disks; not to forget her opaque pearls.

One afternoon, not able to restrain herself, she screamed at the children, "Get out, Get out!" waving her arms wildly so that they scattered like a flock of pigeons or birds of paradise or—rainbirds, the shy piping wrens that hide among the leaves.

"Get out!"

While Godfrey looked on in alarm, remembering in one gulp of memory for he swallowed it quickly, how Beatrice had "raised her voice" on the day, *that* day when he visited the Tourist Office and sat afterward in the Queens Gardens resentful of the pressure of the wide gray sky on himself, the buildings, the trees and the salt-white city. He felt that he knew the city more clearly now through being absent from it; it was to him now a city viewed over water and like the songs composed to be sung on the water the view contained innumerable echoes and depths and distortions of light.

"You're raising your voice, Beatrice," he said gently.

"We've touched rock bottom," she said. She was apt to speak now in a confused mixture of metaphor and platitudes.

"Rock bottom. But there's fire below the rock isn't there, Godfrey?"

She was pleading. Too much sherry. He hated her to plead with tears in her voice that gave her voice a misty quality like the clouds that moved across the seven hills bringing the rain in their white and gray mantlefolds. Also, she had that medical smell now, caught from being in Dr. Ireland's reception room. And when she came home she had the habit of putting on her white smock as if she were still at work. The meals she prepared had a dietary smell and tasted like ether and disinfectant but when Godfrey complained she looked at him sadly out of

242

Mum Muldrew's aging eyes, "You're thinking morbid thoughts again, Godfrey."

Usually she stayed home in the evenings and both sometimes watched television and suffered much under the accusing eyes of the panel members and the newscasters and from the stings of scorpions and the lashing claws of the tigers; the birds too pecked at them from the powerful shimmering paid-for screen. And when the program was finished they would go to their separate rooms and Beatrice would lie in the dark listening for Godfrey's heartbeat and imagine she heard it through the wall, pounding, pounding until it filled the house; but it was only her memory of the drum-music on television and the refrigerator throbbing and the rain knocking rhythmically upon the corner of the roof. And if she slept her sleep was full of nightmares of pigeons and peacocks and birds of paradise crowding to find and keep their place upon a small square of reclaimed land.

Godfrey's winning of the children had no single explanation or reason. It was only in the little boy's dream memory when questioned by his mother that there had been sweets. Godfrey had no sweets to give, no stories to tell. The children had many questions to ask, mostly concerned with Godfrey's crippled state and when he did not answer they were happy, after a swift Ole Cripply, Ole Cripply, to talk to him. Their questions and their glances were cruelly without mercy like the scouring chilling glance that a winter night gives to the earth and the plants and trees.

"You're mad, aren't you?" they said to him. "Mad, mad."

It was only a matter of time, if time could be given any substantiality or density or weight, before a deputation of citizens visited the mayor.

"Our children are being corrupted, alienated. Our children, the country's heritage, are being claimed and possessed by a crank who has spread the word that he died and returned to life when who knows what really happened? There he is masquerading as a cripple, luring all the children in the neighborhood to his home by his gift of sweets and his fantastic stories and promises. The Child Welfare have managed to rescue his own two children —what about ours? His wife couldn't walk the white line if you asked her. If you had her blood analyzed any hour of the day or night you'd find . . ."

What?

"Blood is one of the last privacies; the stations of the blood to and from the heart are nameless and secret; we acknowledge that; yet her blood, faithless like the rest of her, would talk and tell."

"This is a democracy," the mayor said, fingering the chain he wore in preparation for a civic reception to the overseas visitor with the transplanted brain.

"This is a democracy. Live and let live."

At first at night there were three or four stones flung on the roof. Then a few nights later a dozen.

"It's people throwing them," Beatrice said, separating them in her mind from thunderbolts and pieces of colliding planets.

Godfrey spoke possessively. "It's not *my* children."

He can't have forgotten Teena and Sonny, Beatrice told herself. He can't have put them entirely out of his mind. She dwelt emphatically upon this as a means of repelling its converse that came to her in almost every haunted moment of the day and night. Sonny had promised to write letters. It was not advised, the Welfare people said. In these circumstances. In other circumstances, yes. Teena had said she would write a long letter about up north and Aunty Lynley and new Uncle Matthew and his chain of cinemas and Gloria, whom Lynley in the anguished telephone conversations that passed between her and Beatrice when the arrangement about Teena was being made, had promised to provide with a new infant cry. "I can have a record installed in her, too," she had promised, "a transistor or something to make her say Hello, good-bye, I'm hungry and goodnight."

Beatrice had thought dazedly, Why choose those, why of all words, Hello, good-bye, I'm hungry, goodnight?

Teena had not written. Lynley's letters were brief and limited in expression almost like the chosen speech of the doll: All is well. Teena is happy. I'm so glad. Lynley's formal transistor had been implanted deep and was not likely to wear out or break.

"What more sacrifice do they want?" Godfrey asked. "They? I?"

He looked at Beatrice. The stones spattered on the roof. "Are you afraid?"

Beatrice shook her head. The estrangement was complete. She knew it from Sonny's final Welfare glance and Teena's good-bye when she boarded the plane and from the first night the stones were flung on the roof. Perhaps after all they were thunderbolts or colliding planets?

"We can get the police," Godfrey said. "Complain. It will be the windows next. And once they break in—."

"No, I'm not afraid," he said, answering Beatrice's glance, "but the idea of the windows broken—I like to have glass there between myself and the city especially now in winter."

Beatrice spoke dreamily. "Yes, it is winter now isn't it? And tomorrow is the weekend again."

Godfrey did not ask her where for the past year she had spent Sunday afternoons. She had never talked of it but he knew: the children told him. That night he heard her crying out in her sleep but he could not make out what she said and he did not try to; he felt immensely weary but for the first time since he woke from the dead he was conscious of warmth flowing into his body as if from a secret outward reservoir. He sank into sleep as into a warm bath and did not hear the stones on the roof and woke the next morning with the eagerness, alertness and excitement of a child and though it was winter the sun was already hot against the windowpane searching to enter, to touch and reclaim his skin. He felt reluctant to share his new abundance of warmth and life. It belonged to him only; he stood complete once more upright on the earth his space secured.

It was not till late in the morning that he found Beatrice in her room, dead, her throat cut with one of the newly sharpened silver knives; she seemed to be floating, surrounded by lilies of blood.

35

IT ALL HAPPENED MANY YEARS AGO NOW BUT people remember it and will talk of it if you ask them. First they will show you the press cuttings of Teena Rainbird, Dunedin-born-and-bred actress. Every item about her is welcome news. Then they will mention with pride that Melbourne's town clerk is Dunedin-born-and-bred Sonnleigh Rainbird. They will show you the Godfrey Rainbird Children's Ward of the Hospital, donated by some who remembered Godfrey from their childhood.

And if you happen to be visiting Dunedin with an afternoon to spare you might like to go to Andersons Bay Cemetery to see the grave of Godfrey and Beatrice Rainbird. The brochure put out by the Tourist Office will tell you which bus to catch and give you the exact location of the grave. The brief biography includes a mixture of fact and fantasy about the life and death of the Rainbirds and you may not know which story to believe but it does not matter does it?

The cemetery is beautiful in summer. The grave overlooks the sea and the long sweep of coast from St. Kilda to St. Clair and you can sit in the sun on the low rock wall surrounding the grave and look at the ocean breakers rolling in, or you can close your eyes and dream but do not dream too deeply in case, awakening, you discover that the yellow and gold flowers, geraniums, marigolds, nasturtiums, snapdragons, all that Beatrice planted and tended during her weekend visits to the grave, have merged one with the other, have changed their warm bright yellow and

247

gold to become a floating mass of red lilies; but that is only if you visit in summer; if you go there in winter you will have no help with your dreams, you will have to experience for yourself the agony of creating within yourself the flowers that you know and feel will blossom there in summer.